Rough Play

Also by Christina Crooks

Sweet and Dirty

Published by Kensington Publishing Corporation

Rough Play

CHRISTINA CROOKS

APHRODISIA

KENSINGTON PUBLISHING CORP.
www.kensingtonbooks.com

APHRODISIA BOOKS are published by

Kensington Publishing Corp.
119 West 40th Street
New York, NY 10018

All Kensington titles, imprints, and distributed lines are available at special quantity discounts for bulk purchases for sales promotion, premiums, fund-raising, and educational, or institutional use.

Special book excerpts or customized printings can also be created to fit specific needs. For details, write or phone the office of the Kensington Special Sales Manager: Kensington Publishing Corp., 119 West 40th Street, New York, NY 10018. Attn. Special Sales Department. Phone: 1-800-221-2647.

Aphrodisia and the A logo Reg. U.S. Pat. & TM Off.

ISBN-13: 978-0-7582-6137-3
ISBN-10: 0-7582-6137-3

First Kensington Trade Paperback Printing: September 2011

10 9 8 7 6 5 4 3 2 1

Printed in the United States of America

1

The noise sounded a little like a mouse scratching behind a wall. The strangeness of it pulled Charlotte's gaze from her budget calculations. Daytime was when the apartment's mice should have the sense to sleep instead of scratching loudly enough to draw a predator's attention.

Charlotte looked back at her white plastic laptop. She frowned at the clicking-whirling noise it made. Maybe the computer had made the scratching noise? She hoped it wasn't about to break. She relied on the old laptop for her struggling matchmaking business.

The sound again. A metallic scratching.

The fish tank? She looked at it with a frown. No, the noise wasn't coming from her cloudy freshwater aquarium or its quiet motor. She needed to clean the water again, she noticed.

Her door rattled slightly.

The front door.

Someone was messing with the lock. Not the landlord. He had a key. Besides, he'd knock.

Charlotte's hearing zeroed in on the tiny scrapes, the metallic jiggling. Picking the lock? Breaking in to her second-floor home.

Her heart sped into a staccato beat and she leapt silently to her feet. She paced the tiny living room in a tight circle, trying to prevent adrenaline from fogging her thinking. What to do? "Okay," she whispered to herself. "Okay. Yell for a neighbor, call a friend, a boyfriend, anyone. No. There's nobody."

Nobody.

The realization stopped her steps. Half a year after her divorce finalized, and she was still solitary. She knew she should've forced herself to get out more, to meet people. To date. The solitude now impaired her options. She didn't know her neighbors, and aside from the ex himself, there was no one to call.

"Okay, okay, okay. No, it's not okay. Shit."

She started pacing again, and her mind started working again. "Gotta do something. Call the police, of course."

Following her own advice, she dove for the small flip phone next to her notebook. Its rounded edges squirted from her sweat-slicked grasp, falling to the hardwood floor. The crack of plastic, then the clatter of the battery projecting out across the room sounded calamitous.

The scratching sounds stopped.

Charlotte held her breath until small black dots swam before her vision.

She strained to hear. When she couldn't stand it anymore, she tiptoed to the door. She brushed it ever so lightly with the pads of her fingertips, leaned toward the peephole.

The door shuddered under a blow, jerking a scream from her. Charlotte stumbled back without having seen the pounder. The fist-slam against the door told her he was strong. She hoped her door held under that level of assault.

What if it didn't hold?

She curved into the same pacing circle, passing the broken phone. She braced herself against the next loud noise, but it didn't come. She whispered to herself in the ominous silence, "Okay. Okay. Dead phone. Lunatic outside door. Go out the back sliding doors, jump. Crap. Go." Obedient to her own instructions, she'd half climbed over the balcony's wrought-iron railing when she heard the sound of knocking on the front door.

Polite knocking, not pounding.

She paused.

Was it a trick? As if she'd be stupid enough to just open the door.

Still she paused, with a reluctant glance down. It was a long way to a hard landing.

Another polite knock.

It wouldn't hurt to look.

This time she didn't tiptoe to the door, but stomped. "I own a gun! And my boyfriend'll be back any minute! And I have a vicious attack dog!"

She peered through the peephole.

"Dogs aren't allowed," her landlord said. He waited, lanky and familiar, his lean body propped against the iron railing on the concrete balcony. It was the exact same type of railing she'd just been climbing over in the back.

The guy couldn't be more than thirty, but his frown made him look old and mean. She hoped he wasn't feeling mean. She didn't have the full month's rent.

She also didn't have a boyfriend, gun, or an attack dog. Hoagie, her little brown and yellow mutt, wouldn't dream of biting anything but his toys and bones. He lived at Cory's anyway.

Her ex got the sweet little dog. She got the goldfish.

"Oh, man. Okay." Charlotte calmed her breathing, smoothed the front of her shirt. It clung to her sweaty skin and revealed more than she wanted to show her landlord, so she peeled it away and fanned the material to cool herself down. Her hands stopped for a moment. "Can I ask you something? Were you pounding on the door a couple of minutes ago?"

"No." He sounded impatient. His impatience convinced her he wasn't the same guy.

"Okay, just a sec." She walked toward her desk, stepping over the phone pieces, and quickly wrote out a check.

She opened the door with caution, looking past the landlord. "Did you by any chance see anyone? A man running away?"

"No," he repeated. He stared pointedly at the check.

"Because someone was trying to pick my lock," she continued, not to be deterred. "Whoever it was tried to break down my door." She held her check folded in one hand. "Could you please look at the lock?"

He sighed. He examined the lock. "Scratches. Could be from keys." He gave a cursory glance at the door. "The lock's intact. The door's undamaged. Seems fine now. Did you call the police?"

She bit back a number of replies. The police weren't high on her list of good guys lately. They hadn't managed to find her stolen car in the past months, and their swaggering presence while writing traffic tickets or sprawled in uniformed groups inside that donut shop down the road didn't do much to deter the brisk local drug trade. She often heard gunshots at night.

She frowned unhappily. Other than Cory, cops were the only lifeline she had. She really needed to get out more. It was past time.

At the moment, she shifted from one foot to another, wondering how to manage the landlord situation. "Yeah, I was about to call the police. But then, you showed up." She smiled brightly.

"Uh-huh." He held out his hand. His left hand. She noticed he wore no ring.

A man of few words. She could work with that. "The check

is short. I'm sorry. The thing is, I have a small business I'm growing, and I can make it up to you in service. It's a match-making business. To help people locate dates and true love. I have many happy clients." A slight exaggeration. She'd *had* many happy clients. Now they were happily paired-off former clients.

His scowl deepened, but he withdrew his hand.

"So, what do you think of that kind of service?" she prompted. She offered him the check, a gesture of goodwill.

He glanced at it without taking it, then transferred his gaze to her. His scowl faded to a look of speculation. His thin hair hung in limp, unwashed straggles over his broad forehead. Nice eyes, though. And he had the body of a man who did some physical labor.

He suddenly closed his calloused fingers over the insuffi-cient rent check as if afraid she might attempt to snatch it back.

He looked at her in a way she didn't like.

She spoke quickly. "Or, if you prefer, I'll just get the rest of the money to you in two weeks. That's when Burger Town pays me. Things have been tight, hours have been cut. And you know my car was stolen. Right out of the parking lot down there."

He didn't even look. Were thoughts of eviction crossing his mind? "Think about what I'm offering. Just consider it. I mean, you're not wearing a wedding ring. You're single, right?"

She noticed his slow smile and tried to ignore the glances at her body. "I'm a fabulous dating coach. Dating coach," she re-peated when she saw the gleam in his eyes. "I help people meet people. I'm good at it. I charge a reasonable fee. Very reason-able."

"You're good at it, eh?" His nice smile turned into a leer. "In exchange for the rest of rent?" He eyed her apartment's door again, and she knew he wasn't thinking about her intruder. "Sounds like fun."

"Dating coach," she said again. "Nothing more. I don't do sex stuff. You seem like the kind of guy who could use a good woman." As his scowl returned, apprehension fluttered in her belly. "Okay, a not-so-good woman? An easygoing and fun one. Hmm."

"What, I look desperate?"

"Of course not! I just want to help—"

"I never need help when it comes to women." He pocketed her check. "I ain't interested. Besides, if you were any good at your business, what're you doing living here and working in fast food?" He gave her a pointed look, then turned his back. "Two weeks, then I get the rest of it. No excuses."

She felt her lips tighten into a grimace. He was definitely feeling mean. Too bad for him.

Too bad for her. Flipping burgers, even part-time, bummed her out. Though it was only until her business caught on. She had a gift for matchmaking. A real, honest-to-God gift.

She spent every spare penny on advertising her matchmaking business. But people didn't believe her when she claimed a 99 percent success rate of making matches that resulted in permanent relationships. They surely wouldn't believe her if she told them how she did it.

Nothing excited her as much as using her special skill. Nothing felt as satisfying as trusting her instincts and her prescient visions. Nothing thrilled her like consulting her X-rated imagination to hook up her clients. Well, almost nothing.

Her dangerous personal fantasies with always-faceless ravishers didn't count, she told herself. They didn't count at all. Those were strictly and permanently for fantasyland only.

She gave a brief shake of her head, dismissing the thoughts.

She watched the landlord's departure with a professional's assessing stare. He descended the worn steps of the fourplex with a furtive but muscular grace. Lower blue-collar. Very single. Probably frequented Riverport's numerous strip clubs. But he had a nice gruff voice, broad shoulders, tapered hips, and the smudged jeans and easy gait of a man who spent a bit of time outdoors. Not bad. Not her thing, but not bad. Who'd be into him?

Like images on a jackpot's spinning wheel, faces of women she'd known and counseled turned over in her mind. Jill, Vickie, Tina. All taken now, thanks to her. Tamara had moved to Southern California. But she could've totally seen Tamara being into him.

She asked the question of her special intuition, then watched the answer: Tamara getting it on with the landlord.

Charlotte stared into the stairway's handrail, its metal imperfections coalescing into the magic visions.

In her mind, Tamara rubbed against the landlord's strong body, clawing his jeans off with only a little less desperation than his own feral dive for her nipples as he shoved her shirt up over her breasts, jammed her bra up, too, and took first one breast then the other into his mouth. No finesse. But Tamara liked it. Rough and straightforward, a little dirty but nothing too kinky.

Charlotte leaned against the rough stucco of her building with a sigh and made the movie in her head stop.

Tamara was gone and the landlord didn't want to pay Charlotte for her matchmaking services. That was a problem. No one was currently paying her. She'd hooked up all the clients.

Well, all but the last woman. The difficult woman who represented Charlotte's only failure.

Charlotte pushed herself from the apartment building's rough stucco wall, ducked inside to grab her mailbox keys and outgoing mail. Maybe a check or a client referral would be waiting in the box.

Her maiden name listed on her mailbox still had the power to bemuse her. She should never have married Cory. His face had never appeared in any of her visions.

Nobody's had, for her.

A breeze gusted, propelling a chill that lifted the hairs on her arms. Sweat cooled under her shirt. The wind probably heralded another of Riverport's frequent fall rainstorms, though the sun still beat down with noontime vigor.

Who'd dared to attempt to break into her apartment in broad daylight?

Would they have succeeded if she hadn't switched shifts at the last moment with a coworker? What if she hadn't been home? She supposed she'd have returned to find her few remaining belongings stolen. The divorce hadn't left her with much—she hadn't wanted much, just the dog, her exotic fish, and a little money to start her business.

Cory gave her the money and fish but convinced her to let him keep Hoagie at the house. Said the little dog they'd both raised from a puppy would be happier with his own backyard. He offered visiting privileges on weekends.

To her surprise, he'd honored her wish to stop by for a brief visit every weekend. Even more to her surprise, they got along better as friends than spouses. They'd never be close, though. Not after what he'd done to her.

Today she could've used Hoagie in her home. The little pup's barking might've scared off the lock picker.

She shivered again when she realized she might've returned home to find the intruder already inside, waiting for her.

She looked around with a careful, vigilant gaze.

Nobody.

Freaking herself out over nothing. The lock picker was long gone.

She opened the mailbox quickly. Bills, bills, ads, bills . . . aha, a big card.

Charlotte pushed in the outgoing mail—bills plus a wedding card to her latest satisfied client.

She returned to her apartment. She dumped everything with

the keys and ripped open the big envelope eagerly. Another thank-you card. It came with wedding photos from some exotic island with lots of sand and palm trees. Charlotte grinned at the sight of the former client wearing nothing but a bikini bottom and a big smile. The card's handwritten message waxed eloquent with gratitude. The woman promised referrals. The clients usually did. Sometimes they even remembered to do it.

Charlotte gnawed her knuckle with the ongoing worry even as she enjoyed Tina's clear happiness in the photo. She remembered watching the couple's first movie. The woman's expression had stretched into sexual ecstasy as that very same smiling gentleman, now wearing colorful swim trunks as he posed casually next to her, had screwed her enthusiastically.

Some women had all the X-rated movie luck.

2

After locking the front door behind her, then checking to make sure it still felt like a solid and secure barrier, Charlotte bent to scoop up cell phone parts.

Battery, plastic backing, triangular chip of plastic, phone. She inserted the battery in its slot. It stuck out a little and the plastic battery cover wouldn't go back on.

She tested the phone. At least it worked.

Which was a good thing since her last client would call any minute. An "urgent" session.

Charlotte snorted. Everything was urgent to Gail. Despite providing full-service phone sessions to the woman for months, mostly on Gail's fickle schedule, no prospects for a match had presented themselves. Charlotte had to respect Gail's urgency. The failure was embarrassing and a little baffling to Charlotte.

So much so that Charlotte had rearranged her burger-flipping job schedule to accommodate Gail's call.

She checked the time again. Any minute.

Charlotte sank onto her old couch, one of the few pieces of

furniture that had made it onto the moving truck with the many boxes of her hastily packed stuff.

Her right hand slid over her thigh, hesitated, then crept to her leg's outer edge. Through the denim, her fingers read the lumpy old scar like a strange Braille communication. It said nothing good.

Charlotte shuddered, forced her hand away from her thigh.

She thought of her decrepit neighborhood and shabby apartment. She'd expected more success in her business after the divorce. Her matchmaking skill was unique.

She had to grow her business. Her ads, her networking and fliers, nothing worked well enough. Word of mouth had netted her a steady trickle of clients, but even that was drying up.

The good news: All her other clients were deliriously happy, and the fact delighted her. The bad news: Gail was the one who remained unmatched.

Charlotte peered at her phone. Late again. *C'mon, Gail. Let's get it over with.*

In the near future, she promised herself, she'd have so many clients she'd have to beat them away with a stick. Nicer clients than Gail. Which wouldn't be difficult.

As if conjured, the phone rang, flashing Gail's too-familiar number.

Too many months, too few repeat dates.

It wasn't the woman's looks, at least not completely. Gail was a pretty, well-preserved thirty-five-year-old. The few crow's feet certainly didn't create an online-dating deal breaker. Especially with Charlotte's help writing the flirty e-mails.

No, the problem began once Gail met the men. Her attitude repelled them.

Her attitude repelled everyone, including Charlotte.

But Gail always paid Charlotte on time.

Charlotte flipped the phone open. "Hello, Gail."

Gail's brisk voice drilled into Charlotte's ear. "Hi. How are you? I'm so glad you were available. I sent winks to all the Heartlink candidates. I sent questionnaires to the Connections ones. Nothing all week. No winks, no notes, no date for this weekend."

Charlotte spoke carefully. "Was there something urgent you wanted to discuss, too?"

"That's not urgent enough? You know the statistic. A woman over thirty has a better chance of being struck by lightning than getting married and having kids."

"I don't think that's quite accurate."

"Trust me, it is. It's definitely getting worse as I get older. Thirty-six next week. Guys simply prefer younger women. Good thing I like older guys, huh? I just wish they weren't so picky. Sometimes I don't know why I keep looking."

Charlotte knew exactly why Gail kept looking. Unlike herself, Gail still believed in love.

Gail added, "I sometimes wonder if he's really out there. My Mr. Right."

The rare wistfulness in the woman's voice tugged at Charlotte's heartstrings. "Okay, look. Everything will be great. We've barely scratched the—"

Gail cut her off. "Enough of the pep talk. I e-mailed you the latest batch."

From experience, Charlotte knew what Gail's irritated tone meant. It meant this would be a challenging session.

Charlotte would've rubbed her temples, but her arm was bent at an awkward angle to keep the phone in position against her ear. She cocked her head to the right, pinning Gail's voice to a spot between shoulder and head. She liked to keep her hands free to type.

Time for Charlotte to say something sweet and enthusiastic. Gail sounded positively sour. "All right, Gail! Good job. I'm sure everything will work out. You're a great catch for the right guy." She tried to ignore Gail's rude noise of exasperation.

"You just need to be patient. Let's see..." Charlotte typed on her notes, then clicked on Gail's e-mailed list of men found on-line.

"Uh-huh. Yes..." Charlotte reviewed the images and pro-files of handsome, young, rich, intelligent single guys.

Problematic.

"These seem awfully, um, athletic for someone like you. You're an 'unashamed homebody who enjoys lounging and cooking.' That first one, Reggiedawg? He looks so conceited and tacky with his shirt off. He has a smug smile, don't you think so? Hmmm," she added as if she'd just noticed. "Most of them are your age or younger than you, Gail."

"You think the guys I pick are too good for me, don't you?"

"I didn't say that. These just aren't, um, they're not the envi-ronmentally concerned, house-handy, pro-family, progressive, activist, children-loving, vegetarian type you want, mostly. But, he's out there, somewhere. We'll find someone wonderful for you. You're smart, funny, you're super cute when you wear feminine clothes that show off your curves—"

"I'm dyslexic, not stupid. I know my limitations. The guy has to have viable healthy sperm—nothing snipped yet—and not already be married, or bitterly divorced and done with hav-ing kids. That means younger. Otherwise I'd be looking at the older guys like I'd prefer. You're supposed to help me with writing notes and flirting. You're brilliant at that part, so let's stick with what you know."

Her words stung. "Whatever you say." Charlotte's cheeks hurt from keeping the smile on her face. Clients said they could hear it when she smiled on the phone. She was afraid if she let the smile drop even for a moment that Gail would hear her ex-asperation.

Everyone has burdens, Charlotte suddenly wanted to tell her. *Even me. Especially me. I'm all alone, too.*

Charlotte quickly rubbed her temples, even at the cost of a

sudden small crick in her neck and an ominous small cracking noise from the phone. Her muscles and her nervous system always objected to Gail.

She'd nearly told Gail exactly what she thought of clients who assumed paying her meant they could treat her like a slave.

She had a low tolerance for people who treated her like a slave.

Every woman has a slave's heart. Cory's words rolled around in her head as if she were still gagged and bound at his feet and forced to listen to his feverish rants.

The ordeal had been her fault.

Charlotte raised her voice, made herself speak aggressively. A little more like Gail. "Didn't you have a date over the weekend with 'Spuntopping'?"

Silence for a moment. Then, unexpectedly, Gail laughed. "You remember how he'd written all about cooking in his profile? And we thought 'Spuntopping' was a kind of pie topping, and we came up with that clever line about cooking? Well. He meant an entirely different kind of topping."

When Charlotte didn't say anything, Gail explained. "Topping, in certain sexual circles, is the controlling activity of the person calling the shots in a sadomasochistic relationship. The so-called 'top,' or 'dom,' is the one who chains you up and whips you."

That wasn't exactly true, Charlotte reflected. Tops and doms did more than whip you. They tried their best to turn you into a slave-hearted woman who secretly craved to be conquered. And if he was any good, he succeeded.

She wished she didn't know quite so much about S and M.

"Wow," she said for Gail's benefit. "Guess that date was a dud, huh?"

"What do you think?"

Something in Gail's voice narrowed Charlotte's eyes. "Was it a dud, Gail?"

"I suppose. There was no love connection with that guy. But..." Gail fell silent.

Uh-oh. "Not a romance then, but friendship?" Please let it be just friendship. Charlotte felt a ball of dread begin to form in her belly. "But what, Gail?"

"But it made me curious."

Nature has designed a woman to know curiosity, to seek out and relish man's mastery.

"Curious about tops and bottoms? No." Charlotte found herself too startled for more than the simple denial.

"I know how it sounds. But I did some research. Did you know women can be tops? They're called dominatrices. And there's something called switches, people who switch from top to bottom depending on their mood, though there's a contingent that believe switches aren't a valid category."

Charlotte stared at the phone. Gail sounded like an encyclopedia entry. She couldn't truly be interested in the fetish scene. Or anyone in it.

But Gail continued. "I've found a dating site catering to the fetish crowd. I've made a profile," Gail declared in her most stubborn voice. "I'd like to date some male bottoms and I need your help."

"Okay. Okay. Oh, boy."

"Will this be a problem for you?" Gail's voice turned icy.

"It might be."

"Really? And why is that?" Any icier and Charlotte's ear would have frostbite. Her mind whirled.

Of the dozens, if not hundreds of normal online men they'd looked at together, none had triggered Charlotte's X-rated movies on Gail's behalf.

It wasn't unreasonable, at this point, to explore fringe groups.

Gail did need Charlotte's help. And Charlotte did need Gail's money.

And none of it had anything whatsoever do with Charlotte's

ex-husband's violent foray into BDSM. Her fingers crept again to the raised scar. Much healthier not to think about it.

Except that Gail was making her think about it.

"Gail, you can't believe everything you read on the Internet. You don't want to get involved with those sorts of people."

"Explain yourself," Gail demanded, her tone of affront all but singeing Charlotte's ear. Icy to scorching in an instant.

Charlotte remained silent, intending for diplomatic restraint to showcase Gail's own rudeness. Didn't the woman hear herself being so pushy? Charlotte hoped she wouldn't need to elaborate.

"I'm waiting."

Vain hope. "Okay," Charlotte began, reluctance making her words slow and heavy. "There are many good men out there. Sweet, emotionally mature, funny, responsible men. Non-deviant men. Non–psychologically abnormal men who have dangerous ideas about pain. I've paired off dozens of men and women who consider themselves gender equals. We don't have to bring sexual power exchange into the dating process. It's not safe."

"You said it might be a problem for you to help me with this. Why?"

Tension sank its pinching claws more deeply into Charlotte's shoulders. Gail was putting her on the spot. Should Charlotte tell her? No. She'd never told anyone about that side of Cory. She never would.

She'd never even talked about it with Cory himself. No need to curdle their amicable split with recriminations.

She pressed the phone to her ear tightly and tried one last, token resistance. She smiled so Gail would hear it. "Bringing torture instruments into the bedroom sounds scary. Things could go wrong. Aren't you worried about winding up at the mercy of some BTK serial killer?"

Silence.

Charlotte dared to hope it had worked.

Then Gail laughed again. "You so need to get out more. It's not like that."

Charlotte closed her eyes.

"And, there are a lot more attractive, available guys at CollaredNow. I want to do this. Can you go there? Now, please," Gail added, as if Charlotte was a schoolchild needing constant firm instruction. "I have a list of possibles."

Charlotte made her fingertips lightly tap the keyboard and she found the site. This was just the Internet. Nothing to be afraid of. In fact, Gail would probably get an eyeful of some hardcore bondage pictures, maybe see some photos of rope suspension or blood play. The woman would come to her senses.

Gail's voice raced ahead of her, directing her on the unfamiliar site. "Let's see. First one: 'Master Martin.' "

With the memory of her own S and M experience fresh in her mind, Charlotte was prepared to eviscerate the candidate to disqualify him. Her arms hairs were raised, and the site's accent photos of ropes, handcuffs, and spanking benches were giving her the heebie-jeebies.

So, she was more than a little surprised that when she pulled up "Master Martin" she had the sudden and visceral urge to keep him for herself.

She stared at his picture. Rich, dark hair allowed to grow unashamedly unkempt and long enough to brush his broad shoulders. A stubborn-looking face too masculine and irregular to be considered handsome—thick brows, large, slightly crooked nose, a lower lip fuller than the upper one but both lips too thin and long and sharply chiseled—but it worked on him. He didn't smile.

He'd never be a model.

He listed "stern, compassionate dominance" as his favorite activity.

He was the most attractive thing she'd ever seen.

"Earth to Charlotte? Hello? Is your phone battery fading? Damn it, I reminded you last time to charge up for our sessions."

Charlotte shifted the slender cell phone to the other ear, careful to keep the battery in place. She massaged her neck. She couldn't tear her gaze from the image on the computer monitor. "No, I'm here. Gail, this one's a dom. Completely wrong for you."

"I don't know. His About Me section is thoughtful and he's articulate about seeking a true mate and friend, a complementary partner of the heart. What do you think?"

"I think you're not complementary. You're looking for a bottom, remember? Or at least a switch."

"Yeah, but . . . there's something about him."

There certainly was.

Charlotte scanned. Aside from his obvious sex appeal, he was politically liberal, he wanted kids someday, he was handy with tools . . . "What about social responsibility? And he doesn't say what he does for a living. And, he's a dom. Red alert there. Dom equals bossy, bad, dangerous."

"I want to write to this one."

Gail didn't understand. "You're a feminist, even more than I am. Dom means dominant. Not just a top. Certainly not a bottom." The idea of this man bottoming to anyone, much less to a belligerent Gail, made Charlotte smile.

Smiling, she found it easier to be professional. Master Martin wasn't for either of them. "You know overbearing men drive you nuts."

"They're all fixers at this point in life," Gail replied plaintively. "Just like I am. Thirty-five years old, not stylish or giggly, not a size-zero blonde. And, you know I have strong opinions."

Charlotte barely kept herself from snorting at the understatement.

"Charlotte, you know I want to be pregnant like *yesterday* . . . that alone probably scares off ninety-five percent of men. And you know I'm not the easiest person to talk to sometimes." Gail spoke with unexpected dignity.

Charlotte made soft demurring sounds.

"You know it's true. So. Cultivating an interest in kinky sex? Not a big deal. Scoping out the weirdo dating sites to find Mr. Right? I'm not the hottest catch myself, so I can't be picky. You should consider being more open-minded about these things."

Charlotte laughed but immediately covered it with a cough. Gail might know herself neurotically well, but she still didn't have a clue about some things.

Then again, what did Charlotte herself know? Last winter had seen her divorce from Cory finalized, and here she was with a dying business, single, and still dateless three seasons later. She told herself she was managing her life just fine, considering everything.

But the way her libido leapt into high gear just looking at "Martin" made her wonder.

Charlotte made herself think of Gail to get her mind off him. Gail, who was insisting on running into the lion's den.

"Gail, please don't be offended. Something just occurred to me. If having kids is the big priority for you, have you considered—just considered, mind you—the idea of artificial insemination?"

"No. I don't want my kids to be fatherless. Let's get me the date, please."

Charlotte scrolled down. Martin seemed to smile mockingly at her.

"Okay. Okay then. If you want this one, we'll get you the date. Just remember I advised you to stick to regular dating sites. You've wanted someone more . . . well, more bottomy. If we have to use terms like that. If we have to be on a site like that. Which reminds me, I've heard of a hot new site, Cupid's Target, that's really popular and getting great results—"

"Nice try."

Charlotte had the thought she ought to feel grateful Gail was so impossible to match up. It was like having insurance.

"Okay, fine. Let me dash out a note to Martin."

Gail's silence acquiesced. Her dyslexia and self-admitted inability to flirt put the communication method firmly in Charlotte's hands for first contact.

Charlotte wrote quickly, trying to avoid looking at Martin's list of preferred sexual fetishes, but every so often her gaze drifted to it.

Belt spanking.

She imagined those curvy lips of his stretching into a sadistic smile as he brought his belt, still warm from being around his waist, sharply down on her bare ass. Not Gail's stubborn ass. Her own, more amiable ass.

Clamps and clips.

Her imagination fired again. Martin tugging gently on the nipple clips affixed with clawed edges, causing a sharp yet delightful shiver of wanting to zing through her body.

Play toy making.

He made his own sex toys? What sorts of toys? Whips? Dildos? He was good with his hands. Charlotte's eyes narrowed in pleasure, imagining those hands manipulating instruments of torture and ecstasy. Working on them, working on her, using them on her. Perhaps a handmade cane. Perhaps just his hand.

Consensual non-consent.

Charlotte's fingers stuttered on the keyboard, forcing her to delete and retype. Holy crap, he was into rape play?

Martin immediately flung her down onto a bed, ripped off her panties. He raised a mocking eyebrow as he waited for her to call a safe word. When she didn't, he pried her legs open.

The violent, visceral images filled her mind like the dirtiest of movies.

Starring her. With a man who had a face. Finally.

Charlotte swallowed, watching the first full X-rated movie with her in it. She experienced everything as if she were there.

Martin spit on his hand for needed lubrication, simply smiling at Charlotte's tearful pleading for him to stop, then shoved his cock deep into her. She screamed, humiliated and hating the way her body throbbed while pinned under his. He thrust deeper, his face twisted into a bestial grimace of pleasure.

The fantasy was so real she could smell their sweat and hear the slap of his body and the thud of the bed hitting the wall.

She made a galvanized movement. Her laptop crashed to the floor.

"Okay, okay, okay. Shit, damn. Okay."

"What's the problem this time?" Gail asked.

Charlotte's vision cleared. She carefully picked up the laptop with one hand, keeping the phone to her ear.

She grimaced, stunned by the force of her reaction. Horrified by what it meant.

And annoyed by the interruption. "Not a thing. No problems here. This note to Martin is done ... proofreading now ... and, sending it to him. I copied it into your in-box like always."

Charlotte shifted uncomfortably. She wished Martin were in her in-box. Flashes of her fantasy were enough to keep her wet.

She forced her fingers to remain on the keyboard. She put a smile on her face. "What do you think of the note?"

"Wow. This is pretty aggressive. Are you sure? We're giving him my telephone number right away? 'I'm very attracted to you'? And this, 'I could be the complementary partner you're looking for, so please call me at your earliest convenience'?"

"Have my notes ever failed to get you a date?"

"Well, no, but—" Gail proceeded to pick apart the note, second-guessing each line.

Charlotte listened patiently. Eventually she heard what she'd expected to hear. "Is that your call-waiting?"

"Huh. Yes, it is." Gail clicked over without a word of thanks.

Charlotte took the opportunity to straighten her phone arm, then rolled her neck to get the cricks out. She sagged, tired suddenly. She stared at the crease where her jeans-covered thigh met the firm sofa.

It had finally happened. Her own movie.

And it starred a dom.

Unthinkable.

Maybe she needed to get away from Riverport. Get away from Martin and all he represented. Maybe the city was too haunted with memories for her to heal emotionally and sexually.

Even as she thought it, she ground her teeth. Her bad luck and her perverse sexual fantasies weren't the city's fault, and she wasn't going to run away.

She thought she'd built a clean and hopeful new life post-Cory, but the buzzing between her legs at the very thought of the dominant Master Martin informed her how wrong she was.

She closed her eyes to a slit, picking at the edge of a loose thread. The sofa's cotton lining suddenly split, cheap foam filler bursting through. Charlotte flicked the foam onto the floor. Trashed. Like her neighborhood. Like her faulty libido. Like her willpower.

She looked up and was captured anew by Martin's picture. She felt hypnotized.

When phone static told her Gail was back on the line, she jumped guiltily.

"Hello? Hello, Charlotte? Anybody home?"

"Sorry. I'm here."

"We have a date tonight!"

Charlotte blinked at the photo of Martin. "Good."

"Don't sound so worried. I'll need a safe call. I nominate you."

"Nominate me?" Charlotte was used to Gail's abrupt about-faces, but this one was new. "A safe call?"

"I read about it online. It's maybe not strictly necessary since I'll be meeting him at a crowded club downtown, not going off alone with him. But it was recommended for the fetish scene, which is what this is. I'll pay you for your time, of course."

"Of course . . . but, Gail. What exactly do you need?"

"I don't have any friends I can trust with this," Gail said matter-of-factly. "One needs a person who's aware of the meeting happening at a certain place, and who will expect a call at a predetermined time. A check-in, just in case. I don't want anyone to know I'm meeting someone at Subspace—everyone knows that place's reputation. So that leaves you." She cleared her throat. "That is, if you don't mind if I call you at nine tonight? I'll pay you," she repeated.

Charlotte's exasperation faded to understanding. Then, reluctant pity.

She was nodding her head, but realized Gail couldn't see it. "Of course. I'll expect your call at nine. You should call on time," she added pointedly.

"Yeah, sorry about today. I lost track of time. I'll pay you for the fifteen minutes I was late."

Charlotte wondered if Gail bought off all her troubles.

She shook herself to get rid of the sudden inexplicable sourness bubbling in her. "I'm sure you'll be fine, Gail. Only, I do want to go on record as telling you the fetish-scene approach is a bad use of your time." Charlotte tried one more last-ditch effort to change Gail's mind. She deliberately didn't smile. "If you're already thinking about safety calls and stuff like that, maybe it's a sign you shouldn't get involved with the S and M scene. Seriously."

"I don't expect any trouble. I'm not getting any younger, you know. After all the dead-end dates you've gotten me over the last few months, I have to try something different."

Dead-end dates? Charlotte bit her tongue against protesting. She wanted to tell Gail it was Charlotte's responsibility to land her the dates, not make the guys fall for her.

She smiled instead. "Your boldness is admirable."

After a few more pleasantries—pleasant on her part, typically brusque on Gail's—Charlotte flipped her phone closed with an exhale of relief.

She snuck another peek at Martin before closing the computer, too. He'd dominate the hell out of Gail. He'd dominate the sensible khaki pants right off her.

Charlotte grinned.

Then her grin faded. Maybe that's what Gail secretly craved.

Foolish woman, Charlotte thought. Then wondered if she meant Gail, or herself.

3

He was dangerous, but the sweet young vanilla—Bambie was her scene name, and "switch" her stated sexual identity—didn't know it, or didn't care. She looked at Master Kartane as if he were chocolate, and she was starving.

Accustomed to the reaction, Kartane gave her his most appealing crooked smile. His chosen scene name was Kartane of Gor. He liked to emphasize his Gorean mindset even though the other, less authentic Goreans at Subspace didn't like him much and doubtless wished he'd go away.

Which just broke his heart.

His smile widened. He was approachable and sweet. He was at Bambie's service. Until he put her at his.

Telling the single fetish ladies he identified as a switch had been a stroke of genius. They all liked to imagine they'd be the one to use him in perfect safety, to play at submission, or to collar and command him if they felt like it.

But Kartane didn't believe in being commanded.

He got hard remembering the look on each of their faces the moment they discovered their mistake. He enjoyed their begging, their tears. He loved the sight of red welts rising on pristine ass skin.

Most sadists did.

And Subspace, with its buffet of masochists, sadists, and switches, was the perfect place for kinksters to hook up with complementary play partners. It just wasn't the perfect place for true Goreans like himself.

Yet.

He leaned across the table to give the hot little thing a whiff of his pheromones. "You keep looking at me with those big, innocent eyes, I might start to wonder what dirty thoughts you're hiding behind them."

Amethyst suddenly swung down into the booth, her warm thigh pressed against his. "No need to wonder. She's thinking the same thing I once did: what a sexy, great-looking guy. She has no idea what a pig you really are." She smiled sweetly at him.

Kartane controlled his fury with an effort. "I don't recall inviting you to sit down."

Amethyst flipped up her middle finger, still smiling. "Sit on this, honey."

Bambie started to scoot away. "Maybe I should go. . . ."

"Sit," Kartane commanded.

Amethyst also spoke to Bambie. "See what kind of macho bullshit you'll put up with? He's no switch, and he'll never be a bottom, babe. And it gets worse, trust me. He's a Gorean. Means he's an oinker straight out of the fifties. Eighteen-fifties. Or whenever it was that men were cavemen and women were property. His wife left him for beating on her. Not the good kind of beating."

Kartane fought for calm. He addressed Bambie as well. "Amethyst, here, wishes she were a man, complete with penis."

"I don't need a penis to complete me."

"No, you need one in your mouth to shut you up."

Amethyst presented him to Bambie. "See? Goreans should come with a sign or a tattoo or something so people know what they're getting."

Bambie scooted off the seat. "Leaving now. Have a nice life, Kartane."

"You fucking bitch," Kartane snarled at Amethyst.

"You think all women are either bitches, or for fucking. When I own this place, you will so not be allowed inside."

"You won't ever own it," he snapped. "Not if I have anything to do with it." Then he shut his mouth. He shouldn't let anyone know his plans. Subspace was nearly his. The perfect location and the perfect recruiting ground. Stupid to jeopardize it by blabbing his plans. His gaffe in revealing too much increased his fury at Amethyst. "You really do wish you had a dick, don't you. To mark your territory? Bitch like you'd piss down your own leg if you didn't squat." He heard the bitterness in his own voice, saw the others who'd gathered around their small booth, and knew he'd lost even before she delivered her zinger:

"True. I don't have two whole inches to point with like you do."

Kartane shoved her aside, pushed through the crowd with reckless disregard. He had to flee the battering explosion of laughter. The taste of humiliation filled his mouth, thickened his throat.

Clenched his fists.

Kartane controlled his rage. Later, he promised himself. Soon, so very soon. The time for disciplinary hitting approached.

He could wait a little longer.

So many things frustrated him lately. Ever since realizing his Home Stone no longer resided in its customary place. And how long had it been before he'd even noticed? Weeks? Months?

He'd snapped at people and been off his game from that moment of discovery.

He supposed his frustration was only appropriate. Such a loss should naturally bother him. With his Home Stone gone, he'd lost his Gorean honor. It was as if the Priest-Kings were punishing him for his mismanagement of Charlotte.

For his softness in dealing with her.

He saw her every week when she visited Hoagie at what had been their home together. Soft feelings for Charlotte still infested him, he knew. Her kindness, beauty, and grace still had the power to render him unmanly. He couldn't help remembering how uninhibited she'd once been with him. How eager to explore the realms of dominance and submission, pain and pleasure.

He had her to thank for introducing him to S and M.

He was pretty sure she had his Home Stone. It had to have been an accidental acquisition. He couldn't imagine her willing to face his wrath over deliberately stealing anything of his.

But when he'd called her the week before, she'd denied seeing the small flat gray rock with a G carved on its underside. He'd described it as a paperweight and let her think it was worthless, just a thing that had sentimental value. She replied she'd never seen it.

She wouldn't lie to him about such a trivial item, would she? During the divorce, she'd remained honorable and proud, not even asking alimony of him. All she'd accepted was a token sum to start her small business.

And yet . . . most women were flaky, greedy, and devious. As he'd discovered over and over again before and after Charlotte, they lacked a man's sense of honor.

Perhaps Charlotte had discovered what the stone meant to Goreans and was punishing him by withholding it? He had to concede the possibility.

Women.

He didn't belong in this feminized culture, he belong on Gor. Where men were warriors and women trembled in fear.

He'd studied the biology of the sexes when Charlotte brought her sexual proclivities to his attention. She'd certainly opened his eyes, though not the way she'd expected.

Real Goreans utilized simple Darwinism: The strong dominated and protected the weak. The natural system worked to everyone's benefit. The misery all around him in the whole country—in this entire modernized society—showed how feminized relationships built on so-called equality made nobody happy for long. Frustration and alcohol addiction and misery for men. Anxiety and bitchiness and desperation for women. That was all the system provided. That was all anyone had to anticipate from the opposite sex.

He was the enlightened one, thanks to Charlotte. Not that she'd known what she'd begun at the time, of course. The rising number of dissatisfied guys attending his Gorean meetings proved it. They were learning a better way. The Gorean way.

Kartane knew what people needed, deep inside. He knew what they were because he'd once been one of them.

Women like Charlotte would ultimately accept their inner desires. And women like Amethyst would grovel on their bellies, fearing the lash and living to please.

He could still feel the lingering warmth of Amethyst's thigh against his, but it was Charlotte's accusing gaze in his mind's eye.

What was this emotion he was feeling? Guilt again? Shame for fleeing Amethyst? He dismissed the guilt and acknowledged the shame's lesson. He shouldn't flee a woman. Ever. Warriors had higher concerns. Such as the loss of a Home Stone. And the unacceptable state of feminine liberties.

Kartane pivoted with a snarl, then headed back to Subspace.

* * *

Charlotte didn't immediately notice the buzzing vibration of her phone in her purse.

Walking to work, putting together cheeseburgers for six hours, then walking to the supermarket, *then* carrying back two heavy bags of groceries as it started to rain...It made her legs hurt and her shoulder ache. It made her damp down her awareness of extremities and her mind just to keep from being depressed. But small spikes stabbed the center of her heels with each step despite her determination and her comfortable Burger Town work sneakers. By the time she neared home, she all but growled. As she hauled herself upstairs she bent nearly in half with strain, hunched and not caring she probably looked like a cranky, bedraggled old homeless lady.

Who had the stamina for this? She wasn't a teenager anymore. Or even in her early twenties. Adding insult to injury, the afternoon shift cadre of coworkers all sported the zits and youthful features of high schoolers. They flipped the burgers and dipped the fry baskets with far more speed and energy than she did. They treated her kindly at least. Probably pitied her for working fast food at her age. Even thin, shy Rollie had talked to her, and he barely spoke to anyone. He seemed a little older, a little more cynical than the rest. A possible friend.

Getting to know him better might be one of the few compensations for working at Burger Town.

Even so, the fast-food job had gone on entirely too long. It was supposed to be a stopgap, a way to get a few paychecks while waiting for the matchmaking business to lift off. If only she'd had more time, she knew her business would already be taking the online dating world by storm. No one else had X-rated visions that came true, after all.

She hauled the bags inside and shut the front door. As she pondered which to do first, unload the groceries or revise her business plan again, she finally felt the vibration from her cell phone.

Gail.

Charlotte wiped off the phone with the dry inside of her jacket. The lingering scent of burgers puffed up from her clothes as she checked the caller ID, then tapped the batteries to make sure they were still lodged where they belonged. She flipped the phone open.

"Hi, Gail. I'm glad to hear you're safe. How's the date going?"

Static.

Then, two thumps.

Silence.

Charlotte pressed the phone more tightly to her ear, but she heard nothing further. "Hello? Gail?" Charlotte waited a few moments, straining to hear something. Anything. Then she held the phone up to stare at it. Blank screen. A lost connection.

She called Gail back.

It went to voice mail.

"Weird." The sound of her own voice in the small apartment was a comfort. Her home stood guard, tiny though it was, against a world wanting pieces of her. Of her body, or of her peace of mind. What sort of game was Gail playing? She'd probably just fumbled the phone onto the ground. Or got distracted with someone else. Gail was occasionally rude that way.

Charlotte redialed.

This time she left a message. "Gail, this is Charlotte. You just called. Um, I guess the connection was dropped. Or maybe your phone ran out of juice."

Gail always kept her phone charged up.

"Okay. Anyway, I'll try to reach you again. Give me a call when you get this, please? Thanks."

The cold from her wet clothes began to seep into her bones. Charlotte shivered violently. Why had Gail wanted to get involved with those people anyway? No reason was good enough.

The most likely scenario was that Gail had pissed off her date within the first few minutes, then stormed home. It had happened before. More than once.

She huffed her impatience. The woman treated her too poorly to put up with this.

Charlotte redialed. This time after the voice mail message, she added, "Call anytime. In the middle of the night is fine. Just a quick call so I know everything's okay. Okay?"

She pushed herself from the door, her aching muscles protesting. She skidded on a puddle of water. She threw her hands out to avoid a fall, and the phone nearly went flying. Her fist hit the corner juncture of the living area and the kitchen bruisingly hard.

She looked up sharply. "Okay, that's enough for one day, don't you think?" She spoke furiously to the cottage-cheese acoustic ceiling, but the only answer was a voice echoing from her past.

Pain is an effective deterrent. A useful training tool for animals. And what is Woman but the most graceful and lovely of animals?

"Shut up, Cory," she muttered aloud.

Charlotte pondered what to do. If anything. Gail *was* habitually inconsiderate. She often called late, cut short sessions, canceled at the last minute, and let Charlotte know in a thousand small ways she considered Charlotte a disposable employee.

But she had her good points. Plus, Gail might be in trouble. Maybe. It was hard to tell.

Charlotte flipped open her laptop. She typed in "Subspace." The screen lit up with definitions.

"Subspace (Star Trek), a medium for faster-than-light communications or travel." Definitely not it.

"SubSpace (video game), a two-dimensional space shooter computer game." Also not what she looked for.

"Subspace (BDSM), the psychological state of the submissive player in a BDSM scene."

Submissives secretly want to be slaves. Subspace is a slave's Heaven, to be attained only when they please a master.

All this BDSM stuff was triggering her unhappy memories of Cory. She fought against the sourness and unease that threatened to befoul her mood even further. Sure, things had gotten bad between them toward the end. But that part of their relationship was done. It couldn't hurt her anymore.

So, why were her arm hairs raised?

Charlotte shook it off and typed in "Subspace BDSM club."

Bingo. "Riverport's provocative fetish-friendly gathering place for socializing, dancing, ghost-hunting (on designated nights), and quality play in numerous subterranean dungeons. Subspace offers top-notch equipment, and our stern host, Master Martin, will welcome you and enforce safe and consensual kinky liaisons."

Charlotte jumped to her feet, then barely remembered to catch her laptop as it slid from rain-damp pants.

He was there.

With Gail.

Maybe with Gail. Charlotte moved, pacing again. Energy suddenly fueled her to bursting, despite the long day and arduous trek home.

She forced her mind from Master Martin to ponder the issue of Gail. Maybe Gail was with someone else, someone more dangerous.

The thought brought Charlotte up short. Why on earth wouldn't she assume Master Martin was dangerous? He was capable of anything, same as any stranger. Especially one in the BDSM scene.

But he didn't feel like a stranger to her. Very odd. Inexplicable.

The fact remained that her client might be in trouble. Charlotte sat again, tapped a nail against the plastic casing of the computer. What was the deal with that dropped phone call? It was probably nothing.

She should go find out.

Excitement and dread bloomed in her. She didn't care to examine the emotions too carefully.

Charlotte checked her phone one last time. No messages from Gail.

That settled it. She was going to Subspace.

Music throbbed, insinuating a sensual rhythm into her body through the soles of her feet even from a block's distance and across the street.

The club advertised itself loudly enough. Charlotte gazed at the way the large red neon "Subspace" sign wrapped the corner of the building, its warm light causing the misting rain to glow. Drivers couldn't miss it, and pedestrians like herself would appreciate the way it lit up a typically overcast night.

The city's downtown grime looked best in the dark. Though tall buildings prevented views of Riverport's photogenic bridges and mountains and the wide, deep Wilson River, downtown offered its own urban beauty. Club-goers and restaurant patrons drove and walked with purpose to their destinations. Others loitered without evident goal.

She couldn't help but notice the Salvation Army service building and other food and shelter centers. The homeless crowded the sidewalks outside each center. Many of the destitute talked on cell phones as they slouched next to shopping carts piled with battered duffels and black plastic bags. Dirty, but definitely not starving. Riverport, she'd heard, had won attention for taking care of its homeless. Downtown represented a kind of mecca for them, and they came from all over the country.

Once upon a time, when she'd worked for Cory but before

she'd married him, she'd gone to the farmer's markets and fairs, pubs and stores, even after dark. Riverport teemed with artists and students, crazies and tourists. She remembered enjoying their open-minded company.

Her comparative suspicion of everyone now struck her. Awkwardness and a sense of not belonging filled her. What was she hoping to accomplish here, anyway? These kinds of people could only hurt her.

Gazing at the club, she backed into a shadow, lifting her forearm to push away a long, moist lock of hair adhering to her cheek. She shoved both hair and raincoat hood back with impatience. She couldn't quite make herself cross the street to the doorway's black mouth swallowing the queue into Subspace.

She was stalling and she knew it.

But just as she'd psyched herself up to cross the street, a hand grasped her shoulder.

Charlotte jumped with a small scream.

"I found you!" He started to drag her with him.

She fought the man. "Let go or I'll Mace you! I'll Taser your ass!"

"Don' worry, Lizzie, I won't be mad."

"You're insane. Is the whole world insane? Do you want to be maced and Tasered and kicked in the nuts and . . . ?" She ran out of ideas for threats. But it seemed to have stopped him.

"Huh? You never had a violent streak in your body."

"I didn't?" She panted, trying to plot an escape vector. "Maybe I've changed. By the way, who are you?"

"I've been watching you." He peered at her.

He was older, grizzled. Rainwater made the slime on his dirty flannel sleeve glisten. His light blue eyes surrounded by red-tinged corneas met hers in a confused stare that rapidly turned demanding. His face was a map of harsh desperation and anger. "You're not her. I thought you were my Lizzie. Have you seen 'er?" A drunk's voice, but terrible with intensity. The hand, insistent, slid from her shoulder to her forearm, then tightened. The man—not a wreck of a wino though he was sour with old sweat, dirt, and booze—reached into his front pocket. He shoved a photograph into her face.

Charlotte batted away the photo. "Stop it. Let go!" She tried to yank back her arm, but the man clutched her, his fingers sinking in painfully.

"She's my daughter. Look at the fucking picture!"

She looked. "Okay, no. Never seen her."

"Are you sure? Are you completely sure?" His grip tightened.

"Yes, I'm sure. Let go!"

"The lady said to let go, Peter." The new deep voice warned of dire consequences.

Peter's grip loosened. "But I'm only . . ."

"Doesn't matter. We've talked about this."

Peter focused on her again. The wildness in his light blue eyes struck her. "Don't go in there."

"What?" She finally succeeded in pulling her arm from him. The man's intense, haunted gaze transfixed her.

"Don't go inside. Some people never come out."

"Okay, Peter. That's enough." Her rescuer had more bulk than Peter, and it wasn't just his long black wool coat that flared like a cape with his movements. Too permeable a coat for Riverport, even with the rain tapered to a drizzle, Charlotte thought irrelevantly. He had dark hair, also longer than normal. Dark eyes. He looked familiar.

"Just a misunderstanding, Peter. Like the last few times. You've got to stop doing this. I haven't seen Elizabeth, man. But I'll keep a lookout. I promise."

Peter nodded, finally releasing her from his piercing gaze. His slumped posture aged him as he shuffled away.

Charlotte looked at her rescuer. "What did he mean, some people never come out? Are disappearances common?"

He stared back with a frown. "A simple 'thank you' might be more appropriate, don't you think?"

She bristled. Arrogant men saving her from jerky men. How exasperating. "I can take care of myself." She heard her churlish tone. "Okay, you're right. Thank you. Do you often help the resident police force handle drunk and disorderlies?" She looked at him more closely. The unruly dark hair seemed familiar. And his large, slightly crooked nose, and his thin but expressive lips. She gasped as she recognized him. "Oh my God. You're Master Martin."

Her X-rated fantasy man. The sexually merciless star of her movie was now also her rescuer. Her nerves felt jittery and raw, even as her body tingled with the proximity to him. Dangerous. Alluring.

"Just Martin for now, please. Resident police force, at your service." He didn't sound happy about it. "Also dungeon monitor, rule enforcer, keeper of the peace, judge, jury—"

"And executioner?" Charlotte's arm hairs rose. He might be the last one to have seen Gail.

She took a step back from him.

"Executioner." His gaze tracked her movement. "There's a game I haven't played."

"You haven't?"

His lips curved into a bemused smile. "I wouldn't have taken you for an extreme player." He glanced at her clothes. "I still wouldn't . . . ?" He posed it as a question.

She wrapped her coat more tightly around her broken-in jeans and plain gray sweater that was a bit too loose for any attempt at a sex-kitten look. Gray canvas sneakers rather than black leather boots further supported her lack of interest in extreme play, she'd have thought. She'd avoided the color black for nearly a year.

The color suited him admirably.

She took another step back. "You're right," she finally

replied. "I'm not into extremes. However, I'm still going inside Subspace."

He scrutinized her face. "May I ask why?"

"I'm actually looking for someone. A friend."

He seemed to digest her comment. Then shrugged. "May I be of assistance?"

"I hope so." She shifted uncomfortably under his gaze. His eyes seemed to look at her from within the fantasy for a moment. His most attractive feature was definitely the eyes. She should've recognized those eyes right away. And the broad shoulders. Beneath his coat, she glimpsed a sliver of white. A nice dress shirt rather than the plain black one in his photo? She had a sudden, visceral urge to see him in just the shirt. To see the crisp white fabric part to reveal skin down to where the buttons started. To trail her fingers over him and feel whether he had silky chest hair or smooth skin.

She blinked, becoming aware of the sensually throbbing music again. Oh boy. She was in trouble.

Time to get away from him. But she couldn't quite bring herself to leave. The danger of the situation was palpable to her just standing outside on a sidewalk, much less actually going inside the club.

Dangerous for a number of reasons. If this man was involved with Gail's disappearance, Charlotte shouldn't make him feel cornered.

She angled her body away from his, bending her knees to give her maximum flexibility in case she needed to dart away suddenly. She could just ask him about Gail, but not reveal she knew they met for a date. Charlotte watched him carefully. "My friend's name is Gail. Have you seen her tonight? She went into Subspace earlier."

He kept his hands by his side. He met her stare levelly. "I've met a number of people tonight, but nobody named Gail." He sighed. "Still want to go inside? You'll need to give me a name."

"I just gave you her name ... oh, you mean me." Had Gail canceled the date? Or maybe she'd used a different name. People did, in these kinds of clubs.

Charlotte looked at him. He still hadn't moved toward her. Except to rescue her from Peter. "I'm Charlotte."

His stare was cool and composed as he nodded. Considering. Courteous but not quite friendly.

His manner seemed the ultimate in self-control. She couldn't imagine him even slapping a woman in anger.

He might slap one for a different reason, though. He might consider it foreplay.

As if hearing her thought, he smiled slightly. It reminded her of his photo. It reminded her of her reaction to his photo.

Her cheeks heated.

He stepped closer, and the warmth of his subtle woodsy musk enveloped her. His proximity and his steady gaze combined to disorient her. Fear stirred. Unwillingly, she again saw the movies in her mind. The remembered excitement hollowed her belly.

If her gift for matchmaking was any indication, she'd just predicted her happily-ever-after with Master Martin.

"Oh boy, okay."

He looked at her inquiringly.

She spoke quickly to cover her discomfiture. "Okay, yes. I'd like your help. As you've probably guessed, I've never been inside a sex club like this before. All those kinky people in one place. It's a little intimidating."

"Only at first." He lowered his head slightly, without taking his gaze from her. "And it's not exactly a sex club."

He started to walk across the street. Turned. "Follow me."

As he led her into the dark entrance, she thought she heard irony in his rich, low voice when he added, "Welcome to Subspace."

4

Down in the dirty, seedy tunnels beneath Riverport, the man wished for the hundredth time his predecessor hadn't left. Gregory had depended on his former partner, he realized, for more than the older man's boisterous, alcohol-fueled loquacity and ease with strangers.

The man had had a carnival-barker's ability to strike the right balance between horror-fear and titillation-fear. Gregory had less skill in keeping a tourist crowd interested in the paranormal without being frightened of it.

His contempt and impatience with the gullible ghost seekers probably came across, at least to the more sensitive of the tour groups. In addition to making sure nobody wandered off, or slipped a pair of the historic, dusty shoes into an oversized bag, or had surreptitious sex in a century-old bed, he had to dredge up enthusiasm for haunts and spirits despite having zero belief in such fairy tales himself.

But the tour guide biz paid well. Especially now that he had it all to himself. There was that.

Gregory gritted his teeth and tried not to think of the tons of cement and earth and steel above his head. It seemed to threaten to bury him and the ghost hunters alike.

Their fear was contagious sometimes. He sneered up at the unfinished ceiling. Contempt clenched his belly. The money these fools coughed up on a weekly basis astonished him.

Such an impressionable lot. His gaze darted with distaste to the darker crevasses, the filthy, dust-choked subterranean sections of Riverport.

Was that a chill pocket of air he'd just passed through? A teasing breeze, like cold fingertips? Surely not.

Even as he led the twelve people down another steep, narrow stone staircase, farther into Riverport's infamous tunnels, he found he needed to sternly remind himself not to succumb to their garden-variety superstition. The sheep could stare and whisper fearfully, point their flashlights and take pictures. He was above such ghoulish fascination. He had to be to remain effective. Or at least as effective as a soft-spoken man of above-average intelligence could be in such a position.

However, during the last few tours, he'd heard strange noises. Unexplained noises.

Gregory cleared his throat. If the undertunnels disturbed him on occasion, well, there were worse fates.

He began to speak in a soft voice very unlike his predecessor's booming tone. He noted with satisfaction how people had to strain to hear him talk about each chamber of horror and the ghosts reportedly still trapped inside. He showed them the holding cells, the woman-breaking rooms, the bloody remnants of glass strewn by unscrupulous crimpers.

Against his will and his wishes, Gregory's ears stayed cocked for the new sounds. Echoes and cries and thumps that owed nothing to the nearby sex club's bass music or perverted clientele. The odd new noises didn't belong down in this old, dirty tomb.

Gregory didn't believe in ghosts. His rational mind refused

the notion. Just the same, he felt his arm hairs rise when he heard the sound of a crimper's whip. The abductors-of-old employed cruel methods indeed. *Riverport's grimy past should remained buried*, he thought, then put the superstitious nonsense aside. He had money to make.

But when a woman's distant shriek stabbed the dark, he gasped along with his group. The scream sounded inhuman in its despair, yet muffled, as if time itself had smothered and filtered it. It had been ten long decades since sailors reportedly suffered abduction onto seagoing vessels and ladies disappeared without a trace. He heard the sound of a soul in torment.

Gregory cut the tour short, even as the morbid crowd murmured its awe. He hurried them out.

He knew the next tour group later that night would be even bigger and more willing to believe in ghost stories.

Gregory wiped sweat from his brow, wondering how he'd manage it.

The industrial rock bass of the music throbbed, bestowing a gothic vibe. Its rhythm demanded a sensual state of mind, as did the warm yellow arcs of fireballs twirled in dual circles by a fire dancer in the middle of the dance floor.

"Okay. Wow." Charlotte stared at the spectacle.

Martin shouted over the music. "Amethyst's talented, isn't she?"

Talented and gorgeous. The woman's hair, pulled back into a thick ponytail, blazed snow white with a streak of violet that glinted in the firelight. Her black leather cat suit hugged an athletic, graceful, and curvy form. The dancer made the fire swirl in time to music. Was she performing the dangerous-looking routine in high-heeled boots, too? She was.

Charlotte didn't know whether to feel humbled or jealous. "She's amazing," she shouted back to Martin.

She looked. Martin was talking to someone else, a large black man who seemed disturbed.

Martin straightened, then leaned toward her until she could feel his warm breath on her cheek. "You'll have to excuse me. There's a situation downstairs." For a moment he looked frustrated. He seemed to want to add more. But then he simply shrugged. "I'll be back in just a few moments. Don't go away?"

Charlotte nodded acquiescence.

The next moment, she was alone, surrounded by strangers. She scanned for Gail. Doubtless the plain, sour-faced woman would stand out among this crowd.

A mass of gyrating bodies packed the floor now that the fire dancer's routine had ended. Bright strobe lights stabbed at the smoky darkness. Among the dancing people, Charlotte saw a lot of black leather, black-ringed eye makeup, latex, piercings, metal collars, and more strategically revealed nudity than she'd have thought legal.

She jerked her gaze down and away from all the unexpected glimpses of clamped nipples and caged cocks and balls. But even people's footwear commanded interest. She'd never seen so many high-heeled, steel-accented, calf-hugging boots on women, and mean-looking, metal-studded Doc Martens on men.

Gail would stick out even more here than she herself did. A sparrow among peacocks. Gail always wore khaki slacks. Just as dull as Charlotte's own gray clothes still cloaked by a concealing raincoat, and her plain, nearly makeup-free face. Where would her client be? The bar? The open vinyl booths?

Charlotte looked as she walked. Exposed rock walls, irregular corners, and rough wood beams under the high ceiling gave a first impression of a large cave, but that was just the dance area. The light brightened slightly toward the bar. In two of the recessed spaces, nearly invisible to her eyes still recovering from both the strobe lights and the dancer's flashes of fire, she saw corroded metal railings that framed deeper shadows of twin stairways curving steeply downward. Where Martin had presumably gone.

"Hey there! Take your coat?"

Charlotte stopped short before the fire dancer, who patted herself on the face and neck with a thin white towel. Charlotte tried not to stare. "You're Amethyst."

The woman grinned, showing bright, even white teeth. "And you're Martin's friend?" She looked at Charlotte with interest, clearly waiting for her name. She finally shrugged. "Planning on staying? There's a coat check. If you want to stay."

"Why would you, of all people, be taking my coat? You're the talent." Charlotte stared back, equally interested. "Highly talented talent. Your routine was mesmerizing. Your coordination has got to be just about perfect. Do you ever get burned?"

"It's a risk."

"An acceptable one?"

Amethyst looked at her. "You could say so. How do you know Martin?"

"We met five minutes ago. I'm not here for him. Okay, honestly I'm not sure I should be here at all." Now, why did she just say that?

The dancer's smile set her at ease. "Now we're getting somewhere. Come with me. Keep your coat, but give me your name." Her arms radiated heat as she propelled Charlotte toward one of the booths.

"Are you always this bossy?" Charlotte didn't actually mind, though. And she could tell Amethyst knew she didn't mind. What a strange conversation, with a strange person.

Charlotte realized she was enjoying herself.

When they sat, Charlotte took another look around. Martin hadn't yet reappeared, and nobody remotely resembling Gail roamed the bar area. "I'm Charlotte," she replied belatedly. "Nice to meet you."

The dancer grinned. "Amethyst. But you knew that. Bet you didn't know I'm going to own Subspace soon. Soooo... hopefully I can convince you to give Martin a chance, and also put in a good word for me. And, to come back often. We need new blood here. Yours looks tasty."

Charlotte took a moment to compose herself. "Okay. Not into the whole blood-play thing. Or, um, girls."

Amethyst laughed. "Your kink is not my kink, but your kink is okay." She peered at Charlotte. "You've never heard that before? And you want to play with Martin?"

"It's a risk," Charlotte retorted, throwing back Amethyst's words. She wasn't sure if she liked the woman anymore. Amethyst had a strong presence, and Charlotte had to work to keep up with the odd conversation.

Amethyst nodded, though, almost respectfully. "It's a good reason. God knows I get off on the thrill of danger. Martin's safe as houses though—physically at least. If you're into risk."

Before Charlotte could ask more about Martin and risk, Amethyst added, "He's a heartbreaker. He lays waste without even trying. But not in an evil way, you know what I'm saying? It just happens. That aloof thing he's got going—women dig it. I warn people off the real predators. There was a dangerous one earlier tonight. So-called Master Kartane." Amethyst rolled her eyes. "Personal experience there. That creep has very strange ideas about BDSM specific to women."

If Amethyst considered him strange, he must be wild in-deed. "Mmm. Men who have strange ideas about women. Been there, done that." Charlotte looked at Amethyst's interested gaze and spoke before the woman could query her last state-ment. "So Martin's no predator?"

A deep, amused voice sounded next to her ear. "Martin's the resident judge, jury, and executioner. Remember?"

Charlotte stiffened, trying to control her reaction to Martin's voice and close proximity. "I do remember."

Amethyst rose, her body sinuous and enviable. "Martin, if you're done abandoning your friend here, maybe you'll be able to get her coat away from her." She winked at Charlotte. "I want more people like her at my club."

"It's not yours." His tone was long suffering. "Go away, Amethyst."

"Not yet, it's not. You'll come around. I can be very persistent. In the meantime, go gently on her. If you remember how. Then maybe she'll give up her ... coat." Another wink, and Amethyst stalked away with a swaying aplomb that made men and women alike rubberneck as she passed.

"Go gently? Were you ungentle with Gail?" Charlotte pinned Martin with a look. It probably wasn't very intimidating with him towering over her, so she wiggled out of the booth and stood facing him. He smelled nice. His face and his powerful, almost intrusive presence still mesmerized her. She wished her nipples weren't hard as little pebbles. What was it about him that drew her so strongly?

"I told you. I don't know any Gail." He studied her. "But your reaction to the idea of ungentleness is rather telling."

In the dark of the club, with the recessed lights making his eyes glitter, he seemed to radiate all the right kinds of danger.

She couldn't tell if the electrical surge flooding her body was adrenaline or attraction.

Not relevant, she told her body. She had serious unfinished business. Though he made it exceedingly difficult to concentrate on it.

He might be dangerous, she reminded herself. "I'm looking for Gail, or whatever name she went by tonight. I haven't seen downstairs yet ... ?" She let her voice trail off, making it a gentle question. She allowed herself one touch of his arm while nodding to the stairs.

He gave a sigh, and his lips quirked into a small smile as he nodded.

He guided her toward the stairs. After they passed through the noise and heat of the dance floor, he spoke again. "May I take your coat?"

She still had to raise her voice to be heard over the music. "No. I'm not here for a tour."

He leaned close to her ear. "I hadn't planned on giving you one."

Her libido leapt at the now-familiar, silky sound of his deep voice. She frowned at her reaction to him and the knowing half smile that appeared on his lips. He was entirely too arrogant. She was going to confront him now, and damn the consequences. "Look. I want answers."

"An interrogation scene? Delightful." At her look, he amended, "We'll be able to ... talk ... more easily downstairs." She felt his breath stir her hair. "May I play the inquisitor?"

She made a small sound of wanting deep in her throat. To cover it, she raised her voice, faced him squarely. "Maybe. I have to find out ..." her voice trailed off as his arms encircled her, grasping her rear as if it was his right.

Her first impulse was to surrender herself into his arms, let him work his fingers deeper into the crack of her ass, encourage him to grind against her front, hope he took her violently the way everything about him promised he would. Cursing her traitorous body, not to mention her insane mind for even considering it, Charlotte danced away. "Okay, hold it right there!"

He paused, hands up innocently. His obedience didn't fool her. Charlotte watched him with suspicion. "First, answers. Then maybe play." Had she just said that? She had. A sinking, melting sensation heated her more than her coat.

"I'll help you." He moved closer again. She supposed he had to, to be heard over the music. Probably. "I'm taking your coat." Fear dueled with want as he leaned in. He tugged at the bulky, concealing coat. The fabric slid slowly down her arms and swung free from her body. She shivered, though she wasn't cold.

He folded it neatly over one arm. He glanced at her body with appreciation. She saw his chest rise and fall in one deep, savoring breath. She wanted its broad expanse pressed against her. She wanted him. As if he knew it, he blinked lazily and brushed a stray hair back over her shoulder. His thumb grazed her neck and she trembled pleasurably. He stepped closer again.

Her body knew what it wanted.

Too bad for it. Her brain had to overrule her body, she decided, placing a flat palm against his chest.

For a wonder, he respected it. "Yes?"

"I thought we were going downstairs to look around and talk. About Gail. You have to help me find her."

"Have to." It wasn't a question. He seemed amused. "I will help you. For a price."

She shoved against him. It was like shoving against a cement wall. A warm, muscular cement wall. She spoke coldly. "You misunderstand me."

"I understand that when I touch you, you tremble like a warm, hungry little baby bird. Your body melts against me, then stiffens up, shivering. Afraid. Fighting against itself. Even your hand is vibrating." She snatched her hand away, but it didn't stop the honeyed torrent of his words. "All that heat and need. You have the kind of tension I know just how to work into an explosion." The way he looked at her made her breath catch in her throat.

She kept her head. She kept her hand to herself. "I'm not interested."

"Liar." He appeared willing to allow it, though. He even shrugged. "No means no, here. Unless negotiated otherwise."

She looked at him.

"It's true." He looked back at her, curious. "You really

haven't been to a club like this before. I wonder what's made you so suspicious. Who took advantage of your submissive nature?"

His proximity intimidated, but she stiffened her spine and didn't back away. "I am *not* submissive. And, for your information, I won't be coming back here."

"What a loss for everyone." He reached out, hesitated a moment. "Tell me yes."

"Okay. I mean no! I mean—"

He laughed too quietly to hear above the music, but she saw it. He grasped her arm. Not hard, but firm enough to make a point. Her body thrummed with a need she thought was gone forever. Fear rode hard on it, an immediate and irrational urge to free herself immediately in any way she could, to run—just so she could have the ecstasy of him capturing her. Claiming her.

She concentrated on taking deep breaths.

When she dared to look at him again, his gaze was soft as a caress. "I see," he murmured. He released her. He spoke with gentleness. "Who was he?"

"My ex-husband." She blinked, felt the surging bass of the music drive into her bones, trying to drive away the anxiety if only she'd let it.

She refused to let it. "It's complicated. The divorce was cordial and we've stayed friends. We share custody of my dog. Everything's worked out fine. Why the hell am I telling you this?" The words had just popped out of her mouth.

"Because I truly want to know. Because your instinct tells you to trust me, to give yourself to me. Because you want to know me intimately." He smiled, confident.

"You're assuming entirely too much, buddy." With an effort, she wrenched her gaze away, though his words continued to tie her into pleasurable knots inside. "I know nothing about you," she murmured.

Somehow he heard her. "It's early yet."

"Much too early for trust." She found she could think more clearly and speak more loudly when not meeting his gaze. Annoying. Unacceptable. She bore down, looked at him squarely. "Would you trust me? Trust me to lock you up so I can ask you some questions? I imagine there's some sort of torture room for that around here."

She expected him to take it as the hypothetical, smart-ass comment it was, but he just looked at her with kindly tolerance. "If it would make you feel better."

She felt her eyebrows lift in surprise, but nodded. "Okay. It'd make me feel better."

He laughed, a sound that heated her further. As he led her down one of the recessed stairways, she had to remind herself she didn't want him for anything except answers. He had zero hold on her, regardless of what he seemed to think. She'd make sure of it.

For someone who wasn't traditionally good-looking, he was awfully arrogant. True, he exuded an easygoing charisma, effortless intelligence, a wicked level of flirting ability, and a masculinity that licked out at her.

It wasn't just her who reacted to him, either. Women and men going up and down the stairs turned to watch him pass as if he radiated a vitality that drew their gaze like a magnet. Greetings were exchanged. He seemed to know everyone, have his eye on everything. Made sense, if he owned the place. Maybe he only managed the place. Not that it mattered one way or the other to her.

The music and noise of the first floor faded further as they descended.

Though the comparative quiet eased the music's assault on her ears, the bass still felt like gentle kicks to the diaphragm. Sexually suggestive rather than insistent. She realized she could hear her own feet thumping lightly on the steps, and Martin's boots, too.

Was that the crack of a whip?

She forced her legs to keep moving.

In the low-lit room they entered, four unfamiliar pieces of dungeon furniture, each positioned under small white and colored lights, claimed nearly half the space. And just in case anyone made the mistake of thinking the furniture was meant for casual lounging, the thick red ropes of velvet kept onlookers and passersby from penetrating into the dedicated play spaces.

Stadium-style seating lined one wall. All seats were filled.

Small vinyl booths and a bar took up a full corner of the large dungeon room, but Charlotte barely glanced at it.

She looked at the performance behind the velvet ropes.

A sadist spanked his victim. The middle-aged woman being assaulted tilted her ample but attractive ass up from a padded bench. The rose and thorns tattoo on her lower back was well displayed as she jiggled and gasped under the severe, two-handed ministrations of the tall, velvet-clad sadist. After a series of spanks, the man gripped a reddened cheek, digging in his long nails for a vicious clawing. He smiled as the woman yelled her pain. Then she wiggled and bucked her ass up for more.

Charlotte saw another performance. A nude young woman, clearly a bottom and blessed with a model's bone structure and thin, perfect build, was buckled onto a large, glossy black T. The dominatrix behind her, an athletic woman with black hair and a leather corset showcasing the muscles of her strong arms, lovingly wrapped a wide, black piece of nylon material over the top half of the bottom's gorgeous head, knotting it in back. The girl held herself as still as a mannequin, as if she was aware of her beauty and the mesmerizing effect of anticipating the poised stillness erupting into abused, galvanized movements.

Over the nylon, the dominatrix slid a snug and silky-looking black sleep mask. She adjusted it. She arranged the beauty's long hair to drape over one shoulder, revealing a creamy white bare back. Charlotte suspected it wouldn't remain that creamy white for very long.

Charlotte stared, hypnotized, until she felt Martin's hand graze hers in a light touch. She was supposed to follow.

But she had to pause again in front of the nude man hanging wrapped in ropes. The asymmetrical position of his body looked as random as if he'd fought the rope only to find himself more tightly bound in a less comfortable pose.

Two men whipped him. One wore a grin as he wielded a crop with no unneeded movement, not even enough to disturb the pale brown ponytail reaching down to his mid-back. He tapped the instrument with easy patience, repeating on one reddening spot of the trussed one's bare thigh. When the whipper paused, reached into a large pocket of his utility kilt to extract two clothespins, his grin widened until he looked a little like a kid on Christmas.

The older black man on his opposite side noticed the pause. He stopped flicking the single-tail whip against the bound one's back. Charlotte held her breath as the kilt-wearer brought the first clothespin to one distended nipple of the nude man's gleaming chest. He stroked the nipple as if it were a tiny pearl, rolling the nipple between two fingers. Making it ready. The man shook his head as much as the ropes allowed, the shaven skin of his face gleaming with tears. "No, no, no . . ." he begged. The sadist paused, as if savoring the moment. Then he snapped the first clothespin onto a nipple.

The victim screamed, then panted, his eyes round and shocked. When the second clothespin snapped closed, his body jackknifed within the ropes like some caught fish. He let loose a growling moan. Of pleasure?

"Okay, wow," Charlotte said, staring. She ignored the hot surge of desire at the raw sadism on display. She similarly ignored the sympathetic twinges in her own nipples. This was hardcore. "Is he...is that man...?" She turned to Martin. "Clothespins can be really tight. He could be seriously hurt."

Martin watched her. Charlotte suddenly realized he'd been watching her the entire time rather than the man in the ropes. "Things are safer than they appear. At least one DM—dungeon monitor—always keeps an eye on things. Also, Kam there is an expert with ropes, and the tension on those clothespins have of course been loosened. Only slightly, admittedly. Looks like they're still pinchy enough to command one's full attention. Wouldn't you agree?" Martin smiled at her with a speculating look that went right to the heart of her psyche.

Charlotte quickly changed the subject.

"This place...how big is it? That bar upstairs, does it serve alcohol?"

He looked at her intently for a moment. "Thought you didn't want a tour. But since you ask, the bar serves beer and wine. There are five dungeon spaces down here, connected by unfinished tunnels made of concrete, wood, and bracings of roughened metal. Four spaces are fully functional. Three have adjacent private play spaces. Upstairs there's a bar, a dance floor, and even a small bath and shower area reserved for patrons who pay a premium for the privilege. The oldest dungeon space is more for historical display, except for special occasions. The tunnels have been around for more than a century, but they're safety-upgraded in case you're worried. Would you like a drink?"

She digested all the info. "Not right now. Thanks."

"Would you like a tour after all? You seem intrigued."

"I am," she admitted. After all Cory's talk about these sorts of places, she'd envisioned a meat market of oversexed men dressed in leather and groping anything female as if entitled. A porn-shop vibe. A décor of latex, cheap bondage gear, and sticky blow-up dolls.

Subspace was bigger. Weirder. Cooler.

Classier.

If whips and chains and dedicated dungeon furniture could be considered classier. The décor and equipment here actually seemed to fit the description. So did the people, to her surprise.

She wondered what Gail had thought of it all.

The reminder of how she'd been distracted from her purpose made her round on Martin. "Will one of the other dungeon spaces you mentioned be less distracting?"

"You're distracted? Interesting."

"Stop analyzing me." She said it with a smile.

"No." He didn't smile back.

The shifting colored light played on faint smoke at the mouth of the tunnel at the far end of the room. He led her to it, through it, the narrow passage rough-hewn as if left close to its original excavated state. But when she touched the wall, her fingertips slid along hard plastic resin rather than real rock and earth. "Nice," she commented, but Martin was already through the tunnel.

She followed, emerging into a darker, narrower room. Its ceiling soared far above. On the ceiling, stars twinkled. She saw a ball similar to a disco ball perched high over the dungeon equipment. It created celestial pinpoints.

"Star room." Martin looked around. "It's an accurate representation of the night sky. Some submissives say subspace feels like flying into space." Martin nodded to someone. "A smaller room. Less furniture." He looked at her. "Less distraction."

She barely noticed the stars, or his words. She'd recognized one piece of furniture behind its velvet rope, a large X with tie points.

Cory had owned one of those.

"Less distraction? Okay. Please fasten yourself to the St. Andrew's Cross, there." She pointed to the X. Unlike the painted black T-cross in the first room, this one was raw, unfinished wood.

She remembered rough wood under her palms. She remembered splinters, and bruises, and pain that was sometimes pleasure. She crossed her arms over her chest.

"Cold? Need your coat?" He offered it. "Or, I could turn up the room heat?"

She shook her head.

He looked at her closely for a moment, then nodded. "The St. Andrew's Cross. A classic favorite." Martin strode to it, tossed her coat onto a chair, then nonchalantly tightened a dangling black leather restraint onto his left wrist with one tug of the buckle. Then he looked at her. "You'll have to assist."

He really was going along with it. She closed her mouth. This was a perfect opportunity to question him about Gail in a manner he couldn't escape or deflect. Or attack Charlotte physically due to a guilty reaction.

Not that she believed he'd attack her. Or even that it was likely he had anything to do with Gail's disappearance. He was too busy running the club, and he just seemed too arrogant to be anything but honest. Too respected by others, and respectful to everyone, to be a woman beater.

He might just be a very good actor, she supposed. Not everyone's inside matched their outside. She was proof enough of that.

She crossed into the velvet-roped area to the section of wood.

He laid his arm against the wood helpfully. He seemed utterly compliant, yet his presence electrified the very air around him. She frowned at him as a reminder she wasn't to be trifled with.

She leaned in to enclose his wrist.

Without warning, his large hand snaked around her head and he pulled her lips to his.

His mouth took instant and firm possession of hers. The iron strength of his hand contrasted deliciously with his lips, firm one moment and soft the next, fitting to her own lips perfectly. He kissed her skillfully, teasing the surface with sensation and heat. When he forced her mouth open with his thrusting tongue she couldn't stop the full-body response shooting through her, mouth to nipples to pussy.

His breath tasted like the rest of him smelled. Sweet and woodsy. She wanted to taste everything on him. She wanted to touch all of him.

He ended the kiss. It left her weak and confused. She found herself lying against him, savoring the feel of his body.

"Not submissive? I'd say you've a fairly thick streak."

It took all her strength to push herself away. She shoved his arm back against the wood with more force than strictly necessary, fastened him tightly.

"My ankles are still unsecured," he said helpfully.

"I'm not interested in your ankles." She felt her face heat after hearing the seductive sound of her own voice. She spoke with more harshness. "I'm not interested in anything about you except your answers."

She bent, quickly secured his legs. His sturdy black leather boots had metal toe guards and wide, rugged lace holes. Too bulky. She had to wrap the restraints around his large calves instead. The restraints could barely close around them, but she wasn't going to waste time taking off his boots. "Now you'll have to talk."

"The inquisitor has entered the building."

"So be afraid," she replied, unable to prevent a smile.

"You should realize you'd be more intimidating with some sort of weapon in your hand. A flogger. A cane, perhaps. There's a collection over there, and a toy box in the corner." He pointed with his chin.

"Are you always this . . ."

"Incorrigible?" He smiled at her. Pure innocence.

"Yeah."

"I've never let myself be restrained on a St. Andrew's Cross before." He moved against it. "Ouch. Splinters."

"Poor baby." Then what he said registered. "You've never been restrained on one of these before? Bullshit. It's the most common piece of S and M furniture."

"Interesting how you know that."

She remained silent.

Martin finally shrugged. "It's true." He looked her in the eyes. "You're my first inquisitor. Be gentle with me."

She turned her back on him. She went to the toy box.

Toys. Play. Was that what she was doing here? Playing? No. It was strategy, this inquisition.

She rested one hand on its red plastic. Her vision was strange, as if the heat in her body had risen to her eyes, making everything brighter.

She shook her head to clear the sudden fever, took a deep, cooling breath. And another, looking past the velvet ropes.

Then she wondered if a fever really had hit her. Was that Rollie? She blinked, staring. Impossible. Her coworker from Burger Town was here? And, Rollie was bald?

He must normally wear a wig. But recognition came from her coworker's slender, almost girlish body, his hunched posture, his unmistakable peaches and cream complexion, his same tight mouth pursed in concentration even though he did nothing more than lounge against a wall, talking to Amethyst. He wore an outrageous cloak and drapey leggings instead of the blue polyester pants. And, bald.

How weird to see him in Subspace. He'd be shocked to see her, too. Probably terribly embarrassed. He'd have to explain his presence here. So would she.

Amethyst said something to him, and he glanced toward Charlotte.

Charlotte pulled her gaze from him, pretending to examine the stars on the ceiling. Then she stole a look.

Rollie was walking quickly away. Amethyst waved to her.

Charlotte exhaled. She waved back.

"Okay." She muttered to herself. "He might not have seen me." In the toy box she found a lightweight wooden paddle slightly longer than a hairbrush. Instead of bristles, it had several small round holes in the wood.

When Cory had first started insisting on running a Gorean household, he'd bought the St. Andrew's Cross. Then he'd brought home other things: slave whips, snake whips, slave bracelets and shackles, electrical prods, cages, leashes, gags, hoods... and, of course, the slave brand.

She dropped the paddle back into the toy box, selected a long, red prod. It hummed when she pressed a button. Battery-powered zapper. She knew a little about this one.

Charlotte presented the prod, putting it before Martin's gaze the way Cory had always first displayed his tools to her.

Martin's stretched-out masculine form tempted her. She wanted to run her hands over it, caress it with tongue and teeth and lips. Not zap it with something Cory had called a slave prod.

But if Martin wanted to play this silly game and make her life difficult rather than simply answering her questions, she'd play. For Gail.

She pressed the button again, experimentally. She could tell he heard the buzz by the way his eyes flicked to the device. "I don't want to do this," she told him. "But I do have to question you, and you'd better be more open with me than you have been. Okay?"

"Sure thing."

She scowled at his tone. "Martin, where did you last see Gail? Gail Luskind. She saw your dating site profile and made arrangements to meet you here at Subspace."

She saw his reaction. Then his eyes hooded slightly. "How exactly is her dating or sex life any of your business?"

Her heart sank. He was avoiding the question. That was a bad sign. "I'm the one asking the questions."

He closed his eyes in a long, slow blink. Now he appeared to be as relaxed as if he were stretched out on a warm, sandy beach rather than strapped to a wooden cross. "The woman called herself something else—I won't compromise her privacy by telling you her scene name. She wasn't at all what I'd expected. It's people like her that make Internet dating aggravating. She was brief and charming online and on the phone. But she was completely differently in person." He flicked his gaze to Charlotte. "I wouldn't have taken the two of you for buddies. She's shrill and pushy and shrewish. You're very different... hmmm."

Resisting the temptation to ask Martin what he considered different about her, Charlotte said, "So, you've met Gail. Did you hurt her? Where is she now?"

"Hurt her?" He stared at Charlotte with a frown. "I don't believe so. But you're not offering the proper incentive for me to talk." He shifted, indolent. Challenging her.

Her gaze dropped involuntarily to the X of his body, to where his black pants would've made his penis size a mystery if the cross weren't positioned directly under a light. The shadows made his facial features more craggy and dangerous, his muscles more defined, and his cock a small mountain.

He caught her glance. "I'm completely at your mercy," he teased. "Do your worst." He wiggled his hands, making the chains attached to the leather restraints rattle. "But I have to warn you, I won't talk. I never kiss and tell."

She lifted the prod. "You kissed her? What else did you do?"

"It's just an expression."

"So, did you kiss her?"

He remained silent.

"You think I won't do this." She made herself think of Gail, and how this smug man before her wouldn't say what had happened to her. Or where she'd gone. Or whether or not he'd kissed her. "You're wrong to think I won't." Before she could think about it too deeply, she made herself press the button and touch the prod to the exposed skin above his manacled wrist.

The pop of static electricity discharging made her jump. There was tiny puff of smoke. The smell of ozone filled her nostrils. The sound and scent brought memories of all the times Cory had disciplined her. How disappointed he'd been in her.

She found herself staring at the small, red welt on Martin's forearm. She'd made that. She could make more. He couldn't stop her.

It felt nice to be totally in control. Completely, 100 percent in charge. And yet . . .

Martin eyed the tiny welt. He sighed. "Is that all?" He still appeared completely relaxed. Maybe the electrical zap didn't sting as much as she remembered.

"No." She hoped she sounded fierce. "There's more where that came from." She stared at his muscles, his body.

She realized suddenly that she felt jealous of him. She wanted to switch places with Martin. She wanted him to torment and toy with her. She wanted him the way she'd once wanted Cory.

This was the correct man to take her brutally, like in her fantasies.

The movie said so.

How utterly annoying.

She quickly drew back Martin's sleeve, exposing more of his flesh. "You started this. I'll keep going as long as I have to. Please, just tell me where Gail went. Did you see her make a call? Did you see anything at all? I need to know."

"I'm sorry. Subspace patrons expect privacy."

"What are you hiding?" she demanded.

"Ah. Now you're starting to sound more like her. Shrill. Bossy." He grinned at Charlotte.

She felt her temper rise. "Fine." She pressed the button, letting him hear the hum of power. She placed the tip of the prod on top of the welt she'd already made. This time he flinched slightly at the spark, but she steeled herself as the puff of ozone-scented air wafted up. She held the instrument still, then listened to the multiple pops as she drew it slowly up his arm. That had to hurt.

When she stopped, she viewed the dark pink line she'd drawn on his arm from wrist to elbow. It stood out against the dark ivory of the underside of his muscular forearm.

He flexed, and the welt shifted. The pink line looked suddenly small and insignificant. But he nodded, approving. "Nice work! I always wondered what that one felt like. Usually I work with canes, clamps, and the more advanced electrical toys. I'm afraid that tiny zapper has been gathering dust for a while."

His praise gratified her, then, swiftly on the heels of the emotion, perplexed her. Tiny zapper? Did he think she was going easy on him?

Why should she care what he thought of her?

She flung the zapper toward the other toys.

He tsked. "Care for the equipment, little one. Treat toys gently. But you. You don't want to be treated gently, do you." It wasn't a question.

"Don't call me that."

"What? 'Little one'? But you are. I'm bigger and stronger than you, and you like that. Your body is so slender, so submissive. So eager to be overpowered in all the best ways."

She started, feeling naked before him. He couldn't know. The core of her clenched pleasurably in response to his strength even as her mind pondered the problem of it.

She glared at him. "Do I need a bigger stick with you?"

He smiled with honest good humor. His laughing eyes, the quick flash of even, white teeth transformed him into something handsome for a moment. She couldn't miss his look of approval. "No, Charlotte. I just wanted to see you in action. You haven't got a sadistic bone in your body. A submissive all the way through. One with special interests. Let's switch places. I promise I'll give you exactly what you crave."

His gaze held hers calmly, in silent expectation. A predator waiting for its prey to offer itself up to him.

The tight, familiar knot within her begged for the kind of release he offered.

It would be the beginning of disaster.

She stared at him, feeling the panic rise. She craved him. She wanted nothing more than to bring the scenes in that movie to life.

She backed away.

Martin's brows knit in concern. "You're pale. Let me out."

"Hell no." She took another step away. "If Gail's here, I'll find her on my own. If she's missing, or if she's hurt"—she turned, spoke over her shoulder—"the police will be the ones interrogating you." She walked quickly away, deeper into Subspace.

5

Gail had to pee.

She drew her legs up tighter against her chest, pushing herself as deeply into the farthest corner of her sheet metal–lined cell as she could. A small, irregular square window at eyeball height let in the only dim light from the larger space.

She'd repeatedly tried the old, narrow door. Rattled it, pulled it, pushed it. Finally kicked it with all her strength. For all its age, it was solid and solidly latched.

She eyed the two buckets near the door. One contained clean water. She'd been instructed to use the other when needed.

When, he'd said. Not if.

Anger, always present in her lately, it seemed, spiked to rage. "I have to use the bathroom!"

No one answered.

The handsome blond with the angelic eyes—Kartane, he'd called himself—didn't answer.

Neither did the heavy-handed drunk jerk who'd tried to haul her away outside the club.

Her intended date, a man who lost interest in her within a personal record of a minute or two, certainly didn't answer.

No one cared. No one had ever cared for her, not for as long as she could remember. Gail sank lower into depression. It had to be her fault. She was the common denominator. Was she repulsive? She must be.

Once upon a time, it hadn't mattered what anyone else thought. People were wrong, shallow, short-sighted, stupid. But the longer she spent alone, friendless and without a mate anywhere on the face of the earth, the more it started to matter. She should've mended all those breaks with family and friends who'd displeased her.

It mattered now especially. There was nobody to look out for her.

Nobody but her dating coach.

Charlotte had tried to talk her out of coming to Subspace.

Well, she hadn't tried hard enough, Gail decided.

Gail leapt to the door, slammed her hand against the metal. It made an ear-splitting gong. "I don't want to pee in a bucket! Let me out of here. Let me out!" Surely the annoying sound would bring someone. She banged again.

The sounds were a cacophony magnified by the near tomb-like darkness. They echoed in the larger underground space outside her cell. She listened but no footsteps approached. She could hear the muted murmurs and occasional spike of laughter from distant people, and the persistent deeper thump of bass. From the Subspace club or from some other building? Too far away to do any good, at any rate.

There were some closer, less identifiable noises. Scrapes and metal rattles and the periodic gurgle of water, perhaps in the overhead pipes? She knew she was still underground. But where exactly?

She turned to squint in the darkness at the two white plastic buckets.

Perfectly ordinary buckets. Useful for basement storage of bulk products, for carrying gardening seeds and supplies, for various and sundry tasks like capturing the bagged crap from the grassy walk where her neighbors' dogs insisted on shitting. She didn't get along with her neighbors. She didn't get along with anyone.

But that didn't mean she should have to piss in a bucket.

At first she'd let Kartane lead her down some stairs and through the club's labyrinth of chambers. She'd been infatuated with his looks, his attentiveness, his sympathy after Martin rejected her.

He'd taken her to that one dirty chamber with the old furniture. A storage room, she'd thought at the time, but on second thought it'd looked more like a dusty museum. Strange shapes. Old things. It was while looking at what could only be an open iron maiden with real spikes that she'd finally come to her senses. Balked. She'd surreptitiously speed-dialed Charlotte.

He'd never even slowed. The phone fell from her hand when he slung her over his shoulder and simply carried her the rest of the way. She'd bumped her head on a sharp edge on a sloped ceiling, but despite the dizziness that threatened to drag her into unconsciousness she heard the sound of wood grinding against rock. A door, a secret door. There'd been a tunnel beyond it, twists and turns, then this place. Wherever it was.

She eyed the buckets. Her scheduled date hadn't been as politically progressive as she was—she found that out right away, since she liked to ask about it first, get it out in the open. It was a priority for her. Things had sure gone downhill fast. She resolved anew never to have anything to do with men who didn't share her politics. It never worked out.

It was all Charlotte's fault. Gail would tell her so right before firing her, then maybe having her arrested by the police who'd show up soon.

Any minute.

Kartane actually expected her to use a bucket. It would be unhygienic. Simply the idea was the most humiliating thing ever to occur to Gail in her entire life. Where the heck were the police?

She jumped at the door the moment she heard the footsteps. "Help! I'm in here! Over here, can you hear me?" She banged her fist against the metal roughly bracketing the thick door.

The door flew open and more light illuminated her cell. She backed away.

Kartane stood, his eyes narrowed. "I believe I told you to be silent." The now-familiar spicy scent of his cologne wafted from him. His shirt was streaked with brown dirt. His blond hair no longer lay neatly, instead tufting up in unkempt little spikes. He still seemed angelic-looking, but like a fallen angel now.

There had to be some mistake. No one so pretty should look at her with such anger and contempt.

His lovely eyes pinned her. "You will do what I say." A simple statement of fact.

He looked at her crossing and uncrossing her legs. His smile made her heart leap inappropriately, and his voice was pure caramel in its amusement. "You have to use the bucket. Proceed to do so."

Gail tried not to be too obvious about squeezing her thighs together. Tried to speak with dignity. "I have to urinate, yes. May I use the facilities, please?"

"Manners. Very nice." Kartane examined his perfectly manicured nails. "A good start. My answer is no."

"Why not?" she shouted. She couldn't help it. Her need was urgent. His denial unfathomable.

"This is your last warning: No more loud noises. I find loud noise in women unappealing unless I'm causing them more directly. To answer your question, because you will leave your old life behind. The bucket is a symbol. One of them."

She glared at him.

He smiled politely. "You thought you were so sneaky. Your phone call to Charlotte failed. She was the only person looking out for you, wasn't she?"

She tried to hide her dismay. "How do you know her? Anyway, no, she's not the only one. As a matter of fact, I have a number of people who will miss me very shortly. My . . . I was supposed to meet my friend for drinks later tonight. She'll call the police."

He smiled more widely. "You're lying. Lying is punished severely."

Gail edged away from him until the wall of metal pressed against her back. "Punished?" She hated feeling so intimidated. She'd thought herself insulated from such unpleasantness as this. Through the ugly fear and the pressure in her bladder, she found the strength to push her body straight and tilt her head up at Kartane with what she hoped was coolness. "Charlotte got my call before you disconnected it. She'll look for me, it's her job. And you, if you're not completely stupid, you'll realize I don't belong here."

Kartane ticked off another finger. "Disrespect. Another punishment." He tilted his head, and the wavy blond hair caught the dim light. "You have spirit. It'll be a pleasure to break you."

Before she could ask what he meant, he continued. "Did Charlotte tell you we were once married? Earth-style, legally and all? I didn't think so. We were meant to be together from the moment I hired her at the magazine." He twisted his fingers together, then turned his interlaced hands so one set of fingers lay on the bottom, crushed by the top. "She was my secretary. Like in the movie? No, of course you haven't seen that one. But I knew when I spanked her she wouldn't quit or sue. She knew when I tied her up and took a whip to that sweet ass I'd never let her go. But then, ultimately, I did," he mused. "I'm beginning to regret letting her go."

"You let her go because she needed something different?" Gail guessed. "She got tired of playing games?" She couldn't imagine Charlotte enjoying being whipped and dominated. Not for very long, not even to stay married to this handsome man. What woman would?

Kartane laughed with abandon. "Tired of playing games? Quite the opposite. I wasn't playful enough for her." His laughter faded. "Not nearly enough."

His gorgeous blue eyes, bright white teeth, and his profile when he angled his head back to check on something outside her cell, astonished her anew. Such a handsome man. He could be a model. He'd sire beautiful children. He'd told her he was politically progressive and that he liked kids and wanted a large family. He couldn't be all bad. Or be that good of a liar. Could he?

She supposed he could. She still had to pee.

She recalled one other thing he'd said. "You'd told me you were a switch!" Switches didn't have to be in charge, they could be the submissive and obedient ones in BDSM. She'd read about it online.

Maybe all she needed to do to get out of this horrible place was show a little assertiveness.

Not a difficulty for her. "You, worm!" She assumed a pose she'd practiced early tonight before her mirror, widening her stance, throwing her shoulders out, and putting her hands on her hips. She knew she looked stern and impressive. "I don't belong in a cage. Get your ass over here, kneel, and beg my forgiveness. Maybe I won't punish you too hard."

Her heart leapt with sudden hope as he immediately moved forward.

His fist crashing against her cheek knocked her sideways. She clutched at the smooth metal walls to control her slide to the dirt floor. She saw stars as she shook her head, trying to focus. Her cheek flared with pain.

She fingered her face experimentally. "You son of a bitch!"

"Disrespect will be punished. You'll learn. Or you'll die." He was as impassive as a cruel master training a puppy. Worse. Puppies were too cute and fragile to hit that hard. She wasn't cute.

Horror began to sink its poison talons into her. She'd miscalculated severely. "I'm afraid," she whispered.

He nodded. "You're not entirely foolish."

"I'm not f-foolish. I'm dyslexic but I have a genius-level IQ." Her voice was subdued.

He patted her on the head, distracted. "The lesson was necessary. You're a spirited animal."

"I'm not an animal." You asshole, she wanted to add, but bit the words back. She looked up at him, cautious.

He nodded again, approving. "Better. And, you're wrong. All women are animals. Men as well. All of us culturally indoctrinated to believe ourselves otherwise. Women are simpler animals with slave hearts. A real man knows his mastery of females. A female such as yourself, who's never been forced to be a woman, will naturally have difficulty adjusting. You have nowhere to run. Eventually you'll submit to me, beg to be my slave, and strive with every fiber of your being to please the one who broke you."

"Broke me?" She scrambled sideways to put distance between them, struggled to stand.

He was on her immediately, his hand tight around her throat as he threw her down onto her belly. His voice remained calm. "Down, bitch." When she didn't stop struggling, his grip tightened.

In her fear, her bladder let go. As she felt the warmth of moisture soaking her pants, she heard him laugh. "Just an animal. A smart and spirited animal. One of an ill-trained lot of runaways, throwaways, and hookers nobody will miss. If you're fortunate, you might aspire to become my First Girl. After you're broken, of course, my silly genius."

He was crazy. Charlotte had once been married to this insane monster? Rage and fear and humiliation hovered in her mind like bees circling each other, buzzing, distracting. It made her thoughts more sluggish than normal. Kartane was no switch. He was nothing she could immediately understand. But she had to try to reason with him. "Please, Kartane. You don't want to do this."

He shook his head regretfully, and she dared to hope again. But when he laced one hand into her hair, pulled her up to her knees, and yanked her head back to examine her face, she couldn't miss the insane light that sparked and whirled in his beautiful blue eyes. "Slaves address all men as 'master.' "

She sealed her lips stubbornly.

"You refuse? Do without dinner." When he let go of her hair she slipped back to huddle in a befouled, smarting ball, snot dripping from her nose, afraid to look up or say a word.

"Excellent." He cocked his head, listening. A smiled played about his lips.

Through the haze of pain and confusion she heard it.

"Master! Master! This girl would serve you tonight."

"Master! This girl would please you better, with a sensual whip dance!"

"Master! This slave girl bellies to you, craving only your touch! I crawl!"

Gail looked up at him slowly, horrified.

He smiled down. "Yes. Others. You'll have to try harder next time if you want to hold my attention. Much harder."

The words popped out of her mouth before she could censor them. "I'm better off without your attention."

"Then I'll simply have to make the alternative worse. Enjoy your evening. I'll return when it suits me. Maybe in an hour.

Maybe in a week." That diabolically charming grin again. "Eventually you'll beg to be my slave. You'll beg for my collar. And you'll beg for my brand.

"Think on it. In the meantime, I have to go look for something important I've misplaced. Good-bye for now, slave."

His steady gaze was the last thing she saw when he closed the door. She jumped when the latch clicked shut.

His eyes floated in her mind long after his departure. The eyes that horrified her now despite their beauty. How could he have fooled her so completely? For all her intellect, all her justifiable pride in her education and selectiveness, she'd been stupid. As dumb as the bitch he'd called her. She'd wanted to believe, but look where it had gotten her.

Her jaw hurt where his fist had connected. She shifted. Her moist cotton slacks peeled away from her inner thighs, leaving an unpleasant coolness.

At least she didn't need to use the bucket anymore.

Gail started to laugh. Quickly it turned to wild tears. She wiped at her face furiously, miserably.

She had only one hope. She whispered it, plaintive. "Charlotte, get me the hell out of here."

6

Charlotte marched away from Martin, but her steps faltered when she saw Rollie again.

Across the sparse crowd of this dungeon's room, behind their own rope partition, Amethyst allowed Rollie to beat her.

Maybe Rollie had seen Gail. Charlotte debated the wisdom of interrupting him at his play.

No question, Amethyst allowed the beating rather than endured it. The rise and fall of Rollie's thin arm with the flogger showed his exertion. It made the sequins on his colorful coat flash like the stars on the ceiling. Rollie seemed to give the exercise every bit of his strength, but Amethyst all but yawned.

The blond woman glanced back over her shoulder at Rollie, her gaze contemptuous.

It brought Charlotte up cold. That expression triggered a familiar response.

Rollie paused and scowled at Amethyst, clearly not liking the way she was looking at him.

Was her expression similar to Martin's? To Cory's? No. It was something else.

It was the X-rated visions. One began to play in Charlotte's mind.

Charlotte swayed as her normal vision faded. She lifted her hand to feel for a faux-rock wall, then noticed too late this one wasn't faux at all as a sharp chunk of granite did its best to cut her palm.

She couldn't care less. The movie played: Rollie sitting naked in a chair, pale legs spread, his erect cock and vulnerable balls the subject of Amethyst's sadistic attention. Colored pins zippered his scrotum in an alternating red/green pattern. As she carefully threaded another tiny, sharp pin through the loose skin at the base of his shaft, Rollie yelled. It didn't sound like a horrified yell, or a complaining one. Just a yell, meant to express his reaction.

Amethyst smiled slyly in response, running a fingernail down the ladder of pins, laughing at his whimpering response.

"Charlotte? Charlotte!"

Martin's voice. Charlotte shook herself free of the vision. She didn't dare look at Martin.

His voice had brought her back to reality.

Amethyst and Rollie? Charlotte gazed at them. They didn't cling together in affection or mutual passion. In fact they'd squared off, facing each other with angry expressions.

"Charlotte!"

It wouldn't be the least bit appropriate to interrupt Rollie and Amethyst now, she realized. Charlotte pushed herself away from the wall, refusing to look back at Martin.

She absolutely wouldn't look back.

Would. Not.

She looked back.

Martin's eyes were hooded like those of a hawk, but she could feel the power of his gaze hit her. His displeasure radiated out in nearly palpable waves.

She shivered, glad he wore restraints.

Sorry, too.

She fled. Purely by luck, she avoided bumping people or hitting her head against the chains dangling from wood beams or knocking herself out on the low ceiling before the doorway to another short tunnel.

She still quivered with desire. She hated herself for it.

He'd called her submissive. Cory had called her that, too. And worse.

Maybe they were both right. What else could explain the erotic tingle of excitement at the thought of being totally at Martin's mercy?

Of his having no mercy.

She groaned softly.

The scar on her thigh throbbed its warning.

That night with Cory's brand had destroyed everything.

Did being a submissive mean she belonged in chains at a man's feet, a slave to his whim? If so, she might be destined to be alone forever. No way she'd let a man do that to her again.

And if her wayward body wanted to fling itself at Martin it was just a damn good thing her brain overruled her body.

As soon as Charlotte disappeared into the short tunnel connecting the second dungeon to the third, Martin reviewed his options.

They weren't extensive.

He glanced about. He rattled his restraints.

Here he was, owner of all he surveyed, abandoned and secured to one of his St. Andrew's Crosses.

His too-slowly fading hard-on pushed the crotch of his pants to prominence. No denying his enjoyment of his kinky diversion with Charlotte.

He enjoyed less her parting words, the ones about contacting the police.

He saw Amethyst still arguing with Ratty. The smaller man did have ratlike features, if one felt uncharitable, which Martin did just at the moment. Not that his grumpiness was in any way Ratty's fault. Ratty wasn't that bad looking, Martin decided. Just a little too small and sharp-featured for common taste. And odd tattoos decorated his bald skull that Martin was too far away to see. Martin wondered what the guy's out-of-scene name was. It couldn't possibly be Ratty.

Was his hard-on going down yet? Slowly, too slowly.

Martin'd call Amethyst over in a moment to release him. Just as soon as his erection didn't declare to all and sundry he'd been ditched at a most awkward time.

He frowned. Embarrassment was the least of his problems.

There was the blackmailer. Normally Martin would laugh at threats to reveal so-called incriminating fetish pictures—he simply didn't play often enough, and God knew there were plenty of wilder people to watch inside of Subspace. He hadn't done anything worth snapping a picture of in ages. But recent unfortunate ones had surfaced, to his chagrin. Ones of Martin testing his newly created adult toys at a brief appearance in a Subspace pet-play scene. The images were cropped to imply bestiality. They made him look sleazy and depraved. In a bad way.

The blackmailer had to know a lot about Martin's schedule. He must've bribed one of the women to secretly shoot the pics. Now the jerk threatened to send copies to the worst possible person: Martin's conservative partner at Pavlov's Pet Joy, the wholesome, mainstream pet toy company he'd helped start long before discovering his true passion.

The older man who was his partner would be scandalized, possibly disgusted, certainly unable to continue with their plan to sell to Savior Industries, a huge company rooted in religion and specializing in "clean, family-friendly" acquisitions. Their business relationship would sour and Martin's share of the company, if his partner was willing to buy him out, would bring a shadow of the profit it should've.

And Martin had to get his hands on a big influx of money.

But unless Martin capitulated to the blackmailer's demands and sold the asshole his club, that's what would happen as a best-case scenario. Adding injury to insult, the sneaky bastard demanded Martin's club for a pittance. A larcenous, token pittance.

Martin scowled, made a galvanized movement of frustration. Chains rattled against wood. How he'd love to get his hands on the blackmailer.

He needed the money he'd make from selling Subspace to Amethyst, plus the money from selling his share of Pavlov's Pet Joy. His mother's third recurrence of cancer was operable, fortunately, but the additional medical bills would break her if he didn't help.

If he didn't figure out something soon, he'd have to raise the money by selling the sweet house he'd finally bought.

Though maybe that wouldn't be all bad. He'd had the thought lately the modern mansion, private and set back on rolling grounds encompassing five lots, might be too big for a newly successful single guy like himself. He didn't enjoy rattling around in it alone lately. He kept busy, but... somehow he hadn't realized just how lonely he'd been until his encounter with Charlotte.

If he found out the identity of the coward who delivered his threats out of those different cell phones—one phone mailed to him per evening, all within the past month—he'd show him pain. He'd show him suffering. He knew exactly where to push and strike and pierce and twist for maximum agony.

Martin bared his teeth. Once per evening came the same bloody call at the same bloody time with the same bloody threat: Sell by the deadline, or else.

Less than a week remained. Martin had collected a motley pile of phones. Stolen probably.

He again felt the temptation to turn them in to the police. He reminded himself, again, that it would only result in those perverse-looking photos going where he wanted them least. Richard Corvine, the hand-picked business partner with his old money and old-fashioned morals, might even have a heart attack when he saw those photos.

Martin closed his eyes to slits, feeling his mouth compress to a tight line. He wanted to sell Subspace to Amethyst for a fat profit.

She was willing. She deserved it.

And he deserved the money.

It wasn't just about money, either. He'd looked forward to unloading the club for a while. The place was too popular now, crowded and trendy, too complex with petty drama compared to the gathering place he'd begun. No more ownership responsibilities meant finally playing like everyone else did. Playing with toys he made himself, adult toys, and actually using them rather than only demonstrating their use, then watching while everyone else had fun. No longer would everyone insist on treating him like an all-knowing Godfather figure, responsible for every little thing. He'd be responsible for his own life and his mom's happiness only, and that was all.

The less weighty lifestyle sounded like heaven.

He hadn't told Charlotte the whole truth. It hadn't been just his first time locked on that St. Andrew's Cross. It had been the first time he'd played in his own club for as long as he could remember.

Far too long. He'd forgotten the exhilaration. Especially with someone as intriguing as Charlotte. How he'd like to give her the rough sex she obviously craved. Hot and straight up in every possible position until she came with tears in her eyes.

There was his stupid hard-on, back with a vengeance.

"Hey, Master Martin. Ratty's being a douche. He's freaking out over those new clamps of yours. Would you tell him it's perfectly okay and I know what I'm doing—"

"Amethyst, shut up."

His words cut her off as effectively as if he'd slapped her.

"What did you say?"

Martin didn't have to look at her to see her outraged body language, her scowl. People didn't talk to Amethyst that way.

"I said shut up. Look at me. Do I look like I'm in any position to mediate yet another conflict? Can't people think for themselves for once and leave me out of it?"

"Sure. Fine. Sell me Subspace. I'll make all your widdle responsibilities go bye-bye."

"I wish I could," he replied, hearing the harshness in his voice.

Amethyst's vexation was evident. "Why on earth can't you?"

"I already told you, it's not under consideration anymore."

"That's not an answer."

"It's not the answer you want. We don't always get what we want." Frustration was making a dick of him, and he couldn't seem to control it.

She gazed at his spread-eagle position, at the bulge of his cock, and a small smile curved her lipsticked mouth. "Nope. Guess we don't." She started to walk away.

"Hey. Wait a sec. Hey!"

Amethyst kept walking.

This definitely wasn't Martin's idea of a good time. He pitched his voice to carry. "Ratty. Hey, Ratty."

The bald young man looked to his right, then his left. "Me?"

Martin shrugged, making his chains rattle. "I don't know of another Ratty, so yeah, you." He smiled with a friendliness he didn't feel.

"We haven't met." But Ratty approached, his coat glittering

and swaying majestically, a small-framed and nervous prince. "You seem to be in a bit of a bind."

"Amethyst was in a hurry to leave."

Something flashed in Ratty's eyes. "Evidently." He looked away, seemingly at nothing. Then back. "As I said. We haven't met. Officially, anyhow." He stuck out his hand, grasped the tips of Martin's fingers, and shook them gently within the wrist restraint. "Hi, Martin. Pleased to finally meet the club owner." He spoke with a precisely enunciated, matter-of-fact self-consciousness that Martin would have found fascinating under other circumstances. Ratty's flowing garments—the draping coat covering long, wraparound cotton pants—didn't disguise his frail body, but the lines bracketing his mouth put him nearer to thirty than the early twenties Martin had assumed. Amethyst liked her subbie boys young. And compliant.

He wondered why she kept playing with this one when it always ended in a fight.

Martin stared back, bemused. "The pleasure's all mine."

Ratty exhaled in a rhythmic snort that Martin realized after a moment was a laugh. "Ten minutes ago . . . sure. Pleasure. With Charlotte."

Martin looked at him. "You know Charlotte?"

Ratty continued as if he hadn't heard. "But now, maybe not so much with the pleasure? Let me guess. The lady left you. And now, you either want . . . to play with me?" Ratty gave an endearing smile. "Or far more likely, you want assistance getting down from your cross." He tilted his head, looking everywhere but in Martin's eyes. He examined the restraints. "I can help you with that last one."

Ratty grasped and pulled on the first restraint. Martin heard the slip of leather and clink of the buckle releasing its grip. He pulled his wrist down. Ratty moved to the other wrist.

The light gleamed on Ratty's bald head. Martin found his

gaze arrested by the tattoos. Now he could see what really gave Ratty his club name. A daisy-chain of lovingly inked gray rats appeared to writhe, linked tail to feet to tail, all the way around his head: a tonsure of rats. The heavy ink and intricacy of detail made Ratty look as if he had hair on first glance.

"That's okay, I can take it from there," Martin said when Ratty dropped to his knees to release the ankle restraints.

"It's no problem. 'Well begun is half-done,' and all that." Ratty quickly finished. He glanced up, caught Martin's stare.

"I usually wear a wig," Ratty offered. "But here, I don't have to hide. I can explore things about myself in an open-minded environment." He gave a shy smile. "Guess I'm trying to say thanks for the opportunity to meet people like Amethyst. As frustrating as they can be." He waited, obviously hoping for some inside information on Amethyst, then stood with a wry farewell smile and shrug.

Ratty turned to go.

"Hey, hold on a sec." Martin kicked away the last restraint and looked toward the back tunnel where Charlotte had disappeared.

He had no intention of letting the woman get away.

At the same time, she might not respond well to Martin's pursuit at the moment. She seemed to believe he had something to do with her friend Gail's disappearance. She also seemed inclined to involve the police. Neither idea was acceptable.

He turned to Ratty. "You've been more helpful than you realize, and I'm grateful. I'm ashamed, too, for not meeting you sooner. You've been playing with Amethyst for a while now. You two have an intriguing dynamic."

"That's one way to put it." Ratty shifted from one foot to another. "She thinks I can't top. She's wrong."

"Amethyst's an accomplished switch. I've seen her go deep on both ends of the whip. But, it wouldn't be the first time she's been wrong." Martin saw the way Ratty looked at him. "Oh, she's my best friend in the world and she has a heart of gold. But she's not perfect. Nobody is." He grinned. "It'll be fun to see you change her mind."

"I've tried." Ratty glared at a spot on the wall, making Martin follow his gaze. It was only one of the lighted stars. Ratty spoke at it. "She laughs at me."

Martin looked at Ratty, evaluating. "I could put in a good word for you."

Sure enough, Ratty's gaze jerked back to his, full of interest. But his words were more cynical. "She wouldn't believe it."

"She might."

"What do you want in return?"

"A favor. Something right away."

When Ratty didn't ask what, or react at all except to raise an eyebrow in inquiry, Martin's estimation of him went up. With such control under his command Ratty might actually be a decent top.

"It's nothing bad," Martin assured him. "Let me lay it on the line. Charlotte—the brunette woman who was topping me— nobody tops me." Martin stopped, marveling at what he'd just said. He'd actually let a woman top him. How strange.

He shook his head, continued. "Well, she got scared. Of me, possibly, or maybe something else. She ran that way." Martin pointed. "I'm concerned about her, and I also have information she wants, but I'm not sure she'll let me near her right now. Will you please tell her I'm harmless and bring her back?"

Ratty looked at him sideways. "Are you harmless?"

"Not completely. But I promise you I won't do anything to her she doesn't permit."

Ratty seemed to consider it. He gave a brief nod. Without another word, he turned in a swirl of glittering clothes and moved with a sliding, self-conscious gait into the tunnel toward the third and final room.

Martin stared after him. Ratty was a strangely interesting man. No wonder Amethyst was intrigued.

He took a step and nearly tripped over the strewn restraints. "Oh, no."

Traditionally, the grateful bottom usually cleaned and reorganized the equipment. Tonight that duty presumably fell to him. Martin muttered, stalking to the discreet cabinet filled with moist wipes and hand towels.

As he cleaned the too-lightly used St. Andrew's Cross and its wrist restraints, he remembered Charlotte's reluctant sadism.

The strong scent of disinfectant overpowered the basement smell of wood, rock, repaired water leakages, and thin tendrils of smoke from the upstairs smoke machine. Martin breathed through his mouth and made a mental note to order Subspace some different cleaning products.

He hoped Ratty fetched Charlotte, but not just yet. Squinting against ammonia-induced tears and wiping ankle restraints on his hands and knees was not the domly image he wanted to portray.

7

Charlotte stared at the woman in the bathroom's graffiti-scrawled mirror. Was that really her own image? Were those her wide, shocked-looking eyes? Charlotte was appalled.

The covered overhead light seemed a spotlight on the way her nipples poked the thin material of her sweater. The blushing red of the walls matched her parted, moist lips and flushed cheeks. She looked wanton.

She felt wanton.

"I want him." There, she'd admitted it.

Not that it mattered. She'd learned her lesson.

She hated how she wondered whether Martin felt the same level of attraction to her.

She spoke sternly to herself. "You are supposed to be searching for Gail. You are in over your head. Maybe you should just call the police, let them find her. Yes, call them even though you don't want to." She nodded for emphasis. The woman in the mirror nodded back, with a look of sadness and regret.

Decided, Charlotte slowly opened the restroom door, letting music and cooler air in. She crept out. Martin wasn't lurking in the narrow hall as she'd half expected despite her leaving him restrained.

When Rollie appeared before her with such stealth, she jumped. He'd seemed to simply materialize, blocking her path. "Hi, Charlotte. C'mon, Martin wants you."

"Whoa!" She edged sideways, carefully in the opposite direction as Martin.

Rollie slowly kept pace. "Yeah. I saw you earlier. I know you saw me, too. This is a long way from Burger Town, isn't it?"

She stopped. "I think you've said more words to me just now than in an entire day at work." Her gaze kept being pulled to his baldness. There were tattoos on his head.

He shrugged. "Nothing personal. That job isn't exactly a social outlet. Besides, I'm naturally quiet with people outside of the scene. Working at that place is just a way to save money for college."

"Well, it's not a career for me either, but I'm not completely antisocial." Then she remembered she was, lately. Frowning, she added, "Don't you get bored, off by yourself with nobody to talk to?"

"Do you? Oh, I see you make small talk, but that hardly counts. They're not our kind of people."

She started. "Our kind?"

"You're here too, aren't you?"

"Rollie . . ."

"Ratty. Here it's Ratty." He cocked his rat-tattooed head. "And your scene name is . . . ?"

"Still Charlotte. Just Charlotte. And I'm leaving. You never saw me here."

"Goes without saying. But maybe you shouldn't leave just yet. North Riverport is pretty far to go without a car. I could give you a lift in a little while."

She stared at him. "How do you know where I live, and that I don't have a car?"

"Uh. Well, you work at Burger Town, which is in North Riverport. And don't feel, like, stalked or something. It's just that I've seen you walking to work." He waved his hand, nothing to see here. "Anyway, don't leave just yet."

"I'm leaving, and if you're smart you'll leave too. There're dangerous things here, don't you know that? Twisted and dangerous. Even that woman with the purple streak in her hair—Amethyst." She was pleased to remember the woman's scene name. "Even her. I can't imagine that movie was right, that you'd enjoy her doing that stuff to you." She recalled the pins piercing Ratty's scrotum, and shuddered. "Ouch." She gazed at him with empathy and confusion. If he wouldn't enjoy it, then maybe her movies weren't always accurate. "You wouldn't enjoy her doing it. Not that." Would he?

"Doing what to me? I'm not just a bottom to abuse at her convenience. She might think so, but I'm not." His anger seemed inappropriate to Charlotte's comment. Everything about this place threw her off.

Another reason she should leave. "Good-bye. Um, see you at work." She rushed off before he could stop her.

She noticed he followed her as she turned left rather than right.

She made her legs pump faster, looking for an exit sign.

She flashed under an elaborate stone archway, then stopped short. There was no back staircase, here. She'd reached a dead end.

She jumped when he spoke to her. "Martin wants to talk with you. Says he'll give you the information you want. Let's go. I've got things to do. People to argue with." Ratty tilted his head, pointing with it, his body language urging her to follow.

"You can tell Martin I decline his offer, because I don't believe a word of it."

"Sorry. I've exceeded message-carrying capacity."

"Then he can hang there all night, for all I care." She beat back a twinge of guilt. "I'm sure someone'll undo the restraints if he asks nicely."

Ratty jumped in front of her. "Someone did." Ratty considered her. "I did."

"You did what! I have to leave. Now." Where was the exit?

She finally noticed the gray and dismal room around them. It belonged in another century. Large and lit only by dim, widely placed wall sconces flickering with bulbs made to look like real flame, the room appeared at first glance to be a storehouse of old furniture, clothing, and piles of dirt and debris. Hardly a dungeon chamber.

Or, was it? She approached a brick wall, with one small barred window placed low enough she had to stoop to look inside. She fingered the rectangular metal bars grown rough and pitted with age. Inside, she saw a single old chair sitting on hard-packed dirt within the small cage.

She slid her fingers back out, careful not to cut them on the metal's edge.

What was this place? Piles of rubble and bedsprings, mostly shoved against one wall. Crumbled brick on the floor.

She approached a half-rotted wooden cabinet with its lid flung open. A porcelain-faced girl doll wearing a yellowed lace dress sprawled on her side within, limbs akimbo. Charlotte slowly reached inside, turned the doll slightly, then dropped it with a gasp. An empty, jagged black gouge replaced one glass eye.

Charlotte tore her gaze from the small cuts surrounding the eye socket.

In the middle of the room, a tall, sturdy wooden post penetrated deeply into the hard dirt. The large well-worn iron ring attached near its top gave mute testimony to victims fastened to it, possibly to undergo punishments far more primitive and vicious than could be found Martin's modern club.

Or was this part of his club? The muted throb of bass could still be heard, but it was faint enough to allow other, softer sounds to register: surges of water in the exposed ceiling pipe and tiny rattles and scrapes of something small behind a wall. The air smelled of dust, iron, rotting wood . . . and rose perfume?

"What is this place?" Even her voice sounded different, dimmer, as if sucked into the cracks and holes in walls or absorbed by the dust and dirt. She drifted toward the middle post.

"Don't touch it. It's evvvil!" Ratty replied with a strange emphasis. He looked at her. "Didn't see *Time Bandits*, did you. Never mind." He shrugged. "This place? It's a basement, connected to what's left of the Riverport undertunnels. The original tunnels are gone. Or so they say."

She turned, looked at him.

He answered her unspoken question. "In the eighteen hundreds, an underground labyrinth stretched from Twenty-third Street all the way to the Wilson River. It existed to move goods from the docked ships to the basement storage areas. These days, the businesses brick off their basement openings for earthquake-proofing and security. Bad for business to have homeless people sleeping in your basement and stealing your stuff, eh?"

"Naturally." Charlotte continued toward the post. She lifted the iron ring, let it fall with a thump against the wood. She felt a chill. "This looks like the real version of what Martin's clubgoers play at."

"Exactly!" Ratty grinned, and she saw his eyeteeth were sharp points. Were they filed or just naturally sharp? "It's a real whipping post. You're standing on old blood."

Charlotte stepped away hastily, looking down. The darker

splotches might've been blood. Then again, Ratty might've been having a joke at her expense.

Ratty lowered his voice to a near whisper she found herself straining to hear. "They also called these catacombs the Goodbye Tunnels. Women were abducted by white slavers to be broken as prostitutes, and men were kidnapped to sell to nineteenth-century ship captains who needed crew. The crimpers—that's what they called the kidnappers and slavers—cruelly drugged and abused the innocents who fell into their clutches. Literally fell, from rigged trapdoors in the bars above in some cases. Then they punished the ones who caused trouble."

He nodded to a pile of dust-covered shoes, old-style men's boots and ladies' slippers. "Captors took their shoes. They sprinkled broken glass on the floor of the tunnels to discourage people from escaping and to leave a blood trail for them to follow if anyone did. Most of it's gone, but you can see some embedded glass glittering there in front of that bricked-over opening in back."

Fascinated despite herself, Charlotte stared. She could see something glittering. "This place should be given to a museum. It should at least be roped off."

"It was," Ratty replied. "You sort of went right through it."

She looked. Sure enough, a thick velvet rope, twin to those partitioning off the play areas, lay on the ground just before the archway entrance. "Oh."

"Don't worry. Those shoes and furniture and accoutrements are mostly just props and thrift-store crap. Some of it's real old though, so, who knows. Martin lets people role-play in here sometimes. And on Halloween he opens it up to everyone. Blood Orange, it's called. Next week. You going?"

"No." She shivered. "Definitely not." Did Martin have a thing for abducting people? People like Gail?

This place was making her paranoid. She'd seen all Subspace's rooms. Gail wasn't here.

Her rude client was probably fast asleep, completely oblivious to Charlotte's investigation on her behalf.

Charlotte looked around, found her path blocked. "Do you happen to know how to get *out* of this filthy torture chamber?"

"There's a shower and tub for Subspace VIPs. Martin seems to consider you a VIP. It has fluffy white towels, soap, bubble bath. The works. You could wash the nasty icky Subspace filth off." He spoke distractedly.

"Sure. Just what I need right now. A bubble bath." She tried to retrace her steps, but the mazelike room forced her deeper into it.

Ratty followed. "When you mentioned movies and Amethyst doing something to me, what were you talking about? What movies?"

Charlotte passed rusty cages hanging from beams between the old, low pipes. Then her fingers reached out as if with a mind of their own to trail along a towering, many-spoked iron wheel affixed to a sturdy pole jutting out from one wall's stonework. What might it be like to be tied to it, and at Martin's mercy?

She frowned, yanked her hand away.

At the far end sat a throne-like wooden chair with its sewn-leather phallus dominating its center. Her inner thigh muscles clenched as she looked at the big thing. Martin sported a phallus like that, possibly just as large, from what she could tell.

The scraping noises seemed louder back here. And, was that a scream? It sounded like someone being whipped or caned or something equally barbaric. Tortured by someone like Martin.

"Charlotte." Ratty placed himself before her again. "What did you mean about Amethyst and movies?"

"You don't want to know. You wouldn't believe me anyhow."

"Try me."

A small hissing sound and the scrape of metal on rock joined the strange sounds from behind the wall. "Do you hear that?" Charlotte touched the wall, tentative. She was pretty sure Subspace was in the other direction. "Think it's ghosts?"

"Enough." Ratty grabbed her. "What do you know about Amethyst? Tell me."

"Whoa. Rollie..."

"I'm Ratty, here. Use my club name here. Now talk."

"Fine. Ratty." She tried to shake herself free, but he refused to let go. He did loosen his grip.

"I have visions," she told him. "Not all the time, but once in a while. They're like watching X-rated movies in my mind. Whenever I see a pair engaged in foreplay or sex it means they're a match. Since I'm in the matchmaking business—when I'm not at Burger Town—my unusual skill has some value." She drew him close by his own grip on her, lowered her voice to a hoarse, confessing whisper that barely carried over the eerie sounds. "I see *fucking* people."

It jerked a surprised laugh out of Ratty, but he didn't immediately release her. "So you say you have prescient visions. Huh. You're really a matchmaker? You tell your customers about your special skill?"

"No, I don't make a habit of telling clients about it. My title is dating coach," she added with some archness. She gazed at Ratty. "Want to hire me?"

"You must not be too good at it, if you're working at Burger Town." His words echoed her landlord's.

"The visions aren't consistent. They happen when they happen."

"You saw me and Amethyst together?"

She narrowed her eyes at him. "You hiring me? I don't give details out for free."

"You're a con." He stared at her with disgust.

"I'm legit! I said you wouldn't believe me."

"You're right. I don't."

"Well, then you won't believe I saw Amethyst threading your ball sack with red and green pins, and you howling for more," she snapped. "Guess you'll have a Merry Christmas."

His grip tightened until she winced. "I'm not a bottom. I'm not a damn bottom. Why does Amethyst and everyone else in the world assume I'm a bottom?" He shook her, his eyes shooting sparks of frustration.

Ratty squeaked and released her when a large hand clamped down on his own shoulder. He looked at it and froze.

They both stared. That had to be one of the largest men she'd ever seen. For a moment Charlotte thought of the crimpers, wondering if a huge, muscular ghost of one were about to abduct her and Ratty both.

"Ratty, my man. Amethyst wants you." The large black man eclipsed a number of furniture pieces with his girth.

The name seemed to galvanize Ratty. "Amethyst, again!" Spittle made Ratty's lower lip shine. His eyes rolled wildly even as his coat's sequins caught the light and sparked rainbows. His scalp gleamed with sweat, making the rats seem to swim.

The bouncer shrugged. "I'd do what she says. She'll own the club pretty soon."

"Amethyst says what suits her. She can go to hell before I'll come when she calls."

Charlotte looked at Ratty. His hyperventilating breaths concerned her. He seemed so disturbed and so frail. She touched his arm. "Ratty . . ."

"Hands off, both of you. People can't touch me whenever and however they feel like. I'm not everyone's submissive. Do I have a sign on my back saying 'tell me what to do'? Push me, poke me, give me orders? Huh? Do I?"

The bouncer made his mistake then.

He tried to propel Ratty by the shoulder. "Enough chitchat. Amethyst wants—ooph!"

Ratty's left uppercut knocked the man's head back, and his

elbow jabbing into the man's diaphragm produced a gruesome retch.

Charlotte stared. Ratty's violence was as effective as it was sudden. The large man fell to his knees, still coughing.

But on the way down he grabbed a handful of Ratty's coat.

"Hands off! Hands off!" Ratty beat at the hand fisting the glittering material.

Charlotte took a startled step back—right into an open iron maiden. The sharp metal points inside the casket pierced her sweater and pricked her skin.

"Ouch!" Reflexively she flung herself forward, away from it. She tackled Ratty.

Who exploded in a frenzy of defensive kicks and punches. "Hands off!"

"It's me—ouch!" she cried out for the second time in less than a minute. Ratty had just punched her. It wasn't a hard punch, but it knocked her off balance. She stumbled back. "But I'm just trying to—" Her words cut off as her head connected with an edge of rock.

The blow to her head gave her the briefest sensation of tumbling into an abyss. She shook her head violently, grimly using the pain as an aid to cling to consciousness even as she clung to the rough wall.

A shadow loomed over her. She flinched, suddenly back in her slave collar, being put through her paces by Cory. For two days and nights he'd held her, "trained" her, punished her brutally for the slightest infraction.

This wasn't that. She had to forcibly remind herself this wasn't Cory come to hurt her again. Those days and nights were in the past.

People who let past traumas rule them, define them, were sad creatures indeed, she mused woozily. This pain was just pain. Some pains could even be combined with pleasure to enhance ecstasy. She had that talent too.

A diminishment to the spirit, on the other hand, had deeper consequences. No way could she allow more damage in the spirit department.

Nobody had better try.

When one of the two clashing shadows got too close, she tensed.

Not ever again.

She thrust herself toward it and swung wildly. She connected only with air.

She heard a familiar deep voice. "Charlotte? Ratty! Oh, for chrissakes . . . Ratty, all of you, stop it this instant. No? All right then."

A third shadow merged with the first two. Charlotte heard the sound of a struggle. Blows. Someone shoved her.

Her head connected almost gently with the wall. This time she didn't even try to remain upright. She slid down, letting the wall's rough surface scrape her. Its roughness seemed oddly distant.

On the dirt floor, she slumped sideways. She was okay. It had been the smallest of taps to her head.

But fast upon it, the shadows grew dark and all-encompassing.

8

Charlotte swam up from unconsciousness. Her head felt cradled in softness and her body stretched out comfortably.

"You're fine. Please keep still for a few moments, if you don't mind."

She barely knew herself, but she knew that voice. Martin's voice. It centered her with its tone of authority. She felt a light hand on her forehead. Stroking fingertips. She'd do whatever he wanted if he'd continue that delightful touch.

"You bumped the side of your head. Over here." The stroking fingers moved over her hair, light as a breeze.

She heard herself make a purring noise of contentment.

"You're lying on an examination table."

"Examination table?" Her eyes flew open, then squeezed to a pained squint. Light seemed to come from everywhere: white walls, white sheets, and various glinting stainless steel instruments.

She struggled to her elbows.

The hand's touch moved to her shoulder. A gentle suggestion. "Don't make a lot of sudden movements just yet."

She looked at his hand—just as large and capable as when

she'd locked it into restraints—then to his face. The compassion and concern in his gaze caused a surge of warmth in her heart.

She tried to ignore her response, craning her neck to look down at her body. The movement made her wince.

"I told you to be still. Stubborn."

She glanced up at him again, her vision still adjusting to the light. He looked good in the light. Capable. Sort of heroic. She blinked. "People were fighting. You stopped it?" She waited for his nod.

His hand radiated a soothing heat. "I'm going to take a look at where you bumped your head. You'll be more comfortable lying down for the moment." His calming voice and warm hand worked an odd kind of magic, and her body started to obey him even before she consciously decided to.

She stopped her body's movement. "Are you a doctor? I mean, of course you're not . . . you run Subspace, not a medical practice . . . but do you have medical training of some kind, too?" She sounded foolish and she knew it.

She lay down.

He was amused. "I've had some training in how to handle certain situations. CPR, first response stuff. This will be a bit bright, but I need to see your eyes. Look straight ahead."

She did, straining not to blink as he shined a narrow light into first one, then the other eyeball.

"Pupils react equally," he murmured. "Now, do you feel any nausea, any weakness on one side of your body?" She shook her head.

His sigh of relief made her smile, which made him smile in return with a cute, completely non-devilish glint in his eyes.

Her mild headache faded under his smile as if charmed away. She shivered, pulled her gaze from his.

She had to remember the danger he represented.

Her first glimpse of his stern look on that dating site had made her body throb. The memory of her fantasies made her tremble. Good thing he wasn't her type. She wasn't of his world and she didn't ever want to be. He was completely wrong for her. Also, he was strange-looking. Maybe not ugly, but way too intense. Not even remotely model material, she told herself a little desperately.

She snuck a peek at him. She had to concede that if commercials and magazines featured nonstandard guys like him, they'd sell more products. Such easy masculinity and commanding charisma paired with that cute smile of his could melt steel.

It certainly melted her. Made her feel . . . willing. And very able.

"Here," he said, offering his arm. "I'd like to see you walk slowly to that door and back, just to be sure."

"I'm fine." But she slid off the table. She shook her head briefly at his offered arm. She walked to the door, placed her hand on the doorknob. She should keep going. For the sake of her hard-won equilibrium, she should keep going.

Her hand tightened on the knob.

Then her hand slid from the knob.

He spoke as if he hadn't noticed. "We need to ensure you don't have coordination and balance issues, or any persistent feeling of being confused."

"I was confused before, so no change there."

"Yes. About that."

She turned until her back was pressed against the door.

From behind the door came the beat of music and, more faintly, the sound of voices, reminding her she wasn't in a real examination room.

She touched the smooth white door with just her fingertips. The room had a long countertop, just like in a real doctor's office. She recognized some items on it. Bandages and tape, speculums, a Wartenberg pinwheel, tongue depressors, reflex hammers, scopes, needles, thermometers . . . Even the examination table looked real, with a fresh paper gown at its base. Right above the foot stirrups folded discreetly underneath.

She lifted her gaze to his. "And now I'm more confused than ever. What's this room all about?"

"You can't guess?" His smile teased. He put on a white coat, raised an eyebrow.

"Doctor-patient role-playing?"

At his nod, she shrugged. "Not my kink. I don't trust doctors." She considered. "I don't trust many authority figures anymore," she added. "But I don't imagine you rescued me only to chop me into little bits. Thank you, by the way. For the rescue." She smiled and crossed the room, all the while keeping one eye on Martin. Even as she spoke she settled herself onto the table, nowhere near the stirrups, her butt making the white tissue crinkle. "It's very authentic in here. I feel as if you'll present your thermometer any second."

He raised a brow. "Interesting choice."

Charlotte felt her cheeks heat. "By 'thermometer' I meant a temperature-taking device."

"So did I. What kind of doctor do you take me for?" His mock outrage made her smile again. "Thanks for the compliment. This exam room is one of my more inspired additions, according to the feedback."

"I'm sure." Her awareness of him crackled like a force field between them. Every tiny movement of his, every nuance of his voice, she tracked with fascination. Maybe he'd elaborate on the delights this room offered people. Maybe he'd show them to her.

He only looked at her. Then, "So, what do you do for a living?"

She had to laugh. "Small talk? Aren't we past that?"

"I don't know. Are we?"

"I want to learn about you."

"It's good to want things."

She felt the pleasant tension of sexual frustration. "More fencing."

"You seem to enjoy it."

She sighed. Surely he could sense the arousal in her, the magnetism they both resisted. "I used to be a secretary." She found herself telling him about her short-lived job working for Cory on the men's magazines. How she'd fallen for the handsome CEO, moved in with him, married him. Then found out they weren't as compatible as she'd thought. How he'd eventually agreed to give her a divorce. How since that time she'd focused exclusively on other people's relationships. "So now I'm single and I'm a dating coach with not enough clients," she concluded.

Which reminded her of Gail.

She moved, restless. "I don't belong in this club any more than Gail did."

"How weren't you and Cory compatible?"

Charlotte's gaze whipped up to meet his. He'd gone straight to the heart of the matter.

Panic fluttered in her chest. What was she doing? Why was she even still there? "It doesn't matter."

"I think it does. I think it matters a lot."

"Pushy." She slid to the edge of the table, stood up. "Are you this annoying with your other patients? You'll drive business away." Her heart seemed to be doing acrobatics.

His voice became brusque, businesslike. Almost like a real doctor's. "You exhibit no signs of concussion from my visual inspection. I'd like very much to examine you more thoroughly. However, you can go anytime you like," he repeated.

When she lingered, he added more sternly, "You left me restrained and unsupervised. That's a pretty serious breach of safety protocol, not to mention bad manners."

"Guess I was raised wrong." Charlotte felt her energy surge, riding on a crest of fire. "You could've helped, you know."

"Helped, how?"

"You wouldn't tell me where my client is."

"Your client." He spoke. "That woman was your client. Not a friend, a client. You set her up on the date with me."

She just looked at him.

"You must not be a very good matchmaker. She wasn't my type." His eyes glittered dangerously. "You are."

She felt his proximity and her body's reaction to it. "I'm quite good, actually. I know very well I'm your type."

She felt reckless and lightheaded. She wanted to provoke him into doing something dangerous, to find out if he merited trust. She had the urge to run and see if he chased her. She wanted ... crazy things.

He didn't move, only looked at her with that damned knowing gaze. "What are you afraid of, Charlotte?"

"You," she whispered.

"I won't hurt you." He considered. "Much."

"Stay away from me."

"Okay."

She panted where she stood. After a moment, she began to feel foolish. "That's it? Just 'okay'?"

"What did you expect?" He gave her a mocking smile. "I like the way you think, but this is the wrong room for a rape fantasy. All we've got here is this examination table." He patted it. Paper crinkled. "Let me examine you."

She felt her mouth twitch, wanting to smile. She didn't let it. "What happened with Gail?"

"I don't know, exactly."

Charlotte folded her arms. "What happened with her, inexactly?"

"We didn't connect on a meaningful level. Or on any level. Have I mentioned she's shrill and annoying? She paired off with someone else."

"Who?"

"Ah, that's where it gets murky. See, I truly do feel an obligation to protect patron privacy. I can tell you she didn't leave right away, and I can tell you I didn't actually see her leave. She looked fine when she went with him downstairs to the dungeon play spaces."

"With *who?*"

"Privacy."

"Screw privacy. I want to know."

"Why?"

"Gail called me. An arranged safe call." Charlotte looked. Martin nodded, encouraging. "Then the phone went dead. She hasn't answered my calls, and she hasn't called again. I'm not sure what to think. I wonder if I'm overreacting."

Gail often sounded urgent, brusque, ready to pick a fight. Charlotte allowed the bad behavior because she needed Gail as a client. But wasn't it possible the disconnected call meant nothing at all?

"So it might be urgent. Or it might not." His decisive tone and small frown enhanced his appearance as a doctor. "You came here and you've looked all over the public places. All three dungeons. The bar, the dance floor. A bathroom. The play spaces." The ghost of a smile touched his lips. "Having met the woman myself, I'm betting she didn't hit it off with the dom she ditched me for any better than she did with me. In fact, I'm certain of it. He wouldn't put up with a woman like her for five minutes. She obviously left. She's not in Subspace now." He shrugged. "What more can she expect of you?"

"The world," Charlotte muttered. "On a platter. She's demanding and rude." She gazed at Martin. "She left you for another dom? What a foolish woman." She heard the breathy sound of her own voice. Her tongue was thick in her mouth. Her sex felt heavy and warm. She'd never wanted anyone so much.

"Foolish," he agreed. "She didn't belong here."

"And I do?"

"Is that what you're worried about? Something happened to you." He cocked his head, examining her without touching. "Something to do with your ex, probably." He moved, a slow pacing revealing an animal-like stride. It unnerved and excited her. "Something that makes you afraid of this place, of the kinds of people here. Of me. Yet you don't leave. I can help you. The table's over here."

He grinned, patted it. Paper crinkled again. "I'll do my best to help what ails you, but I'll need your cooperation. Your full cooperation." His gaze took her in from the tip of her head to the tips of her feet. He turned, walked to the door. His heat and scent, the fabric of his white coat brushing lightly against the sleeve of her sweater, made her weak in the knees.

He faced her and stretched, casually placing his hands up against the doorjamb. Blocking the exit? It certainly showcased his broad shoulders as much as the St. Andrew's Cross. "Please remove your clothes. There's a paper gown for your convenience."

Her breath caught in her throat. Fear and desire surged in her, making her almost painfully excited.

"I don't..." She plucked at her clothes. She saw his eyes track the movement. "I'm not sure..."

"I am. Doctor knows best." His evil grin hardened her nipples. Did he have to be so damn appealing? He made it difficult for her to think straight.

He would examine her.

New dirty movies rolled in her head.

"Turn around," she said.

When he did, Charlotte found herself stripping her clothes off, everything but her panties and bra. It was too warm anyway. Probably not the fault of the cozy exam room, she thought as she pulled the paper gown over herself.

She fingered the ties uncertainly. "Should I... that is, am I supposed to...?"

His calm voice, aimed at the door, carried just the right tone of dispassionate professional. "Do you require assistance? I can call in a nurse, if you prefer."

He probably would. A male nurse perhaps? To hold her down for an injection? A big, thick injection? What was she getting herself into? And why did she feel so exhilarated?

"I can't believe I'm doing this," she muttered.

"Excuse me?"

"I'm decent now." She noticed he didn't turn around until she'd settled onto the long section of the exam table, her legs swinging freely.

"What's up, doc?" she quipped. But when she glanced up at him, the knowing look in his eyes hit her like a shock. The air seemed to ignite between them as he crossed to her. Her awareness of him grew and grew, knowing he'd soon touch her.

She'd made herself helpless in a flimsy paper gown, and he'd touch her at any moment.

She looked up at him, schooling her expression to blankness. She needed this, and she didn't even know exactly why.

All she knew was his proximity made her jumpy in the most delicious ways. She wanted him hard, and vicious, and dirty. Just the sight of him watching her, taking his time, wakened senses long dormant within her.

When he let a full minute go by, torturing her just by gazing at her, she bit back a groan.

She had to speak. She couldn't help herself. "Martin, I'm not sure this is exactly what—"

"I have an extensive background in the treatment of many different types of afflictions, certainly including yours."

"Afflictions?" She blinked. He thought something was wrong with her?

Martin leaned in, let his large hand rest next to her bare knee. The very image of casual authority.

"I can and I will help you. For the rest of this session, you will refer to me as 'Doctor.' You will do anything and everything I say. If you don't wish to, you're free to walk out of here now. Is that clear?"

9

She considered leaving. For about a second. "Yes, Doctor."

"Very good." He lifted the hand to pat her shoulder warmly, then slid the paper of her gown up her arm. He wrapped a heart rate monitor around her bicep. He punched some buttons into the device's holder on the wall, and the encircling band tightened. She felt as if the air in her immediate vicinity constricted around her as well.

"Breathe normally," he commanded.

"Easy for you to say." The beeps began to sound in time with her heart.

"We need to give you a safe word, don't we. How about 'red,' for stop? Say it."

"Red."

"Yes. Notice how I stop touching you, step back, and check in with you. That's what saying 'red' accomplishes. Would you like me to continue this examination?"

She looked at him, knowing her mouth was hanging open. She shut it. "You mean, you'll stop. Just like that. If I say so."

"Yes, Charlotte." He gazed at her, his eyes penetrating and

wise. He nodded. "I see." His lips tightened and his gaze sharpened further. She could tell from the intensity of his stare he was selecting and discarding different comments. He clearly debated what to say next. He finally shrugged. "You can't tell me what to do, of course. Doctor knows best. But you have the power to stop me with the word 'red' unless we negotiate otherwise. I think your treatment is proceeding well so far, don't you?"

He'd stop. He actually meant it. Unlike Cory. She honestly believed she could make Martin stop anytime she liked.

It changed everything.

"Yes, Doctor." This time her response was heartfelt. The beeps of the machine came faster.

He raised an eyebrow. "Very, very good. But I see we have a problem."

A problem? She cast a quick glance down at herself, at the band which gripped her so tightly. It all looked normal to her. She still felt giddy about having control over any part of this, control over making him stop. She didn't have a slave heart. Cory was wrong. "What's the problem, Doctor?" She could get into this.

"I asked you to remove your clothes. But you're still wearing your bra and panties. I'm afraid I don't tolerate difficult patients in my office. We'll have to punish you." His hand came off her shoulder, landed again on the tissue-covered padded table next to her with a loud whap that made her jump.

Punish?

The beeps raced.

Then ceased as he ripped the band off her arm. "Normal," he said as if bored. "Are you a hypochondriac, Charlotte? Do you pretend to be ignorant, weak, and fearful? Or is there a deeper problem here? You crave a man to give you what your body and your mind demand. Don't bother to protest. You need someone stronger than you, and that's not easy to find, is it, Charlotte?"

She stared at him.

"That's what I thought. On your belly. Now."

The static of fear in her mind rose to a shriek, freezing her for a moment. It seemed to shout at her to go, to get out while she still had any sense of control. Cory had abused his power. Martin might, too.

All she had to say was "red."

But her body throbbed and yearned toward what he offered.

Her voice trembled, that of a stranger. "Yes, Doctor." She turned herself over, knowing she was giving herself into his hands. It felt as exhilarating as she imagined paragliding off a cliff would be: a leap, then simple hope and faith that what followed wouldn't be a disaster.

She felt his hand on her lower back, firm and impersonal. It drew all her attention.

His voice sounded distracted, a jaded doctor instructing his patient. "This may smart a bit, but I want you to hold still for it. Hold very still. Do you understand?" He waited for her to nod.

He pushed aside her paper gown, then pulled down her panties with the same smooth, firm movement.

Smack!

His hand landed with more noise than force on her bare rump. He left it there, pressing firmly. She gasped at the insult to her more than the mild pain. The sharp heat radiating out mesmerized her with its intensity, and the surge of humiliation changed swiftly into something else, something deeper. Something familiar.

The sensation of willing helplessness was a homecoming.

She squirmed with delight.

"I told you to hold still. If I have to restrain you, I assure you, it will be done." He landed another blow, this one landing in the crease where her buttocks met upper thigh. He let it stay for a moment. And another, harder.

She thought, briefly, of her safe word.

Red.

The word danced in her mind in opposition to the delicious craving for more of Martin's stern manhandling. Then it disintegrated, blown away by sensation as he spanked her hard once more.

Where his hand met her ass a delicious heat spiraled inward, making her clench pleasurably. It was as if there was a direct connection between the sweet spot where his hand made contact and her aching pussy. Her need forced soft moans from her. A languor rose, steady and strong in response to his firm spanks. He could do anything he wanted to her, anything at all.

Martin suddenly stopped. "The patient has to want to be helped. I can see you're making some progress, so I hope we can continue without further delays. Strip. Everything but the gown." He fiddled with something under the table, then turned his back on her to give her privacy.

"Everything?"

"Of course."

She struggled onto her side, then to sit up. Her ass tingled with warmth. She checked to see his back was still turned. She quickly wriggled out of her bra and panties.

Even with his back to her, his deep voice easily came to her. "When you're finished, place your feet in the stirrups."

"In the ... ?"

"Will that be a problem?"

"I don't think I can."

"You'll have to trust me to determine your tolerances, Charlotte. Unless you have a certain word to say ... ?"

She swallowed. "No. Of course not. Doctor."

"Then stop wasting my time."

She toyed with the edge of her gown. "But I can't just—"

That was all she got out before he whirled on her. He took two steps, then lifted her easily by the waist onto the table. "Enough." He positioned her at the table's end. His hands moved past her, pulling up two matching wide, white winch-strap style restraints. His hands moved firmly on her, encircling her thighs with the wraps. He tightened them with practiced ease.

He'd positioned her legs open enough she could feel every stray breeze on the moistness between. Heat rose to her face.

"This isn't necessary," she pleaded, horribly embarrassed. Yet her breath came faster. She tested the bonds. She shifted in a vain attempt to hide her exposed flesh.

He tightened one strap further, then patted her leg dispassionately.

Her only warning for his next action was a wicked grin.

Three long strides, and he was at the door. Opening it wide.

Everyone could see her!

He ignored her cry of protest and the crackle of tissue as she jackknifed forward to try to hide herself, then try to undo the tight straps. When both failed, she placed her hands over herself.

She looked up. She recognized the man standing in the doorway. "Ratty." As she said his club name, her face heated further with embarrassment.

"You're getting into the swing of things," Ratty observed. The brighter light in the exam room illuminated every curve and shading of the rat tattoos on his head.

She realized with mortification she was equally illuminated. "Okay, if you tell anyone at Burger Town about this, I won't leave you any balls left for Amethyst to pierce."

He finally averted his gaze from between her legs. "Excellent."

Martin watched with amusement. "Ratty's been waiting to find out how you are. He was concerned about you."

"Ratty can speak for himself," Ratty said, brushing imaginary specks of dust from his coat. "I was waiting to find out how you are. I was concerned about you." He spoke to the bare white wall beyond her. "I apologize for my inexcusable behavior earlier. I think I hit you . . . ?"

She'd forgotten. Her hands started to her face automatically before she remembered what they were covering. She kept her hands in place. Her jaw felt only slightly sore when she spoke. "Not very hard."

Ratty's own jaw worked, clenching and unclenching. Finally he spoke. "I don't know what came over me. I'm so sorry. It's utterly unacceptable. Amethyst made me lose it tonight, and then it was like people kept flinging her in my face. She makes me question . . . well, never mind. I should just stay away from Amethyst."

"Probably," Charlotte agreed. "I would. She'll hurt you. I suppose you like it, though." Was he ever going to leave?

Ratty's shoulders slumped. "I know. Your visions. Just let me know when I can ever make it up to you . . . ?" He looked at her, noticed her expression. "Yeah. Okay. I should—" Ratty waved his hand in the air in the direction of the club.

When he'd left, Martin closed the door again. Charlotte kept her hands in place. "You had him standing outside the door this whole time?" She looked at Martin accusingly. "You could have covered me, you know."

"I chose not to." Before she could process that, Martin added, "Ratty waited to apologize to you."

"He should apologize. He was out of control."

"Would you like me to ban him from Subspace? I could, if it would satisfy you. But I'd prefer not to."

"Why would you prefer not to?"

"Because he was willing to wait to apologize, possibly for hours, as penance for his actions. And because he's still outside the door keeping an eye on things for me so I can have some time alone with you. Furthermore, I believe he's good people. Troubled at the moment, perhaps. Currently struggling with his sexual identity, definitely. Amethyst is, of course, not helping him. Amethyst could provoke the Dalai Lama into a rage," he confided with a smile. "So, it's your choice. I can ban him immediately and permanently. Or . . ."

Martin walked, ever so slowly, back to the table. He spoke softly. "Or we can let him play guard, while we play doctor-patient."

"That last one." She breathed in his warmth and scent.

"I thought so. But first. What is this 'visions' business in regard to Amethyst?"

"What do I say if I want to change the subject? Yellow?"

"Yellow means to pause, check in, possibly stop. Do you want to stop?"

She looked at him. "No."

"You're very distracting like that, you know." His voice, deeper and more sensual, sent a ripple of awareness through her. "I don't want to cover you up, Charlotte. I want to uncover more of you. Explore you." His fingers grazed her neck, pushing the paper gown down her shoulders, her arms, until the garment pooled uselessly at her elbows. Only the outside of her thighs were still covered.

It reminded her of her scar.

She kept her hands in place. "I suppose you want to finish examining me."

"Astute of you." He grasped both her slender wrists with one large hand. He lifted them above her head.

She felt a gasping sensation of pleasure at his dominance. He made her feel so exposed, so small before him, so helpless. So entirely turned on. "Please," she whispered, even as she twisted and tested the strength of his grip.

"You want this, but you fight me." He tightened his hold, shook her slightly. Her breasts jiggled, bare as the rest of her, but he didn't take his gaze from her eyes. "You're all but flying into subspace, just sitting there. And I know exactly why."

A pleasant languor suffused her. "Do tell me why."

He let go of her wrists. She immediately felt the loss of his sturdy grip. Her arms remained in the air for a moment, making her cooperation obvious. She lowered them quickly to her thighs. She refused to cover herself like some embarrassed schoolgirl.

"Because you trust me."

"I barely know you." She wished he'd step just a little closer to her. Being handled that way by him had her in a state of arousal she'd never experienced before. If only he'd take the one tiny step to close the distance completely, put that delicious-looking bulge between her spread thighs.

"Doesn't matter. You can tell I'm not like your ex. No." He arrested the movement of her hands to cover herself after all.

She raised her chin to him, rebellious yet nervous and curious.

He patted her hands gently. Too gently.

She craved . . . something overpowering. Something beyond the physical thrust of his body into hers, though that would be gratifying.

"Tell me what happened with your ex."

Her frustrated exhale made Martin smile. "Whatever it is, it can't be that bad."

"It's that bad."

"I'll judge for myself." He stepped closer, as if unable to help himself. She could feel the heat radiating from his body. She tried to wiggle her body closer to his.

"Charlotte?" He tilted her head up to his, looked deeply into her eyes. "Your fear and lust radiate on a certain, special wavelength. People like me pick up on it." He took the tiny step closer, which effectively ended the second thoughts starting to rise in her mind. His enormous bulge pressed firmly against where she wanted it most.

"Feel, Charlotte. I know you want this, too, and everything else I can make you feel. So tell me, what is it you keep thinking that makes you frown even when your body's begging for mine? Hmmm?" He thrust against her, once.

She gasped at the pleasure of it. She tried desperately to remain in control. "I'm not a submissive."

"There's no shame in being a submissive."

"There is. Shame and danger. I don't have a slave's heart."

"The ex."

"Yes."

"You're my patient here, tonight. Not my slave." He looked at her, inquisitive. "Charlotte, I'll stop anytime you like. Just say 'red' and all play ends." His body against hers managed to feel both comforting and enormously stimulating.

Then he kissed the top of her head.

Her heart thudded hard in response to the unexpected affection.

This was beyond dangerous. Betrayal, pain, degradation awaited. Most of all, the spirit-shriveling degradation.

The scar on her thigh throbbed, a reminder.

"I can't..."

"Tell me." His voice in her ear, soft as thought. She felt his smile against her cheek. "You can tell me anything. I'm your doctor."

She had to smile at that, then gasp as he moved against her again. "It's complicated."

"Pleasure isn't complicated."

"The fallout can be."

"Not this time."

She looked up. There was a nearly audible click as their gazes met. He stroked her arms, her outer thighs...then his hand stilled. His fingers investigated the skin on her outer left thigh.

She knew he felt raised scar tissue that was almost, but not quite, in the shape of an ornate, lowercase *k*.

Her Gorean slave brand.

10

Gregory held a flashlight in each hand as he led the evening's second tour group down into the city's bowels.

Halloween would be the jam-packed tour. But the weeks leading up to Halloween boasted the next largest numbers of ghost hunters signing up for a late-night thrill, his predecessor had said.

Seems he was right.

Nearly a sold-out group. Gregory had had to shout to convey the spiel to all fifty people. Though most of them seemed to ignore the overview and safety instructions.

It wasn't the juicy part.

The tour promised a "unique, once-in-a-lifetime, authentic" ghost tour.

Gregory should be happy, would've been happy, except, well, the undertunnels were creepy. He'd never realized quite how creepy.

Not, of course, because the old, interconnecting rooms and the pits beneath were haunted. They were just dirty and claustrophobic. Probably filled with rodents and insects. Doubtless the air quality was bad.

He breathed fast and shallow, holding one of the flashlights thrust forward, a sword of light spearing the dusty darkness. He strode farther into the forsaken rooms. They were simply neglected spaces, not pits of doom, and it was no big deal. He did a job. He explained the remnants of clothes and furniture. He told stories.

Dark fairy tales.

He listened to the murmurs and nervous laughter of the record-breaking crowd in between stops.

As Gregory reported instances of people hearing odd noises, he listened to the murmurs and laughter die down as they tried to hear the noises, too. He pointed out the remains of prison cells in one dreary room. He elaborated upon the bloody history behind the pile of rusty old bedsprings.

Oh, yes, his crowd was affected. Maybe he wasn't half bad at this gig after all. They wanted to be titillated and scared, and he was delivering the goods.

Though there were some inexplicable noises.

He preferred not to think about them.

Gregory cleared his throat, continued the tour. The group huddled close, the occasional camera flash capturing portraits from the previous century—a small china doll, an old stain in the shape of a body, and numerous broken pieces of furniture that may or may not have been used by the abducted men and women imprisoned there.

Perhaps the ghost hunters foolishly thought the strangely random, moist blasts of air were the exhalations of disembodied spirits.

Gregory didn't. He did, however, hold the other flashlight closer to his body. He liked the heft of it, and he really liked the beam of light illuminating the perfectly ordinary dust.

Other beams of light from other flashlights arced past him, around him, congregating on the holding cells. All the moving lights were making him feel strangely dizzy. Or maybe it was the poor air quality.

It was when they arrived at the deepest, most remote part of the tour that he heard the noise.

The distinct sound of a whip being applied to bare flesh. And, the shriek of pain on impact.

His speech stumbled.

Everyone grew silent. He let the silence stretch.

Gregory knew it was only someone inside the fetish club. Those people did odd sexual things, perverse and dangerous things, to each other. They enjoyed it.

But even as he smiled a showman's smile, wanting to feel smug, Gregory felt a chill crawl up his spine and freeze his rehearsed speech. The fetish club should be too far away to hear so clearly.

The crowd of ghost hunters marveled at the acoustical emanation of tormented souls.

The whipping had stopped. The sound of a woman crying—a desolate, heartbreaking expression of grief—could clearly be heard.

It sounded real.

It sounded . . . haunted.

His crowd milled uncertainly. Gregory could feel panic in the air.

He suddenly realized they might stampede, hurting each other. Hurting him. Definitely hurting his business.

Gregory improvised desperately. "The century-old ghost of an abducted woman, named Lilli, is rarely heard. It seems she has, she really has revealed herself to us." Gregory licked his lips. His voice trembled, but that only enhanced the tale. "Once captured and bundled away from daylight and everyone she'd ever known, Lilli refused to submit to her captors. They tried the usual tactics employed in breaking a woman: withholding food, leaving her in isolation and darkness, applying dreadful indignities to her person. Still she rebelled, until they decided to make an example of her."

The room was silent except for the ghostly echoes of a woman sobbing.

"The most evil of the crimpers, a man named Dunthor who prided himself on the creation of docile prostitutes, stripped her naked and bound her facedown to one of those mattresses." He pointed to the pile of rusty bedsprings, which was all that remained of the beds. "He proceeded to whip her mercilessly with a very cruel weapon, a cat o' nines embedded with sharp slivers of glass. An inappropriate tool to use on even the most mutinous of shipboard louts, he used on her poor flesh until skin and muscle was nothing but raw hamburger." Did they have hamburger back then? Gregory didn't know, but he could hear the shocked gasps of women in the group and figured it didn't matter.

He aimed a beam of light at the ceiling, at a square of old wood. "The brave, spirited Lilli didn't have a chance. But though she screamed herself hoarse, she never broke. Rebellious to the end, she cursed Dunthor. He finally gave up. Furious and humiliated, Dunthor dumped her body, still alive, down through the trapdoor you see above, into a pit. Into this pit, as a matter of fact.

"In time—no one knows how long—she succumbed to her injuries. But her ghost lingers."

Gregory felt a strange tightness in his throat and nausea in his belly. He'd made it up, every gruesome detail. The trapdoor was real, but everything else pure invention. And yet his body quivered with panic and an enormous sadness. It felt as if he were channeling something real, some insistent soul's story . . . which was ridiculous! There was no Lilli!

The crying woman had finally fallen silent.

"I'm sorry, Lilli," he whispered. His words echoed.

Thoroughly unnerved, Gregory pushed through the group, which parted in silence.

"The tour is completed," he announced. He spoke over objections, launching into the closing spiel and cautioning them to watch their heads as they ascended steps under low cement blocks and exposed pipe. "There will be another ghost tour tomorrow night," he concluded. "And, of course, the extra-spooky Halloween tour. Tell your friends."

He knew they would.

The whipping and crying had sounded real.

Gregory held two flashlights before him, twin lightsabers of reason. When the last of the group departed, he shook his head and all but ran up the narrow staircase leading to the fresher air above.

11

Charlotte remembered the smell of burning flesh, fragrant like a kind of meat. The skin on her leg had sizzled, the hot iron brand hissing. The kiss of pain progressed relentlessly, penetrating with each microsecond into deeper and deeper agony.

She remembered screaming.

Helpless in Cory's ropes, knotted tightly like an animal, she'd still managed to jerk away from the hot brand.

Lodged within her flesh, the iron had ripped her open, ruining the brand's precise edges.

She'd been marked for life.

White with shock, Cory had apologized. He'd helped her to the bathroom to vomit. He'd held her as she'd choked and sobbed.

When she asked for a divorce, he'd let her go without the fight she'd expected. He said he was sorry he couldn't give her what she needed sexually. He'd said he forgave her for being the way she was.

He forgave *her*.

Martin tapped his finger on the raised flesh. "What is this?"

She felt her lips thin and tighten. "What does it look like?"

He gazed at it. "Like...a two-headed kangaroo in quicksand? No?"

"This isn't a Rorschach test."

He heard her tone. "I know it's not. I'm just trying to minimize what appears to be its tense-making effect on you." His thumb caressed her. "Where'd you get the scar, Charlotte? I really want to know."

She couldn't help smiling a little as she threw his words back at him. "It's good to want things."

He gave her a stern look. "You trust me, but not completely. It won't do."

He moved against her, ever so slightly. "I'll just have to distract you." The length of him throbbed against her. She leaned into him as far as the thigh restraints would allow. He felt so good.

"I will get to the bottom of you."

She shivered at the promise in his words. Her body yearned for his despite her vigilance. He'd seen her gruesome scar and he wanted her anyway. Impossible to disbelieve; his erection pushed at her.

The tense core of tightness inside her relaxed further.

She wanted more of him. All of him.

At the moment, she wanted Martin to unzip his pants and shove his cock inside her. Just like the movies of the two of them together. Was that too much to ask? She looked at him under lowered lids. "I'm very sick, Doctor. I think you've realized I like men who are rough with me. I'm not sure we have time for a pill. You'd better give me an injection."

"Self-diagnosing is frowned on in my office." But he leaned in for another teasing fabric-covered thrust. His dark pants were wildly tented now. "You're being a very difficult patient."

"Cure me," she invited. She tried to thrust back at him, but the restraints held her by the legs.

"Naughty Charlotte. I think it's time you remembered who's in charge here."

With economical movements, he fetched a small blue jar from the counter. "This should help you focus." He held it before her.

"Vicks VapoRub?"

He opened the top of the jar, dipped a large finger in, scooping out a small amount of pungent white jelly.

She began shaking her head. "Oh no you don't."

"Oh yes I do." He rubbed his forefinger and thumb together, spreading it thin. Then without further words, he applied it between her legs.

At first, the slippery sensation electrified. Then it ratcheted up to a turn-on too quickly. "Oh!"

"Your mind's in the right place now, isn't it?" His fingers were deft, stroking, massaging all around her clit without quite touching it. She trembled, every inch of her yearning for him. Her belly felt deliciously fluttery as he continued above, below, in sensual circles that made her sigh and gasp with pleasure.

The menthol scent and Martin's devious smile seared itself into her memory. He'd somehow managed to relegate her scar, and all it represented, to unimportance. She knew that whatever else happened between them, she'd cherish this moment for the rest of her life.

Her heart softened further toward him. A need beyond the physical craving spread through her body. He'd awakening an ache of longing inside her that encompassed more than sex.

Distracted by it, she suddenly realized the stimulating sensations had ignited. Everywhere his fingers went, the coolness heated. Heat on heat. Almost burning.

"Oh." She shifted, unsettled. "That's ... wow."

He tapped his now-empty fingers on her leg. "Yes. Where were we? I was asking you where you got this scar."

"Oh, that's intense." She shifted again. It felt like liquid fire. Not like the brand's agony. More like a prickly sunburn. Charlotte shifted. Martin was correct. Her mind was now quite focused on the fire between her legs.

"I'd also like to know why you abandoned me to hang in my shackles. The first woman I play with in ages, the first woman I've *ever* let lock me onto a St. Andrew's Cross, and she runs scared the moment I mention she's a natural submissive. Now why might that be? Charlotte?"

"What?" She shifted again.

"You aren't paying attention."

She bared her teeth at him. "So punish me."

He grinned back. Then lowered his head. And blew on her.

She squirmed at the sudden icy chill in her nether bits. "Oh, no! Cold! It's cold!"

"Yes. That's without putting any directly on your clit. If I have to take an extreme therapy method, I assure you I will do that, and more." He lowered his head, but instead of a cool blast of air, she felt the warm, moist tip of his tongue touch her where she was most sensitive.

She shouted. How had he managed to bring her right to the brink so quickly?

"You're not playing doctor, you're playing inquisitor!" she accused when she could. She considered. "Which isn't necessarily a bad thing."

He laughed. To her great mortification, she realized she could feel new wetness between her legs. Her muscles clenched involuntarily. The sight of his head between her legs, his tongue so near, had her aching. "Oh, come on!"

He stood up instead, watching her with a mocking smile. "Tell me what you're afraid of," he suggested. "Why'd you run from me? Does it have to do with this?" He leaned to the side, caressed her scar with his tongue. The raw eroticism made her catch her breath. The tenderness tugged at her heart. She could feel his mouth's heat.

"Please," she whispered.

"Please what?" His voice, a low whisper. His fingers drifted across her thigh to her center, grazing lightly. In their wake she felt the flare of menthol. When his thumb began to gently circle her clit, a steady glide that teased, she moaned.

"You know what," she finally managed.

"Say it."

"You. I need you."

"You need what you fear."

"Yes." The tickle from a single rivulet of sweat ran down her chest to her belly, disappearing into the narrow shaved triangle of her pubic hair.

"But I haven't given you anything much to fear." He smiled. "Yet." His gentle tone didn't alter, but she shuddered, her pleasure spiking.

He lifted his thumb immediately, moved his hand to her throat. Then stroked down, his hand trailing sensuously over her throat, across the expanse of her chest, up the swell of a breast to rub her nipple slowly and rhythmically between thumb and forefinger. "At my mercy. But guess what?" He leaned in, sharing the nimbus of his warm scent and the hint of musk already so familiar to her on such short acquaintance. "I have none."

His murmur, paired with his clever fingers, made her shudder again.

He brought his other hand into play, on her other nipple. He tweaked it, bringing a gasp from her. "Just testing the nerve endings of your breasts. Pressure. Pain tolerance." He pinched hard with both hands for a long moment, and she cried out.

"Normal."

"No. I'm not." Her twisted fantasies couldn't be normal, or

healthy. But she was here. She wasn't saying "red" despite his sadistic touches.

"Let's try something new and exciting, Charlotte. Well, exciting for me." He opened a drawer nearby, brought out two small clips shaped like the heads of reptiles. "They have little teeth, see? Like an alligator. I like to make my toys unique." He snapped one onto a nipple with practiced ease.

She yelped.

"A little painful, isn't it? Like the little creature has your teat in its tiny jaws. It won't damage you, the tension's adjusted . . . but you can say 'red' anytime if this gets too much for you. Personally, I think you can take a lot more. You need a lot more. Don't you?" He snapped the second one onto her other nipple. The sharp, sweet pain shot through her body like lightning.

Her brain began to feel pleasantly buzzy. "I need . . ."

"Let's focus on symptoms, shall we?" His professional tone and the sudden coolness on her perspiring skin brought her back. He was fetching a stainless steel tool from the counter. Something sharp? She craned to look.

"A Wartenburg wheel. A legitimate medical tool, not one of my creations. See? Just a small, spoked wheel with needle-sharp points. Professionals like myself use it to test skin sensitivity." He ran it up her leg from knee to groin. She jerked, then stilled. Ticklish.

"You're thinking it tickles. It's supposed to. But the more firmly I press, the stronger the sensation. See?" This time he pushed it harder and moved it more slowly, letting her feel each one of the sharp points as it traveled down her thigh. "Hold still," he commanded when she squirmed.

She did her best.

Something he said sank in. "You make these? Fetish toys?" She craned to look at her nipples. The unique clamps and delicate chains glittered like jewelry. "Cool."

"Thank you." He flicked the chain, punctuating his words with more biting sweetness. The ache between her legs grew to a desperate yearning.

The tiny wheel's needles didn't rest in any one spot long enough to truly hurt, but they pricked her with rapid-fire stings as Martin rolled it down her body. The more she tried to block it out, the harder he pressed, the stingier it got. A sweet itch seemed to spread from each point, pain turning to relief turning to pleasure. She lost herself in contemplation of the sharp sensations, examining the tiny hurts as if they were something outside of her.

She wondered anew how Martin could call her normal. A normal person would be screaming bloody murder for the discomfort to stop, not analyzing it. Certainly not transmuting the little pains into pleasure.

He stopped. "Normal."

She hissed with frustration.

He laughed again, opened another drawer.

With a deft flick of each wrist, he withdrew and slipped on black gloves that clung like a second skin. He presented his palms: an array of small sharp points sprouted from each glove.

"This is one of my latest toys. When I release your leg restraints to turn you on your side, you will not resist or struggle in any way." He did, and as he turned her onto her side, she felt the glove's pointy nubs.

The clamps tugged at her nipples. The slippery skin between her legs ached. She'd lost all will to resist. Floating in a kind of euphoric daze, she merely waited for the next sensation.

The table's paper bunched up under her body. "This may pinch for a moment. Or possibly more than a moment." He proceeded to spank her.

Though his stroke wasn't hard, the sting was fierce.

She struggled. He immediately pinned her with his left hand. "No."

Yet when he started spanking again, the tiny spikes drilling into the skin of her buttocks, the pain had her howling within moments.

"Are my vampire gloves too much?"

"Too much?" She panted, lying on her side. Her ass blazed its pain. And something more. Her vision was blurred, her eyes hot and wet. It took her a long moment to realize they were wet with tears. "I don't know. I don't know anything. You can't hurt me. Nobody is supposed to hurt me."

"Hurt you? I'm trying to help you." He waited a moment, then spanked her harder. She groaned helplessly. "To reach you." He used one hand on her ass and brought the other up to her chest to tap her breasts, jiggling the alligator teeth.

Between the bite of the clamps and the tiny needles of the gloves pricking her breasts, and the rough spanking, she felt enfolded in pain. Then nearly overwhelmed by it. "To solve the mystery of you, Charlotte."

Though she tried very hard not to cry out, the spanking soon had her gasping, her tears flowing freely.

"Would you like to be helped, Charlotte? Are you ready to talk about it? Will you tell me why you ran from me? Will you tell me how you got this?" His sadistic glove scraped her scar lightly.

"No," she breathed, desperate, full of a delicious tension. She didn't want it to stop. She was wetter than she'd ever been. She felt inflamed and fierce with a desire to shock him, rock him, provoke him.

She needed more. What the hell was wrong with her that she needed more?

What more could there be?

12

Of all his five trained slaves, Kartane liked Talia the best. With her supple dancer's body and long red hair, she never failed to catch his eye or raise his temperature. She was a tease and a brat, yet when the flirtatious vixen trailed her fingers over his flesh, then sucked in a quick feminine breath as if in fear of her own audacity, his body thrummed its response.

So when Talia sometimes elbowed the other slaves and lorded it over them with an arrogance unbecoming in a slave, he let it pass.

Talia was a bitch, but she was the best of the lot.

An alluring female. But not Charlotte.

His mood curdled. He didn't want to think of Charlotte. It was that stupid new slave's fault for bringing her up, making him miss his ex again.

Kartane reclined to watch his five women rush here and there, cleaning and making the too-large conference room more hospitable for a Gorean gathering. Soon there would be a sixth, then a seventh woman...then more. His warrior friends would eventually bring their own to these gatherings. This

126 / Christina Crooks

place wasn't quite a paga tavern, but it would have to do until the Gorean movement caught on.

He decided to test his slaves.

"Wine!" he demanded.

While the others stood staring vacantly, Talia leapt to serve, taking up a bottle of wine with calculated grace and pouring carefully. Amazing how she displayed her servility so beautifully. Kartane stepped back from himself to observe the two of them doing what they did best. A woman serving, and him ruling over her. Dominate and submit. Taking all her training and applying it to serve her master. As nature intended.

Talia approached, the red silk of her dress swaying with her slow, seductive movements. She knelt back on her heels, knees widely spread in the dictated position of the pleasure slave. Holding the goblet with both hands, she pressed it against her body, pushing inward against her belly beneath her navel. Then she raised it to her face, touching her lips to its side, kissing the goblet lovingly with her eyes closed.

Then she extended her arms, lifting it. "I offer you wine, Master."

He took it with a small grunt of acknowledgment, watching her narrowly as she bowed her head and retreated with as much grace and decorum as she'd approached.

Such beauty and fire. Such a well-trained slave. Like Charlotte could've been.

He turned his sudden frown on the other women, who began to clean faster under his fierce scrutiny. "Finish preparing this place, then kneel facing the chairs where your masters for the evening will be seated. Nadu position," he added, knowing that maintaining the shoulders-straight, chest-out, belly-in rigidity of the kneeling position for hours would be a form of punishment.

It was no more than they deserved, the stupid cows.

He still wanted Charlotte.

The realization annoyed him.

He shouldn't want her. He had slaves like Talia, and soon he'd have Amethyst, and then many more.

But for all his women's pleading looks and tears that seemed as right and appropriate as the sun rising in the morning, it didn't replace what he'd almost had with Charlotte. Had he given her up too soon? Setting an enslaved woman free went against the Gorean code. Mostly because the code didn't account for slaves *wanting* to go free, not after fully tasting the glory of being a slave, of being protected and treated in a way that satisfied their biological needs. After the initial shock of becoming a slave, most women adapted, even thrived. The normal ones did. The rest, well, they generally weren't considered worth preserving. Biologically flawed, after all.

But Charlotte hadn't been flawed.

She'd been the one to bring him into S and M. To pain and pleasure and dominance and submission. She had a slave's heart. But she denied her own urges.

Because he'd loved her, because he'd been so remorseful and confused, he'd let her go.

Maybe he shouldn't have.

Their bodies had sung together so well, once upon a time.

Kartane's gaze went to the four red-clad slaves. They knelt in an orderly line, branded thighs well on display, each woman positioned before a still-empty chair. Talia hummed as she tidied the wine and glasses, the undisputed queen of the bunch. Charlotte easily rivaled her in beauty and grace.

The idea struck him suddenly: Why not reclaim what he'd so rashly set aside? Why not simply take what he wanted? First Amethyst.

Then Charlotte.

What more could there be?

Even as she asked herself the question, Charlotte's mind

presented the X-rated movie images: a savage Martin ravishing her, merciless, hurting her, bestial in her fantasy. So unlike Cory in every way that mattered. Martin's hard, driving use of her—as she pleaded for mercy—would send her over the edge.

"Please," she begged. She couldn't tell him about something so depraved.

He stopped, removed his gloves. Opened yet another drawer. Withdrew yet another teasing instrument of pleasure and pain.

Would he ever be done toying with her? She was coming apart at the seams.

"Martin, please. I want you so much."

With a sudden brutality that shocked her, he reached between her legs, grasped her clit, twisted it between two large, smooth fingers. "That's 'Doctor,' to you. Say it." His fingers moved in a key-turning movement. Back and forth.

She couldn't speak, all her awareness focused on the shrieking nerve endings between his fingers. Pain. Pleasure. Intense pain. So much pleasure. "Doctor!" she gasped. She was going to come if he didn't stop instantly.

For a miracle, he did. She panted, bereft and relieved both. "Jesus."

"No, just 'Doctor.' "

It startled laughter out of her.

"Impatient patient," he chided with a smile. "Open your mouth."

"I'd rather you gave me an *injection*," she tried again suggestively.

"Open your mouth." This time he didn't smile.

She stared, rebellious, but complied. Expecting a tongue depressor, or possibly a thermometer, she frowned in consternation at the length of hard rubber he forced into her mouth.

The thing nudged against first one cheek, then the other. He pushed it in until she started to gag. Then he withdrew it completely. "Very good." He held the spit-moistened thing up for both their appraisal.

The gag was almost penis shaped, except for how it tapered at the tip, and tapered again at the base.

She saw Martin reach for another container alongside the small blue one near them. As he stroked the object's wet surface, she realized he was adding to its slick coating. His large fingers returned to the jug of Vaseline, then, as if as an afterthought, to the Vicks VapoRub.

"Incorporation of patient participation is generally a significant factor in the resolution of her complaint. But in this case, I think the opposite applies. I think your cooperation is contraindicated. Isn't that so?"

She felt a pleasurable frisson of panic. She looked at him, then down at the thing. She hadn't liked being gagged.

"Time to take your temperature," he said briskly. He bent between her legs.

It wasn't a gag.

He wormed one of his slick fingers into her ass.

"Hey! Oh! Not there! That's not . . . I didn't think . . . I can't . . ." She tried to close her legs, but his hands pried them apart.

"Either say your safe word, or cooperate. Or fight me. I'd prefer you fight." He waited a moment, then brought his thumbs into play again, rubbing her clit as he violated her ass. It felt more invasive than painful, but she couldn't help struggling. His thumbs brought a sudden, intense pleasure as he stretched her.

Her face flamed with embarrassment at what he did to her. It was so degrading. How could it feel so good? She couldn't let herself accept his probing touch. She fought, trying to squeeze her thighs closed, to roll away from him.

"Naughty." He slapped her clit, making her yelp with surprise.

Then he pinned her arms to the table with such force she knew she'd have bruises. He replaced his intrusive finger with the blunt, moist head of the object at her opening.

It nudged, threatening and exciting. It felt cool, and wet, and totally unfamiliar. Most of all, it felt far too large for where it was intended.

"You can't! You wouldn't!" She began to struggle harder.

He wouldn't dare. Would he?

"Are you ready to tell me your dirty secret? Or does this go in?"

She stared at him, fear and lust battling inside her. She heard the tremor in her voice. "Please. Martin, don't..." Please don't? Is that what she really meant? If it was, the proper word was "red" and she knew it. She panted, fearful yet rocked by lust. Tears rose to her eyes, unbidden. "Please, you can't do this to me."

Martin shook his head, mocking. "Wrong. In goes the thermometer!" He shoved the rubber dildo into her ass with a sadistic grin.

He pinned her as she made a galvanized motion of resistance at the outrage he inflicted on her.

He gave her a cheerful grin. "It's easier to simply do as I ask. But I'm glad you don't. You know why I'm glad, don't you? Because I'm a sadist." He paused, considering. "A fairer kind of sadist than you've known, I suspect."

Charlotte barely heard him. The thrusting probe filled her rear, hard rubber stretching her inner walls to the point of pain. She twisted, trying to get away from it, to rid herself of the object.

He held her down. "No."

She panted.

His grip remained firm. "How does it feel now?"

"How do you think? It feels..." But even as she tried to

maintain her outrage, the sight of his amused smile and her own body's responses undermined her.

It felt exciting. Forbidden. His calm dominance was a turn-on, too.

Martin wiggled it a little, twisted it back and forth. With each twist, his thumb brushed against her clit.

"Stop!"

He ignored her desperate plea. He worked it in farther. Suddenly, the largest section was inside her and she felt her sphincter clamp around the smaller, tapered part. "There," he said with satisfaction.

She tried but couldn't push it back out.

He'd succeeded in penetrating her. And in such a way! She barely knew him. She couldn't understand how the deliberate obscenity of his action increased her attraction to him to a near-desperate level.

She looked at his stern look of concentration and wanted him with an aching need that shocked her more than the invasion of her body.

She shook her head, appalled at herself. Cory was right. She was just a demented sex slave. No wonder he hadn't been able to satisfy her, even after she'd driven him to extremes. Nobody could.

Her mind whispered that she was wrong. Martin could.

Martin frowned, stood. Holding her body pinned with one strong arm, he quickly scooted to the head of the table, where he reached underneath. He brought out a long chain with padded forearm cuffs, which he enclosed around her arms, locking them behind her.

He walked to the sink, washed his hands in a leisurely manner. He spoke over his shoulder as he dried his hands. "You haven't worn a plug before, have you?"

He crossed back to her, looked down at her. He tapped her

legs. "Open." When she didn't, he trailed his fingers back down her body to the neat triangle of her mound. Then lower.

He wormed his hand between her sealed thighs, prying them apart. He moved his fingers in slow, sensuous circles around her clit, occasionally pushing the bottom of the plug. Each push was a jab to her insides that caused her to suck in her breath.

She hadn't realized how it would feel. That there'd be the perverse connection between the nerve endings in her rear and the other erogenous zones. Especially with him working her with his fingers.

With her hands bound, there was no possibility of escape. He'd caught her. He could do anything he wanted with her.

The sinking pleasure made her moan.

"Tsk, tsk." He seized her clit, twisted brutally, ignoring her shocked yell. "I asked you a question."

She gasped. She tried frantically to gather her thoughts, but they danced away from her. He masterfully inflicted enough pain to make her straddle the fine line dividing pleasure from hurt. The idea of disappointing him seemed to hurt her almost as sharply as his cruel grasp, and that added to her pleasure, too.

Charlotte slid more deeply into the pleasant zone she'd felt earlier. Nerve endings all over her body tingled to exquisite life, even as her insides whirled pleasurably. Pulses of pleasure in between the pain brought her a sensation of floating. Of flying.

She looked at him with all the desire and submission offered up in her gaze. "I'm sorry, Doctor. What was your question?"

"I asked if you've worn a plug before."

The act of thinking was like trying to wade through warm, thick molasses. "I thought . . . it was a rhetorical question."

His response was instantaneous. *Twist.* She cried out. "I'm not asking you to think. I'm asking you to answer a simple question. Yes or no."

"No! No. I haven't worn one before."

His pincer-like grip eased, transitioned to a stroke. His voice turned silky as well. "That wasn't so hard, was it?"

She was quick to shake her head. "No. Not hard." A slick, startling sensation grew in her ass. Icy one moment, hot the next.

He'd added the Vicks to the lubricant, she realized. Diabolical.

He nudged the plug hard, stabbing it into her bowels. "How do you feel?" The glint in his eyes told her he knew exactly how she felt.

"Feverish. Hot and cold. Achy." She looked at him from under her lashes. His gaze didn't drop to her clamped nipples, which she knew stood out in hard little nubs.

"Then you'd better talk soon, my responsive little submissive."

"I'm not a submissive." She wanted desperately to believe it. "I just . . . I don't want to say."

"Why'd you leave me in shackles, Charlotte?" *Twist, twist nudge.* "Why'd you run? When I couldn't chase you, bring you down, and fuck you hard. The way you want me to so badly." Twist, flick, rub. NUDGE. "Why do you have a botched brand on your thigh, Charlotte? You can tell me, I'm a doctor."

"Stop it! I'm not . . . oooh!" Her orgasm felt imminent. She squirmed against his fingers, hot tears of frustration wetting her face.

He stopped. He pinned her legs so she couldn't rub them together, couldn't come. He grinned.

She stared her resentment at him.

"Hurting you gets me off," he explained unnecessarily. "I'm the flip side to you. I can honor what you are even while I lick the tears off your cheeks." He proceeded to do so. The surprising warmth and tickle-sweetness of his warm tongue called up a surge of tenderness within her that brought new tears to her eyes. Conflicting emotions warred within her, feeding her lust and increasing her fascination with this man. He did honor her. She could tell it from the stern and gentle touch of his hands and tongue, from his words, from the sound of his voice. His palm traveled up her belly to caress her left breast. He brutally yanked off one alligator clamp.

She howled.

He laughed, yanked off the other.

She cursed him with the same amount of creativity she put into her clients' dating-site profiles, though with a very different intention. She meant every word. How could he be so cruel?

How could she be enjoying it?

"You might even be ready for the chain trick. Or maybe I should save that one for later."

"The chain trick?" She looked down. Her nipples felt lacerated, alive to every air current, too sensitive. Reddened. But perfectly healthy and still peaky, as if asking for more abuse.

She scowled at him, not knowing whether to shout her safe word or beg him to mount her, fuck her hard, relieve the burning need he'd stoked inside her. "I think I hate you," she told him.

"Excellent. We'll save the chain trick for later, then. You need punishing, not rewarding."

"I do not!" She thrashed in frustration. Paused. Then again, curiously, "What's the chain trick?"

"No." Martin delved into yet another drawer. He pulled out a long rectangular black strip of stiff leather. Two pieces, joined at the handle.

"Never you mind about the chain trick." He slapped the paddle into his palm. It made a double whapping noise. "Are you familiar with slapper bats?"

"Actually . . . yes."

She closed her legs tightly as she watched him move to the foot of the examination table.

"Explain."

"I think it's obvious."

He slid the slapper bat up the inside of her legs, right up the middle. He pried them apart. "You're so very vulnerable right here. Such an exposed sensitive area." His fingers opened her, exposed the tiny pearl of her clit. He rested the narrow leather against it.

A wave of apprehension swept through her.

He spoke with stern dispassion. "Do you want to apologize for your disrespect? Tell me how you experienced a slapper bat. Tell me how you got that scar on your leg."

13

She tensed, her thoughts in a riot. Tell him? She couldn't! Not about the scar. Even if it meant the kind of pain he implied. Especially if it meant the kind of pain he implied. Would his playing finally get rough? "An apology under duress wouldn't be worth much."

"I'll be the judge of that. Such a smart mouth you have. Such a dirty girl." He flicked his wrist, and the double slap of the bat impacting her clit made her jerk. The first slap thudded down, the second one following immediately to make a snapping sound of leather meeting leather. The paired impact drummed into her. Not too painful, she thought with relief and regret.

But he wasn't finished. Smiling as if he knew her thoughts, Martin gave another deft flick, slapping it down again. Then again.

The stinging impacts, backed by the relentless thuds of the echo-slaps, developed a fiery rhythm that soon had her squirming, then making small animal noises as the pain increased and deepened.

Without stopping the cruel hits of the slapper bat, Martin

brought the fingers of his other hand into play once more, pushing the plug in cruelly with each slap.

The biting sweetness of the leather impacts paired with his clever fingers pushing the hard rubber repeatedly into her ass sent her hurtling off the edge with a shout.

He kept his rhythm fast and hard, shattering her soul into a thousand glowing pieces even as his eyes narrowed and his lips tightened with cruelty.

He didn't stop.

Even as her orgasm faded and her oversensitive clit broadcast messages of pain undampened by pleasure, he didn't stop.

She yelled her pain. She was going to have to say "red."

Or she could capitulate. "Okay! Okay! I'll tell you."

He stopped immediately. "Speak."

Rather than dirty or used or guilty, a deep sense of satisfaction pervaded her. Aftershocks thundered through her body, little echoes of the pleasure and pains he'd caused. Relaxation unfurled within her, almost as intensely pleasurable as a second orgasm. Every inch of her radiated a kind of bliss, too deep and all-encompassing to last more than a few moments.

And yet it did.

Her eyes focused slowly. "Wow."

He tapped her with the bat once more.

"Ouch! Okay, damn it." She spoke quickly to get it over with. "I married my boss, even though I never saw any movies with him and me. We started playing fetish games, at my instigation. Master-and-servant stuff. I liked it, I've always had a secret taste for a little bit of pain and dominance, but I wanted more dominance and aggression than he was willing to give. Neither of us were in the fetish scene. I just liked it when we played those games. But something was missing. Sex was sometimes unfulfilling for me. Then one day he read some weird novels. He did some research. And ... he changed. He went from uncertain and frustrated to arrogant and cold. From playing to dead serious. Women were biological slaves, he said, and he meant it. The next time we played, things went wrong. Terribly wrong. I taunted him, just in play. You know?" She darted a glance at Martin but barely registered his calm presence. She was back in that house, being a brat, smarting off to Cory. Instead of starting a dominance game, though, he'd backhanded her. Casually. As if the action meant nothing to him.

It had succeeded in shocking her, making her wary if not respectful. Being hit that way was outside her experience.

She continued. "Then he put a tight metal collar on my neck. He tied me up and treated me like an animal. For two days. He made me kneel, and crawl, and dance for him until I ached, then service him in every imaginable way. He punished me frequently with whips and his hand and tight rope. He made me eat from a dog bowl. Then he . . ." Her voice failed.

She took a deep breath. "He heated an iron and he branded me. He said he wanted a slave with his brand. The bastard branded me. Despite the ropes, I moved around. I jerked away. The brand came out wrong. It hurt and damaged me more than he'd expected. He saw it, too. I watched him turn white with shock." She laughed, a little wildly. "He doctored me then, Doctor. Salve and pills and chicken noodle soup. He knew by then I didn't like what he'd done. I hadn't responded to it the way he'd expected. Not at all. Not even a little. He apologized over and over again. I asked for a divorce. We're still friends. The end."

The catharsis of telling someone, finally, made her sag in her bonds. Her body shuddered with the force of her emotion, with the jerking sobs.

He removed the padded forearm cuff restraints and the plug efficiently. His gentle fingers stroked her, lifted the paper gown to cover her.

The warmth of Martin helping her to sit up, then wrapping his arms around her in a gentle hug, was an unlooked-for rapture.

She clung to him, tears running down her cheeks.

Just a postorgasm effect, she told herself, even as she marveled at the lingering bliss and resonating feelings of relief, fondness, respect, and fulfillment from exactly what Martin had given her.

Such emotion. She rubbed her cheek surreptitiously against Martin's shirt, inhaling his scent and feeling a deep languor totally new to her. Tears seemed a natural response. She knew they were tears of profound release. "Thank you," she breathed.

He nuzzled her hair.

She basked. "You. That was magnificent. Superb. Wondrous."

"Stop, I'll get a big ego." He hugged her tight for a moment, then gently, rubbing her back with a savoring touch, as if he enjoyed touching her as much as she did. "Mmmm." His nose in her hair and his deep growling exhalation of pleasure gave her goose bumps. "Thank you for your trust, Charlotte."

She tried to gather her thoughts. She should feel shame. That's what she'd always felt after her desires rose up. Shame as a constant sexual paradigm.

But she didn't with Martin. "This feels so good. Right now. I got a massage, once. It made me feel a pale echo of this. It's delicious."

"It's aftercare."

She hadn't heard the word before. "It's very nice."

Martin cradled her. "Submissives love aftercare."

Martin still thought she was a submissive. Cory had, too.

She felt some of her tension return.

A few minutes ago, she'd taunted Martin, trying to inflame him into a kind of rough rage so he'd fuck her hard. She'd done something similar to Cory, and look where it had gotten her.

"Why do you keep calling me submissive? I'm not. Not like that."

"Like what?" He leaned back just enough to look at her.

"Like a slave. Like someone who has a servile heart, 'yes, master,' 'no, master,' and all that."

He frowned. "We played a game. A fun game, I hope?"

She smiled, tentative. "Definitely fun." She still tingled from the slapper bat, her nipples ached, her legs had the slight soreness that heralded bruises, and her labia and the inside of her ass felt icy and hot. *Alive.* "It is fun. It's just..."

"Yes? This has to do with your ex. And the scar. And you mentioned something about a movie? You can talk to me, Charlotte. I hope you know that. I haven't met anyone as interesting as you in years."

"Thanks." A twinge of appreciation and pride shot through her. She interested someone like Martin. "You're a good listener. I just didn't think I'd ever do anything like this again, after the divorce. Too dangerous. The scar reminds me. Cory does, too, when he talks about Gorean philosophy...what?" She'd seen Martin start.

"Nothing. Please continue."

"That's it, pretty much."

Martin had taken control and pleasured her with the intensity she craved, without making her feel like some kind of slavish subspecies. It made her want more of him, all of him.

All that the movies promised.

The truth was she wanted full rapture of rough sex with someone who'd have no mercy, but, conversely, someone who made her feel safe.

Someone exactly like Martin.

Dread and hope warred within her. Would Martin respect her perverse cravings, or was it too large a risk to take?

"And the movies? What about the movies, Charlotte?"

She opened her mouth to confess everything.

At that moment, the door swung open and Amethyst walked in.

14

"Hey, big guy, got a problem—oh."

Amethyst noticed he had company. Martin ground his teeth. How like her to barge past Ratty. How rude.

He looked at Charlotte. She just blinked for a moment, still deep in the relaxation of aftercare. So cute. He watched as she finally moved to pull the exam table tissue up around her fun bits. She smiled at the intruder. "Hi, Amethyst."

He didn't feel so kindly disposed toward his friend. "You're interrupting a scene." He scowled at Amethyst.

Both women looked at him. "Well? Do you *mind?*" he asked the one with the purple streak in her hair.

Amethyst's timing was atrocious. He finally felt as if he was getting somewhere with Charlotte. The woman had appeared in his life so unexpectedly and touched him so deeply in such a short period of time. She piqued his ardor and his interest in ways he'd all but forgotten were possible. Not only was she the sexiest woman he'd ever played with, she represented mysteries he wanted to solve. And depths he craved to explore.

Soon.

Now would be preferable. He walked toward the door, intending to usher Amethyst out. "Where's Ratty, he was supposed to watch the door."

"I told him to fetch me a drink, that I'd wait here and play guard dog for him. I think he enjoyed the thought of me as a guard dog."

"I'm sure he did," Charlotte said.

Martin looked from one woman to the other. They'd only just met but spoke as if they already knew each others' secrets.

Women, he thought with exasperation.

He looked at the wide-open door pointedly. "You're doing a great job of guarding."

His sarcasm bounced off her. "You need to hear this."

"I don't need to hear anything right this moment." He gave her a quelling stare. "Please go."

Amethyst continued as if he hadn't spoken. "Kartane's back, picking up fresh meat like it's going to spoil overnight. He even put the serious moves on me again, trying to get me to play downstairs! How many times do I have to tell you he's bad news? He's going to hurt someone, get my club closed down. You have to toss him out. And not let him back in."

"I don't have to do anything. And it's not your club." From the corner of his eye, he could see Charlotte getting dressed. Charlotte was pulling on her sweater.

The scene was ending poorly. Damn it, he was just getting Charlotte to open up! He glared at Amethyst. "I'm sorry Kartane's sexist attitude screwed things up between you two. I regret his being here upsets you. But it's time to quit running to me whenever you have a personal problem."

"Personal problem?" Amethyst glared back. "I don't run to anyone. This problem isn't personal, you jackass, it's professional. He's bad for business. Bad for Subspace."

"Not your concern."

"Not yet, maybe . . ."

"Not ever." The regret tasted bitter. If he could only sell Subspace to her. But he couldn't. He sighed. He could cheerfully strangle the blackmailer for putting that look of frustration on his best friend's face. "I'm sorry, Amethyst."

Charlotte spoke up, clearly trying to ease tensions. "Kartane sounds like a real jerk."

Amethyst was already nodding. "You have no idea. He's involved with some weird science fiction shit, which is fine, and some nonconsensual stuff, which is not. Goreans are into total power exchange, but even the regular Goreans think he's way the hell out there. What? What is it?"

"Kartane's a Gorean?"

Martin watched Charlotte's throat work as she swallowed. Suspicion was confirmed even as he heard her speak the words. "Is Kartane a blond guy with light blue eyes, really good-looking, dresses a bit too formal for most occasions . . . ?"

"Holy shit. You know him?" Amethyst stared at Charlotte. So did Martin. "Oh, you poor girl."

"We're kind of friends now. Only friends. Now." She stood with her arms wrapped around herself, leaning against the table. She wore her jeans and sweater once more. She looked paler than she should.

He went to her. "Are you okay?"

"Checking in on me?" The vulnerable smile she offered him made his heart beat strangely, strong and fierce. He wanted to protect her from everything.

"That's right." He looked deeply into her eyes, evaluating. "Amethyst," he said, turning back to his friend. "You might have a point about Kartane."

"Hallelujah. The man sees sense."

"If he's an irresponsible player, he could be dangerous to the newbies in the fetish scene."

"That's what I've been saying, if only you'd listen—"

He continued, overriding her. "It's my responsibility. I'll

talk to him." He looked forward to talking to him. He'd ask the guy how he could look at himself in the mirror after what he'd done to Charlotte. He'd tell him in no uncertain terms his kind wasn't welcome here. He'd kick his ass out and then ban him for life. Maybe he'd throw in a parting punch in the face in payment for the brand. That'd be only fair. That'd be—

"Well, this looks cozy."

Charlotte paled further. She stared past both of them. "Hi . . . Kartane."

Martin whipped around in time to see Kartane's blue eyes widen with surprise. "Charlotte? What are you doing here? You told me you never went to these kinds of places." He stared at her, then shook his head with vigor, as if trying to shake out water. "How do you know my club name? Could I have been so very wrong about you? No, I couldn't have been." He visibly recovered even as he spoke, until his expression matched his perfectly tailored clothes: smooth, appropriate, attractive.

She clearly wasn't recovering as quickly. Seeing Cory / Kartane here, now, obviously didn't fit with her concept of him. Martin remembered her tale of her ex's regret, his tears of remorse after the branding. Doubtless she'd been convinced he'd have nothing to do with fetish activities ever again.

She'd been wrong. Of course she'd been wrong. She'd put the guy on the road to S and M, after all. Why be surprised he'd kept exploring it?

Charlotte's arms wrapped more tightly around her own body. "I'm not exactly a regular."

Martin edged in front of her, his muscles tensing as if for battle. His loathing for the guy narrowed his eyes and made him hyper-vigilant. He was surprised to feel Charlotte's slender hand on his arm, a quelling gesture. He looked at her questioningly. She kept her gaze locked on Kartane.

The guy leaned against the doorway. "It's just so surprising. Charlotte, what do you think you're doing here?"

"Same thing you are. Kartane." She said the name slowly, as if tasting it.

Amethyst sneered. "Picking up women by the truckload, dumping them, then coming back to restock?"

"Don't take it so hard, love." Kartane gave Amethyst a quick dismissive wink. "Dominant women—like you're playing at being, at the moment—aren't my type."

Amethyst marveled at him. "You have King Kong–sized balls. For the record, you aren't *my* type. You use women without the slightest regard for what they want."

"That describes most guys here. But, not me." He stared at Charlotte. His voice turned gentle. "Are you okay? This can be a rough place."

"You're the expert on rough." Martin heard the growl in his own voice. Kartane was Cory, the guy who'd hurt Charlotte with a brand. Her ex. What right did he have to speak to her in that lover's tone? The throb of Martin's own heartbeat pounded in his ears with barely controlled rage. The strength of his detestation of the man shocked him.

Kartane glanced at Martin. "Rough for its own sake isn't my area of expertise. I'm not a part-time play sadist. Like you."

Martin's fists clenched.

But Amethyst wasn't done. "You're completely full of crap. You don't care what women want in the slightest."

"I don't care what they say they want, because I already know what they really want. Each one of them secretly wants a strong, steady hand. Every woman nurses a biological longing to surrender to a master who makes them feel fully like a woman. It's the natural order."

Amethyst made retching sounds.

Kartane gave her a lazy smile. "You know it's true. Search deeply inside yourself."

"I'm sick of you trying to get deep inside every available female in a square mile radius and then dumping them hard afterward. Leaving them broken!"

"Both of you, give it a rest." Martin glowered at him.

"It's not." Charlotte's raised voice made everyone turn to look at her. "It's not the natural order. Women as slaves? Seriously? You still believe it after what happened with us? That isn't something from nature. That belief just makes you a garden-variety misogynist."

"Amen, sister!" shouted Amethyst.

Kartane stared at Charlotte. "Don't believe the rumors about me. At least one source is highly biased." He glanced briefly at Amethyst. "Charlotte, your desires got me into the scene. You might not frequent the clubs, but even you know there's too much gray area inside this world to call me a misogynist." The very intensity of his look seemed to almost compel her agreement. A creepy sort of charisma radiated from him.

Martin's skin crawled watching Kartane at work. The jerk was good. Really good. Like a high-dollar lawyer. Or a used-car salesman.

"Feel the truth of what I'm saying, even if you don't want to admit it. Might you have a little bit of a slave's craving, Charlotte? You're here. You're playing at submission. You enjoy being dominated and controlled, toyed with and conquered. I failed you there. I still had much to learn. You may not like hearing it, but my research does show that despite this world's traditional relationships, the evidence is overwhelmingly in favor of natural female servitude to some degree or another. There are occasional exceptions." He glanced at Amethyst. "Aberrations. Women who remain in deep denial. But normal, healthy earth women like you simply won't be completely happy lacking a strong master."

"See!" Amethyst pointed at Kartane, while looking at Martin. " 'This world.' He talks about it as if there really is a planet of Gor. A planet of barbarians and pretty slave girls. An adolescent fantasy of horny little boys. He takes it seriously and inflicts it on naïve submissives."

"You don't run with the usual Gorean crowd here," Martin said. Kartane bothered him for more reasons than he could count, but a new reason began to stand out. "A small Gorean group meets at Subspace each week. I've never seen you there."

Kartane shrugged. "Ceremonial and online role-play Goreans don't embrace the full spectrum encompassed within John Norman's novels. Gamers focus on some valid things, but only when it suits them: integrity, honoring the Home Stone, caste loyalty ... ways for a man to live a truthful and fulfilled existence." He smiled, warming to his subject. "Of course, they also spend quite a bit more time on issues of slavery, slave etiquette, slave dances, slave punishments. It has a strong BDSM flavor, don't you think? Masters and servants, dominants and submissives. Their so-called slaves submit but don't ever fully surrender. Everyone plays the game, then steps out of the role to go on with their lives. It's false. They aren't true Goreans." He gazed for a long moment at Charlotte. "I have you to thank for introducing me to the possibility of a Gorean lifestyle even though it didn't work out between us. I presented it improperly, and for that I have regrets."

"All year ... every week when I visited Hoagie ..."

"You had no idea I still craved a household full of kajirae, and all that other Gorean nonsense?" He grinned, boyish, and Martin saw Charlotte's nod and answering smile.

She took a step closer to the guy. "You're always nice to Hoagie. And to me. You've been nothing but supportive and kind."

Kartane reproved her with a soft voice. "Maybe Goreans aren't as bad as some people would have you believe?"

Martin intercepted a quick glance from Charlotte that she couldn't control.

Kartane nodded. "It's true that for me it's not a game, it's a lifestyle. But I respect your discomfort with the subject. I will always regret mishandling that part of our marriage." Kartane looked at Charlotte with a knowing gaze that had Martin itching to slug the guy. "Maybe one day I'll convince you of the need for a strong Gorean master to conquer you. That anything less than a slave's full surrender isn't authentic and won't completely satisfy you."

Charlotte looked shaken. Repugnance and recognition warred on her face, the expressions trading places. "Maybe you're right," she whispered.

Enough.

"Kartane. I think it's time you left. Now."

Kartane ignored both Martin and Amethyst. He looked at Charlotte thoughtfully. "I should've never let you go."

Martin made a small sound of fury.

Kartane oozed toward Charlotte.

Intolerable. Something snapped in Martin. He took a single step forward, swung his fist at the man's face. His knuckles connected with the strong chin, driving Kartane back.

"Stop!" Charlotte leapt between them even as Kartane rebounded from the wall with icy fury in his eyes. "If you want to just talk to me, we'll talk! This isn't necessary, or civilized. Or legal. This isn't Gor, Cory!"

"Thank God," Amethyst said.

"Kartane," Cory corrected.

"Whatever," Charlotte said. "We're all friends here ..."

Three snorts met that statement.

"... and so there's no need for violence. I'm talking to you, too, Martin."

Martin's head snapped toward her. Outrage coursed through his veins. "I'm trying to help you."

"By punching people? Don't you think there's been enough testosterone-fueled aggression tonight?"

"'Cory' is past tense," Kartane insisted. The man breathed hard as he glared at Martin, his control obviously straining.

He wasn't alone in that. Martin had broken up his share of conflicts, been the one responsible for preventing uncontrolled violence within Subspace and subduing flare-ups. Now he wanted to fight. Had this bloodthirsty lust for battle lurked beneath the surface in him the whole time? He'd never before felt so close to losing himself to rage. "Get out."

Kartane slowly smiled, touched his own jaw where Martin's fist had landed. "Your inner warrior wants to play. Gor welcomes strong fighters. Consider it."

Oh, he was asking for it. Marin ground his teeth. "Out."

"Gladly. Charlotte? I'll give you a ride home."

"You can stay here," Martin assured her. He touched Charlotte's arm.

She flinched. Stepped closer to Kartane.

The tiny rejection actually made Martin step back. He scowled, suddenly uncertain who most deserved his anger. For he was still angry. Deeply angry. "Fine. If he's what you want."

Amethyst looked at Charlotte with some concern. "You think it's a good idea to go with *him*? Are you feeling okay?"

"Peachy." Charlotte gave a despairing sort of laugh. "I know him better than both of you. He won't hurt me. But, thanks for your concern."

Martin didn't like the sound of Charlotte's laugh. It sounded a little hysterical.

What was he supposed to do about it? Slap her, like some barbarian Gorean slave master? Force her to stay?

She should want to stay.

He tried to keep the anger stoked high, needing the emotion's warmth. It held his hurt at bay.

"It'll be okay," Charlotte said in a low voice to him. "I just have a lot to think about. I was only here to look for someone and I got distracted." She spoke as if trying to make sense of her own words. "I shouldn't have gotten distracted. True, the phone call was dropped. It happens, connections are dropped all the time, right? But she's still missing. We . . . Kartane knows where I live and he can take me home easily. It'll be okay," she repeated more loudly.

"Of course it will." Kartane looked at her, the very image of a caring friend. His voice radiated sincerity and solicitude.

It was hard not to believe him, even knowing what Martin knew. It was those baby blues and clean-cut blond good looks. No wonder so many women fell for him. No wonder Charlotte had.

Jealousy gnawed. He ignored it as a totally unworthy and inappropriate emotion. If Charlotte still had a thing for her ex, it was her business. He barely knew her. He didn't want to know her, he told himself.

He ignored the little voice inside that laughed at that. He clung fiercely to the anger instead. "Well? Get out. What are you both waiting for, an escort? That can be arranged."

He watched a little shudder run through Charlotte. He'd caused that. He'd given her pleasure and pain, and now a different kind of pain.

Martin felt a twinge of remorse. Belatedly, worry rose up in him again. But as he searched for the right words to say to make her want to stay, Charlotte went to Kartane. "Let's go."

Without saying anything more, Kartane turned and left, seemingly confident she'd follow.

She did. Without a single glance back, she did.

"Well, you handled that one like a champ. Not."

He glared at Amethyst. "Real mature."

"How could you let her leave with that creep?"

"Was I supposed to throw her down and sit on her? Tie her up again? Strap her to the St. Andrew's Cross? Do you want me to beat him senseless and get my ass sued penniless?" He was yelling. With an effort, he got himself under control. "Shit."

"He is."

Martin stared at her. "He dumped you hard, didn't he?"

"Fuck you. If you want her undamaged, emotionally and physically, you'd best keep an eye on them. I'll handle Subspace. It'll be good practice for when I own it."

Martin gave an exasperated sigh, but his mind was on Charlotte. "We'll discuss it later. I don't have time to argue with you." He threw off his white coat, then grabbed his keys and wallet.

He spotted Charlotte's coat. Good. He had an excuse for following her now.

He rushed, wanting to keep the couple within sight.

He hoped they weren't a couple.

He nearly slammed into Ratty in the room's doorway.

"Whoa!" Ratty danced back, nimble, not spilling a drop of his two drinks. "What's the rush?"

"Later! No time!" Martin ran.

Ratty looked at Amethyst. "Sorry I took so long. I didn't mean to make you guard the door so long. There was a line at the bar. So, what was that all about?"

Amethyst plucked one drink from his hand. "Charlotte left with a Gorean. *That* Gorean! And Martin let her. Men can be so stupid," she snarled. She drained the drink in one long gulp.

She held the empty out to him. "Here."

Instead of taking it back, Ratty poured his own drink down the front of her tight dress.

"Hey!" She stepped away from him, staring at her sodden dress. "What the fuck did you do that for!"

"Because I'm stupid." Ratty turned, his cloak flaring in a swirl of color and sequins, and went after Kartane.

15

Kartane made sure to reveal none of his elation as he left Subspace with Charlotte in tow.

Things were going his way.

He saw Charlotte darting surreptitious glances back, as if longing for Martin to give chase. Kartane looked over his shoulder once, but all he saw was that angry older guy still pestering people for news about his missing daughter.

Amethyst would soon be kneeling at his feet. So would Charlotte. Martin would soon be completely irrelevant.

He savored the thought.

Charlotte walked by his side, just like old times. "Dearest, would you mind terribly if I made a quick stop at the office? There's something I should attend to."

He noted the way she started at the old term of endearment.

"But the office is all the way across town."

"Not anymore." He looked at his ex-wife. It bemused him, how different women could be. How distinct. They truly were treasures, and Charlotte was the treasure he'd let get away. He remembered her writhing, limber little body. He inhaled, savoring. From her scent to her colorless suburban clothes to her plain but long brunette hair starting to frizz in the night mist the way it always used to, she reminded him of how they'd been once upon a time.

Before he'd grown up into the man he was now.

"It's only a few blocks away. I decided to move headquarters downtown. More traffic, more open minds, more opportunity. Are you cold?" Without waiting for her answer, he pulled off his own jacket and offered it to her.

"Oh! I forgot my coat. I should go back—"

"No." He walked on when she didn't take his coat, confident she'd continue walking after him. After only a tiny pause, she did. He smiled inside. She truly was a submissive. And so much more.

Such a shame he'd rushed things. He'd branded her prematurely. That should've gone very differently. But, he'd sensed her distance and dissatisfaction. He'd been afraid of losing her if he didn't dominate her totally, conquer her utterly.

He'd made a mistake. He'd misjudged the proper moment.

Her feelings for him changed irrevocably the night he'd branded her. They cried together, after. They'd remained civil. They'd even remained friends, of a sort, sharing a few hours of time on weekends with Hoagie. But the marriage was over the instant they both smelled her flesh burning.

He'd been scared. He could admit it, now that he was a man who took responsibility for his weaknesses. Scared he'd lose her, then afterward scared he'd have to explain her terrible burns at an emergency room, scared he'd be put in jail, scared he'd lose not only Charlotte and his marriage but his business and his freedom.

Her request for a divorce, though it broke his heart, seemed a reasonable alternative at the time.

But now he could admit to himself he'd been a coward.

He'd been punished, though. He'd lost his Home Stone along with Charlotte.

The loss of a Gorean Home Stone was considered the most heinous shame a Ubar—a leader—could endure. A Home Stone *was* a Gorean's home, more than metaphorically. It was his pride, his center. Theft of one, or simply misplacing it like some senile elder, that was a kind of sacrilege against manhood itself. He'd first found his Home Stone while reading the Gor series of science fiction novels. He'd been thinking about founding his own city of "Gorr" on Earth, and the stone simply appeared in his path on a nature hike. Walking and day-dreaming, it had caught his eye. The small gray stone with its smooth edges seemed to call to him, and after he'd touched it and turned it over to see the faint, natural lines of a rough G, his blood surged in his veins and he gave a shout of victory. A sign!

It had to be a sign, a sanction of authority from the Priest-Kings themselves . . . if those godlike beings still influenced Earth to such an extent. Kartane still wasn't certain about that particular detail even after studying many of John Norman's books.

But the acknowledgment from the more forward-thinking of the local Gorean community that he was Ubar to the new city of Gorr empowered him, gratified him, and reinforced his position as a Bringer-of-Change. Soon Gorr would be a reality. A much-needed reality for so many men.

Or at least it would be a reality if he could find the damn stone. So far he'd managed to keep its disappearance secret, but a secret like that couldn't be kept from his warriors for long.

When Charlotte disappeared from his home after the divorce, the small, flat stone with the plain initial G carved into its underside had disappeared, too. She had to have it somewhere.

He stopped under a bright streetlight illuminating the familiar men's magazines logo of three overlapping triangles. He took out a fistful of keys, flipped through them, inserted one into the lock.

"Business must be good."

He saw her studying the old, well-kept building. Ornate

stonework and painted carved-wood trim framed each window and doorway. Surrounded by similar sturdy structures in the active part of downtown, it loomed over the others. Its architectural details pleased him.

Its expensive location pleased him more.

It would make a good Gorr city center—a worthy fortress—when he had the money to buy it outright. Which would be soon.

He smiled. "It's been around for a century. Has character, doesn't it? I rent the entire first floor, which has plenty of room. As you'll see."

"I don't mean to be rude, but this won't take long, will it? I'm pretty tired."

"I'm sure you are."

She looked at him. "I hope you're not mad. Or jealous."

He laughed. "Of Martin? He obviously has no control over his impulses. I pity him. He plays the part, but he's not a real master. Most men aren't. Not even most Goreans. Only the honest ones. Coming?" he asked as he held the door.

He saw her shiver, a delightful tremble. Yes, he'd made a mistake letting this one go.

As he entered the building, he heard them.

"Ubar has returned! Tal, Kartane!"

He grinned at the number of people he heard in the background. And at the music. It was perfect.

Kartane gave her an impish smile. "You'll be safe with me, I promise. Just a quick peek in at the party. I promised them I'd come. And you know I always honor my promises. Five minutes, then we can go. If you want." He winked at her.

"You've changed," she said suddenly. She scrutinized him. "I didn't realize how much. It suits you." She shrugged, smiled. "I'm glad we've stayed friends."

Pride swelled inside him. Certainty grew. He was Ubar of Gorr, chosen of the Priest-Kings, and he had the power to make his vision a reality. A vision that included Charlotte. Even Charlotte sensed it. "I'm glad, too," was all he said. He waited a moment. "Come inside."

"Okay. Yes." She entered.

Charlotte was so lost in thought she barely noticed the vaulted entryway with its glass receptionist desk and the hall beyond with its enormous framed photos of Old Riverport. Her ex-husband's presence didn't frighten her at all. He seemed content with their platonic relationship. Plus, Cory . . . no, his club name was Kartane, and he preferred the club name, she had to remember . . . did always keep his promises.

His Gorean friends, however, were an unknown.

While he went to greet them, she turned and surreptitiously twisted the front door's latch to the unlocked position.

She'd seen and experienced too much violence in a single night.

Some of it had been directed pleasurably at her.

Just remembering Martin and his exquisite, sadistic touch made her knees weak.

But the last bit, Martin punching Kartane, was too much.

She needed to think.

She'd avoided thinking about her desires for too long.

The passion in violence both drew and repelled her. In some circumstances, it provided a rare and wonderful spice. The rapture of being conquered and tamed dominated her fantasies completely. But in reality, it didn't work. The wildcard of violence could flare into something horrible.

Or heavenly.

She'd done violence of her own too this evening. She'd hurt Martin with his torture tools. Well, she'd halfheartedly tried. She smiled, remembering his bored eyebrow raise.

Then the smile left her face. He'd called her a "submissive all the way through."

Was it true?

A submissive was acted upon. A submissive agreed to give up choice, control, shame, and honor. A submissive seemed just another type of slave.

It definitely didn't sound like the type of person who'd build a successful matchmaking business.

Why did her movies have to pair Martin with her?

She noticed Kartane was halfway down the hall. She hurried after him. Five minutes of socializing, she promised herself. Then she'd be able to go home and make sense of it all.

The noises grew louder. How many Goreans were at this party?

She felt her forehead crease in a frown. A Gorean gathering here, at midnight? The men's magazines had always been a bit on the wild side, with models traipsing through, photos of legs and panties and boobs and bondage gear plastered over all the production layouts. The subject matter ensured a certain amount of political incorrectness in the workplace.

So long ago. So much had changed in the two years since she'd first laid eyes on the blue-eyed boss and lost her heart. And yet it suddenly felt like just yesterday. Things had been so much simpler before her sexual proclivities ruined everything.

How big was Kartane's business now? It had grown. The cubicles went on and on, and one glass-walled conference room was bigger and stranger than she'd have expected. It might have been a converted warehouse, it was such a surprisingly open space. The only furniture was a bunch of chairs and a few tables curved in a half-circle around what all the men watched with avid fixation.

Women, of course. Women on furs. Women dressed in short, skimpy red silk dresses. About ten women posing and preening.

"A midnight photo shoot?" She looked from Kartane to the other men.

He cleared his throat. "May I present Charlotte, a free woman!"

Chairs scraped and mugs frothy with beer thumped to tables as the men stood. All of them. There were at least thirty of them, most around Kartane's age. "Greetings, Free Woman!"

They seated themselves again, courtesy executed.

"All right. That was weird," she said under her breath.

"Come on," Kartane said, amused. "They salute your status. On Gor, free women are honored. Though, of course . . . all free women secretly crave to be slaves." His eyes twinkled.

"You're nuts," she said, but with affection. If he wanted to role-play with willing partners, who was she to judge? She'd indulged recently herself.

The men had gone back to talking among themselves, darting glances at the women. The music faded, then began again with a new beat. One man stood. He carried a bullwhip.

No one carried cameras and lighting, or a video camera. "Not a layout or an ad shoot then," she murmured to herself.

"No. Watch," Kartane said, even as the music increased in volume. Its rhythmic drumbeat reminded her of Subspace. "The Whip Dance is starting."

"Wouldn't want to interrupt the Whip Dance," she grumbled. When Kartane gave her quelling stare, she stuck her tongue out at him. His lips curved into a cute smile, reminding her why she'd fallen for him.

"Quiet, you," he commanded gently. "I promise I'll take you home as soon as you ask to go. But you'll want to watch this." He indicated the woman rising sinuously to her knees, then her feet. "Talia's quite talented."

It was on the tip of Charlotte's tongue to ask to go immediately.

But just then, a sharp crack filled the air, making her jump.

The bullwhip.

She stared at the spectacle despite herself. The woman moved with the lithe grace of a trained dancer, gyrating and undulating with a restrained sensuality far more effective than blatant bumping and grinding. With each crack of the whip, she flinched with a different part of her body.

"He'd better not miss."

Kartane's eyes remained glued to the slave girl. "He won't hit her. Yet."

"Yet?" She turned to look at Kartane.

"She doesn't currently merit discipline." His face was flushed, his eyelids lowered to the half-mast she remembered indicated lust. He watched the dancer for a moment, then checked Charlotte's reaction. His expression changed at her look. "Don't worry. She's willing."

The beat changed, increasing tempo. Charlotte looked at the other men.

The man with the whip wore a leather vest and wielded the weapon with a savage smile. His ash gray hair and craggy face indicated maturity, but his body seemed as fit as a man in his prime, especially the rock-hard bulge of his biceps and ropy muscles and tendons of his arms.

The other men lounged in their chairs, the very image of barbarian gentlemen of leisure. Some wore jeans, others kilts, and some seemed dressed for a Renaissance festival with leather pants and chainmail, but all had an air of arrogance she associated with power. The Goreans came in a variety of ages and shapes, but all seemed a little fitter, a little healthier, than the normal guys she knew.

Charlotte noticed four of the women knelt at four different men's feet, their heads lowered, long hair falling loosely. Their hands lay palm-up on their parted and bared thighs.

Charlotte's gaze sharpened. Each thigh sported a slave brand. Real ones, if she was any judge, and she figured she was. "Kartane," she began.

"Unless you're choosing to leave now, please be quiet? It's rude to talk during a performance."

Did the women not mind having the brands? They didn't seem to. In fact, as Charlotte watched, one of the men patted a blonde on the top of her head as if she were a pet. The red-clad woman leaned into the man's caress, giving every indication she savored his touch.

Crack!

The dancer yelped, danced faster. She spun away from the whip, her dress swirling up to show bare butt cheeks. Sweat gleamed on every inch of her body.

Charlotte looked from her to Kartane, who now frowned. She wanted to ask what had happened but feared to provoke a reprimand.

Crack!

The dancer stumbled, then spun the other way.

"Clumsy woman," Kartane declared.

The dancer heard. Not stopping her dance, she tossed her red tresses, retorting, "You'd be clumsy, too, with this oaf whipping you for no reason!"

The men gasped. At her audacity? Charlotte saw their appalled expressions. Yes, appalled she'd addressed the insult with one of her own.

"You should take a whip to her in earnest," one man declared.

Another shut off the music.

In the sudden silence, Charlotte heard the whispering hiss of leather as the man with the whip coiled the weapon and hung it on his belt. He looked to Kartane.

Who nodded his head. "Tie her for punishment. She dislikes it." He addressed the men, but rather than waiting, he strode to where different lengths of rope, color-coded, hung on the wall. He selected a short length, tossed it to the nearest man who caught it with a smile. He rose, stepped around the woman kneeling before him. Younger than the whip-wielder, with dark hair glistening with too much oil and dirty jeans that reminded Charlotte suddenly of her landlord, he approached the haughty dancer with eagerness.

His kneeling woman remained in place, still as a statue. All four of them were.

Charlotte frowned, on the verge of protesting. Was this for real? Or was it role-playing?

Watching as the dancer had her dress ripped from her and thrown aside as if it were trash, then forced roughly to her knees, Charlotte was shocked to find her body responding warmly to the violent scene.

"Okay. That's not good," she muttered, backing away slowly.

Competently and without a wasted motion, the man forced the girl's forehead to the floor. "Kneel to the whip."

"A punishment position," Kartane explained unnecessarily as he returned to Charlotte's side.

Incredibly, the woman laughed. She ground herself sensuously against the furs, twitched her glistening ass at the men. "There's not one among you who can conquer this girl! Do your worst. All you can succeed at is the spoiling of beauty. Silly men." She stretched sinuously within her bonds and laughed again at the sharp inhales of all the men. One approached with a short, straight whip Charlotte had seen before. Two feet long and wicked-looking. A quirt, Kartane had once called it.

Kartane's voice rang out sternly in the quiet. "There's nothing beautiful about a rebellious kajira. I suggest you punish her severely."

"I agree wholeheartedly, Ubar." The quirt met the flesh of her ass. The woman made no sound.

It impacted again, harder, and she flinched despite her obvious effort to remain still.

And again. The woman panted, and then: "Is that a little boy? It must be a weak boy, with a limp little weapon."

The laughs of the men were a goad to the one with the whip. He rained down blows but failed to win from the woman any further sound.

Her ass bloomed with a crosshatch of dark pink welts.

The slave yawned and stretched, making a show of it. Her

162 / Christina Crooks

taut, well-muscled body extended in deliberately provocative ways. She made the rope wrapped around her wrists seem an attractive accessory rather than a forced restraint.

Incensed, the man threw down the quirt. He unzipped his pants, then lowered them to expose his enormous erection.

The slave glanced over her shoulder. Tensed. "You can't do that." She began to struggle in her bonds.

Kartane shook his head. "You're his for the punishing. He can do what he likes."

"Not in front of everyone!" She wriggled, her face flushing with effort and shame.

The man—the woman's owner? or was Kartane her owner?—slapped her ass. "Be still and don't fight me, and maybe I won't pass you around."

Immediately the other men started hooting and shouting. "Fight him!" "Kick him in the nuts!" "Fight him, kajira! He likes it!"

She did fight, but there was only so much give in the rope. She fell awkwardly to her side. The music started again, but this time she wasn't dancing. Her struggles made her body spasm in frantic, violent ways unrelated to the music's beat.

The woman seemed to wilt, shaking her head. "Please, Master. Please, no."

The man positioned himself behind her, his erection rubbing between her legs, to the cheers of the others.

Charlotte's body seemed locked into place. As the simple whipping changed to a threat of violent sex, her own response confused her. The struggle and the dominance turned her on. The woman was just role-playing. So were the men. And yet . . .

Defeated, the woman struggled weakly one last time.

It was completely not okay.

Charlotte had to swallow twice before trusting her voice. She managed to shout, "Stop! Right now!"

16

Her voice was loud with the power of her dismay behind it. She hadn't intended the shrill, desperate tone. It served its purpose, however.

Kartane looked at her.

The man looked at her.

All the other men looked at her, and even the kneeling slaves momentarily glanced in her direction before returning to their statue-like positions.

But it was the bound woman who spoke first. "Who the hell do you think you are?"

The man poised behind her added, clearly gritting his teeth, "Free Woman, if you don't like what you see ... please leave!"

Charlotte trembled with outrage and something more. "You can't rape that woman."

Kartane walked to her quickly. "Charlotte, enough."

"Enough? Look! Do you want to go to jail? Do all of you? Huh?"

Unexpectedly, Kartane smiled. Knowingly. "Why don't you ask the kajira what she wants." When Charlotte hesitated, Kartane gave her a little nudge. "Ease your mind. Quickly, if you don't mind."

"Then maybe you can drive me home like you promised," she retorted. But she went.

The woman reclined on her side, showcasing her feminine curves. The long curtain of her hair draped her body fetchingly, feathering over nipples, hips, and slave brand. Her brand, Charlotte noticed, was in the shape of a flower.

The woman's coolly beautiful stare unnerved her.

"Okay. Um, excuse me. I want to make sure you're all right with this. If you're not, we can get you out of here. Right now."

The woman looked at the man, now standing behind her, his pants pulled up. Her eyebrows raised in question. He nodded permission.

She spoke even as she turned back to Charlotte. "This girl is happy to serve. Her master's smallest whim is her highest law. There are penalties for breaking the law." She shrugged, a graceful and economical movement of one shoulder. "You are interrupting."

"Yeah. Real nice. I try to save you and this is the thanks I get."

"Ignorant bitch."

"What? What did you call me?" Baffled, Charlotte stared at the sweaty naked woman at her feet.

The man nudged the slave with his boot. A warning. "She'll be punished for speaking to you that way. A slave doesn't so address the free."

The woman didn't seem worried. Her eyes glittered, avaricious. "Yes, Master."

"Answer the free woman's question."

"Yes, Master." Her gaze pinned Charlotte again. "This girl called you an ignorant bitch, because you don't understand. This girl does not compromise on her femininity as you do. This girl is not confused, or unhappy, or trapped in a maze of societal conditioning with inconsistent directives and standards for women. This girl is not artificially inhibited. This girl has no need to try to become a man, knowing herself naturally a slave, as you do not yet know yourself. Free Woman, this girl is wise in the ways of men, and intimately knowledgeable about her own needs as well. As one of the free, you'll never know true womanhood or the rapture of being owned, body and soul, submitting wholly to a master who accepts no less."

Charlotte blinked. "You don't seem very submissive to me."

"True. This girl merits severe punishment." Her eyes glittered again. She half smiled. "This girl enjoys not-enjoying it. If you can comprehend such a thing. Are you finished interrupting?"

"Okay, all finished." Charlotte backed away so quickly her movements jarred her. She knew she looked comparatively graceless, not to mention stiff and awkward. "Have at each other. Violence galore. Enjoy." She turned, trembling with both recognition and horror.

The saucy slave girl reminded her of herself, at least a little bit.

"Okay, Kartane. Time to go."

He nodded. "If you wish. But things are about to get . . . interesting."

Against her better judgment, Charlotte looked back.

"Master, don't, please! This girl is sorry!"

This time Charlotte could hear the false note in her voice. The slave girl undulated in a seductive arc with the crocodile tears on her cheeks making them glisten. She looked undeniably alluring.

"Not sorry enough," the man said. "Belly position."

She lowered herself to her stomach, every movement graceful with a show of reluctance. She truly was beautiful and talented, Charlotte had to admit, riveted despite herself. She flinched empathetically when the man pushed the girl onto her side with his boot, transforming all that grace and beauty into an ungainly sprawl.

The slave crawled back up into position, weeping. "Punish this girl severely for having disappointed you!"

"You presume to tell me what to do?"

"No, Master!"

"Then you're saying you don't merit punishment?"

"No, Master!"

"I should feed you to a sleen."

Charlotte whispered to Kartane. "What's a sleen?"

He whispered back, his breath warm on her ear. "A six-legged beast with enormous claws. It eats meat."

A creature from science fiction. Gorean fiction. It'd be ludicrous, if it weren't for the very real violence.

"I'd like to see the others on you. You're welcome to her," the punisher invited the other men. They smiled and stirred, many rising with lecherous expressions. Those closed quickly on the nude figure.

"No, Master! Please, this girl wants only to please you!"

He pushed her beseeching hands away. "I know what you want. Not that your wants are relevant. Perform well, and you will please me."

One older man grabbed a fistful of her hair, pulled her back by it. Her body arched into a bow, then she fell again onto the furs.

The woman struggled and cried out when two men held her pinned, one for each arm. She snarled and bit one when his arm came near her mouth.

A third kneed her legs open while unzipping. His breath came hard, excited. The girl jackknifed her body trying to escape her fate, but he shoved her back down brutally, covering her body with his, wormed between her legs.

The crowd of men surrounding her blocked Charlotte's view. She blinked and took a step back in an attempt to make sense of it all. She angled her head away, needing to not see anymore.

She could hear, though.

"It hurts, please," the slave gasped, then whimpered and grunted in time with what Charlotte presumed were the hard, punishing thrusts. "Please, oh yes, please." The woman's voice hoarsened to a slavish, purring moan.

Charlotte raised her fist to her mouth, bit on it. Why the hell was she responding this way? Was she slave-hearted, too?

"I need to go now." When Kartane didn't move, Charlotte realized she'd whispered. She cleared her throat, spoke again. "I need to go home now."

"Yes." His voice was soft, too. When his gaze met hers, she could see the fire in him. The scene had affected him as well.

She had to pull her gaze away. It wasn't Kartane she wanted.

"Of course," Kartane said, as if he'd heard her thoughts. He paused, then shrugged. "Follow me."

She glanced back one last time. The punishment continued. All of it was consensual, she reminded herself. Everyone involved wanted it. Charlotte had zero place here, among these kinds of people.

Or did she?

All the four kneeling slave girls still held their poses, hands on thighs.

All but one.

Charlotte's eyes locked with the most distant slave, a petite dirty blonde whose silky poncho covered more skin than the others, pooling around her thin legs. Her eyes pleaded with Charlotte before she turned her head back to the empty seat before her.

Charlotte stopped. Watched. Did she just see a wordless appeal for help? Surely not. Charlotte had publicly offered to rescue the punished slave on the furs. That would've been the time for the kneeling woman to speak up, to object, to ask for help.

The woman didn't turn her head again. Motionless.

"Kartane," Charlotte began.

He stopped, backtracked. "Yes?"

"Those woman, the ones kneeling there. They're all volunteer slaves? This is consensual play for everyone? Not just the dancer."

His lips thinned. "Yes. It's what they want."

"Because all women have slave hearts," she said, testing.

He looked at her. "Are you coming to believe they might?"

She answered carefully. "I believe some might."

His smile, when he bestowed it on her, was truly warm. "You've come a long way on your own."

"Maybe." She spared one more glance at the smallest slave. Still as a statue. "Maybe not. Don't misunderstand me. These games of yours aren't for me." Her skin prickled with horror at the thought of being bound and branded, punished and used, all at the whim of a man who considered it biologically ordained.

"Aren't these games for you?" Kartane used his softest voice. "Surely a little bit? You seemed quite riveted."

"Not exactly. Not by the ceremony, or the permanent hierarchy you believe is biological." She cut herself off. She glared at him. "You love that part, though, don't you? 'Master' this, 'Master' that. I'm just glad it's consensual, this time." Her voice held censure.

"We've discussed that again and again. I've apologized too many times. *You drove me to it.* No, you listen to me. You taunted me for not being dominant enough. That's difficult, isn't it, Charlotte? Accepting part of the blame?" He held her stare, not backing down this time. "When you brought home toys for me to use that didn't get you off, when you orchestrated scenes of violence and scenarios of abduction and that didn't get you off either, what did you expect me to do? I've never backed away from a challenge in my life."

"I didn't ask to be tied up and tortured for two days. I never wanted a brand," she snarled.

"I regret hurting you. I'm sorry for my mistakes. I only wanted to please you, so I asked around. I found the fetish scene. I found . . . well, it doesn't matter. Done is done." He offered her a small smile of regret, a ghost of its former self. "At least we're friends now."

Suddenly Charlotte felt exhausted. If that woman wanted rescuing, she should be way less subtle; Charlotte was hardly in a position to determine nuance among Goreans, especially after the dressing-down by the dancer.

Her small aches and pains from Subspace plagued her all at once, as if adrenaline and lust had kept them at bay. Now they insisted on being heard.

"Let's go," she said, and let Kartane lead her toward his car. As she went, she realized something else.

Despite all the single men and women in one room together, her X-rated movie vision hadn't paired off any. The movies in her head remained dark and still, here.

At least, they did until she pictured Martin.

A movie snapped to life, placing Martin squarely in the role of slave-chastiser, and herself under him as the naked slave struggling and moaning on the furs.

"Okay. I have a problem."

"Excuse me?" Kartane asked, his familiar voice dispelling the visions.

"Nothing." She marched after him. "Nothing at all."

17

Martin stood outside the building into which Charlotte had disappeared with Kartane. As he struggled with whether or not he should go in after her, Ratty joined him.

Martin stared at the slender man. "You followed me here? What's wrong? What is it?" He looked at the door, then back at Ratty. "Did Amethyst send you?" He didn't have time for this.

Neither, it seemed, did Ratty. "Kartane went in there?" He moved past Martin, tried the door. It started to open.

"Wait! You followed him?" Martin lowered his voice, darting a glance at the door. The beat of music and the sound of many voices wafted out. "Why?" He eased toward the door. "What are they doing in there?"

"To answer your first question first, I followed him because I want some Gorean pointers."

Martin's head whipped back to Ratty. "Huh?"

"To answer your second question second, I don't know what they're doing and I don't care. It's Kartane I need to talk to, and talk to him I will."

Ratty went to push open the door.

"Hey!" Martin was obliged to shout in a whisper. And follow. As soon as they were both in the entryway, he moved swiftly to block the smaller man.

"Is this Amethyst's idea?"

The explosive curse had Martin covering Ratty's mouth. "Shh! Quiet!"

Ratty knocked Martin's hand away. The skin of his face had turned a deep red. His words, when he spoke, were carefully measured, controlled: "It is not Amethyst's idea. It is my idea." He visibly gathered himself together. "Amethyst seems to think Kartane's dangerous."

"I think she's right."

"Amethyst seems . . . afraid . . . of him. Angry and afraid and very aware of him whenever he shows up at Subspace. All her bluster, all her cursing."

Martin nodded. "You might be onto something with that. Why do you want to talk to him then?"

"Because one respects what one fears. I want her to respect me," Ratty said simply. "If it takes becoming a belligerent Gorean, that's what's going to happen."

It was Martin's turn to curse. "You've got to be kidding. She doesn't want that."

"What does she want? Huh? What? I'm having some trouble figuring it out!"

"Shhh!" Martin looked, but the hallway was still empty, and the voices far away. "What does she want? She wants Subspace. She lives for what goes on there—the fire-dancing, the play, the power games—and she'd spend all day and night there if she could. Romantically?" Martin glanced at Ratty. "You think she wants a Neanderthal like Kartane?" He started to smile. "You don't know what she likes to do for extra cash, do you? She's a dominatrix. A pro domme. Guys come to her for abuse. They go to her place, let her kick them around, humiliate them, make them lick her boots. They pay her for it."

Ratty blinked. "Yeah. Well, I'm not surprised. She has a strong personality. But I'm not licking her boots. She can lick my—"

"You don't get it. She's a switch. Playtime means going both ways, top and bottom. She's played with you every night this week. She's into you."

Ratty spoke heatedly. "She's evidently into bootlickers. I don't intend to be one."

The music suddenly shut off.

Both men crouched, ready to flee.

No one appeared.

"We're trespassing," Martin whispered.

Ratty whispered back, "So leave."

"I'm not going until I see Charlotte's okay."

"Awww! That's so sweet. You like her. Martin and Charlotte, sitting in a tree . . ."

"Shut up. Let's just take a look. Quietly."

Martin picked his way more slowly and carefully in the deeper quiet. It unsettled him, until he heard talking. Two women. One of them sounded like Charlotte.

Because it was Charlotte. Martin stared, transfixed by the sight of Charlotte bending over a naked woman laying on furs. Talking to her.

Martin conquered his surprise, ducked behind a stack of file boxes just outside the large room. He yanked Ratty after him.

They peeked around the corner.

Now the naked woman was struggling, being held down by four men. One of them prepared to fuck her. Martin goggled at the sight, jerked his gaze away. Where the hell was Charlotte?

Not fifteen feet away, she stood with Kartane. Her clothes were on and she seemed tense, but not afraid. Was she okay with what was happening? How could she be? But then again, she'd just talked to the woman. If he knew Charlotte even a little, she'd been making sure the woman was on board with it all.

Which clearly she was. Martin's experienced eye picked out the slave girl's real pleasure even as she faked another cry of distress.

Kartane certainly seemed pleased. Martin could see his dick bulging at the crotch, and the little looks he kept tossing at Charlotte. Charlotte didn't notice.

"Please tell me you don't still want to join the Gorean club," Martin whispered. "Amethyst won't respect you for it. That crowd of dorks think of themselves as sword-wielding barbarians. They convince gullible submissive women into morphing on demand into wanton slave girls."

"Sounds kind of fun." Ratty's chin was set in a stubborn line. "At least they get the girls."

"They hurt the girls," Martin countered. "Look."

The action on the furs riveted them both. Martin had to wipe the sweat from his eyes after a minute. Jesus. The slave girl was flexible, he could say that for her.

After a time, Ratty spoke, his voice thick. "She doesn't seem too . . . hurt . . . to me."

Martin conceded. "Not exactly hurt, this time maybe. But you have to take my word for it they do hurt their slaves. They crush their independence totally. It's a total power-exchange type of relationship. There's no switching places, no time-outs, and no relaxing of discipline. And, this crowd?" He indicated Kartane and his friends. "They're extreme for Goreans. They're hardcore. The regular ones at Subspace go too far, if you ask me."

"Maybe I'm not asking you." Ratty's eyes were glued to the slave girl's plight.

"I thought you liked Amethyst. You think she wants *that?*"

"I don't know what she wants!"

"Shh! Well, I don't either completely, but I know it's not that." Martin hissed the words, hauling Ratty farther back into the shadows. "Look. She wants you. She just needs more time." Martin hoped it was true.

Ratty blinked, looking away from the slave girl. "Charlotte saw us together."

"Yes. You and Amethyst have good energy when you play."

"No. I mean, Charlotte *saw* me and Amethyst together. In her movie visions." Now Ratty looked at Martin. "She saw Amethyst performing cock-and-ball torture on me. This coming Christmastime. I don't want to be a bottom." Ratty paused. "At least, not exclusively. But I'm pigeonholed as a subbie little bottom boy, and will remain so if Amethyst can't let herself bottom to me for real. To respect me, trust me. Fear me." He turned again to the Goreans. After a moment, he added, "Maybe all women secretly crave dangerous Neanderthals."

Martin stared. "Charlotte has visions?"

"I thought we were talking about me," Ratty complained. "I might walk right over to those guys any minute. Just go on over and introduce myself. I'll say, hello, take me to your leader. I want to be a Gorean. Or something like that."

"You won't, though." Martin hoped he was right.

"I won't, though," Ratty agreed. His eyes broadcast regret. "I grew out of Dungeons & Dragons years ago."

Martin tensed. "They're leaving."

Kartane and Charlotte were saying their good-byes, which meant Kartane would see them in about five seconds. The file boxes provide inadequate coverage and they had no time to move. Martin tensed, trying to think of an excuse for them being there. The coat. No, not good enough for trespassing. There was no excuse.

Suddenly Charlotte called Kartane back. Martin spared a moment to check. Was she getting together with Kartane now? Had she been enflamed by the sight of the punished slave girl?

Kartane clearly had the same thought, all but skipping back to her. What a jerk. He'd better not—no, Charlotte was pointing to one of the red-clad kneeling women. More Gorean slave girls in short silky dresses. Pretty skimpy outfits for such a cool night, but undeniably attractive on their young, fit bodies.

Martin seized the opportunity to nudge Ratty and tiptoe back down the hallway, turn a corner, and let themselves out the front door. They ducked into one of the recessed alcoves so common in buildings downtown. The alcoves were prized by the homeless. Fortunately theirs was unoccupied.

A minute later Kartane pushed open the same door, holding it for Charlotte. A true gentleman. Martin sneered from his shadowed perch. Ratty rustled, and Martin went still, hoping his alcove partner didn't do anything to reveal their location. It'd still be awkward to explain their presence, and Ratty didn't strike him as particularly diplomatic.

The Gorean held the passenger-side car door for Charlotte. A late-model BMW. The man had money. How nice for him.

Martin didn't breathe easily until the dark blue luxury car had disappeared.

When he did, he inhaled the smell of piss. Cursing, he stepped out of the alcove and let the moist night air seep into his sinuses, cleansing his nose and clearing his brain. "Filthy city. The homeless problem is out of control."

"So, move." Ratty stepped out, brushing at his coat with long strokes.

"I might, after the blackmail situation's settled."

Ratty looked at him quickly.

Martin exhaled noisily. "Never mind. Look, I've been foolish. Going after Charlotte as if I had any right to invade her privacy."

What was he doing, anyway, breaking into a building in the middle of the night? Taking these kinds of risks for a woman he barely knew? A woman who'd chosen Kartane over him? He wanted less responsibility for others, not more heaped onto the towering pile of duty that was his life.

Money. It came down to money, and freedom. Martin had been so close to both goals. Now his choices were being stripped away. Charlotte wasn't a viable choice. Was she?

"Ratty? When Charlotte talked about her, ah, visions, did she ever mention seeing me in them? Me and her, specifically." He tried to sound impersonal and businesslike.

He discovered it was impossible to sound impersonal and businesslike regarding Charlotte under the circumstances.

"Uh-huh. That's what I thought."

Martin bristled. "What? What's what you thought?" He clutched Charlotte's coat to him, scowling at Ratty. Ratty simply smiled.

Why had Martin ever tried to help him? Clearly Ratty was an ungrateful loose canon. Martin should ban him from Subspace to save himself trouble. Amethyst was far better off without him. Ratty had no friends in Subspace. Martin would tell Ratty so immediately.

"I think she must've had a vision about you. She's obviously crazy about you." Ratty grinned.

Martin decided he wouldn't ban Ratty after all.

18

Gail sprawled in her small, dark cell and cried.

It wasn't just the pain, though the whipping had been harsh.

It was fear.

What else was he going to do to her?

Kartane. Such an evil, crazy man.

Without the slightest warning, he'd come back, unlocked the door to her tiny room, woken her up with a curse and a kick. He'd hauled her out, ripped her clothes off, tied her face-down to an old mattress, and whipped her with some kind of heavy flogger.

He hadn't explained why. He hadn't talked to her. He hadn't sexually assaulted her. He'd just punished her.

He'd beaten the hell out of her for nothing.

No more sleeping for her tonight. Unless she passed out. She mewed, rolled onto her side with an effort that had more tears streaming down the side of her face. Her skin hurt. Her muscles ached. Her brain wanted to shut down.

She couldn't let her brain shut down. She had to get out before he hurt her worse, or killed her.

With shaking fingers, Gail investigated her butt and her back.

Cool wetness. That would be blood. Her fingertips traveled as far as she could stretch. Found parted skin. The lacerations were more numerous than they were deep.

Her hand slid, strengthless, to the packed dirt of the floor.

She began to shiver, more from shock than cold. She couldn't get comfortable and she hurt all over.

Her tears tapered off. She sniffed, feeling wretched.

She hadn't done *anything*.

Did that asshole think she was made of leather? She could get sick. An infection. She could die. How could he get away with this?

All she'd wanted was a nice date. Stepping so far outside of her comfort zone, stooping to fetish dating sites because the regular ones weren't working, she'd congratulated herself on being open-minded. On doing whatever it took to find Mr. Right and the elusive goal of marriage and pregnancy.

The guy Charlotte set her up with, the dark-haired one—Master Martin—took one look at her and got an expression on his face she was too used to seeing on first dates.

Sure she wasn't classically pretty. And she hadn't dressed all in black or rubber or naughty-schoolgirl outfits like some of the other women at the club. Maybe she'd come off a little abrasive, when he'd asked her if she was sure she had the right place. Perfectly understandable how she'd be a bit snappish after such a welcome. Overcompensating for her nerves and inadequacies made her act that way, made her need to take control of things.

His declaration that they didn't seem to have the right chemistry was par for the course. Usually, however, her dates waited longer than two minutes.

Gail's lips curled into a snarl of anger, remembering. He'd driven her away, right into Kartane's strong arms.

Kartane, a nice, easy "switch," according to him. Liar! He'd grinned at her, flashed those gorgeous eyes, bought her a drink, nodded his head, and acted gratifyingly attentive when she poured out her story of Martin's rudeness. He'd laughed and called Martin some rude names, which made her happy.

He'd nodded some more as she'd braved her opinions about dating, and about how much she despised overbearing men. He'd given her a knowing smile.

By the time he'd invited her downstairs, she was half in love with the guy.

Not anymore.

Gail clung to her anger, stoking it until her pains faded a little under the onslaught of adrenaline. Her mind filled with simmering rage, then white-hot fury. She launched herself at the metal door.

She pounded on it with all her might.

She didn't hear the small, frightened voice until she'd stopped.

"Please! Don't do that anymore! You'll have us all strung up for punishment." Gail heard fast breathing, like someone having an anxiety attack. Scraping and tapping sounds on metal. Fingernails?

Gail darted to the spot on the wall. "Who are you? Can you get me out of here?"

"Please." A girl. She sounded young and terrified. Tears clogged her voice. Her voice dropped to a strained tone just above a whisper. "We're not allowed to talk, not when we're in these rooms. These are supposed to be like solitary. They're breaking rooms. Don't show you're not broken." Her voice lowered to a whisper. Gail could barely hear her, but she'd heard enough.

"Kartane." Gail snarled it. "He whipped you, too? How many women does he have imprisoned down here?"

"Please keep your voice down!" Panicked.

Gail rose, her skin smarting all over. "Fine," she said, her voice soft. "But I'm getting out of here. You should, too. This place...this terrible place..." Words failed her. Finally she finished, "It's some kind of slaver operation. We're being 'broken,' then we'll probably be hooked on drugs and beaten to compliance, then likely sold to some rich, syphilitic Middle Eastern pervert. I've read about these things." In the perfect darkness, she began to feel around the door, searching for any gap in the metal, any weakness.

"You're wrong."

"Huh?" Gail pointed her face toward the girl's soft voice.

"Our owners live in town. They aren't so bad, usually. As long as you please them, they're very reasonable." Her voice held both certainty and a quavering doubt.

"Says the girl in a box. Your owner, you say? Are you retarded, or just freaking nuts?"

Silence.

Gail shrugged, continued searching for a way out.

After an hour she was trembling with exhaustion and shuddering from pain, and utterly defeated. The cell was a metal fortress all around, with hard-packed dirt and not so much as a rusty nail to use as a tool.

She pounded the door in an extremity of frustration.

This time the girl didn't say anything.

"Hey, you still there?"

Silence.

"What's your name? Mine is Gail."

Silence. Then, "This girl is called Sula."

She had a strange way of speaking. Maybe she was retarded. "Why do you talk that way? Aren't you American? What did you do to piss off your...owner? Is there any way out of these goddamned boxes?" Gail kicked the wall between them with her bare foot, then stumbled, wincing.

Silence.

"Look, I'm sorry, Sula. This is just difficult for me. Okay?"

"The shock of first bondage is hard," Sula agreed.

"You sound like you accept this."

"I . . . this girl only wants to please. My master's will is my will."

"You poor, brainwashed moron. Don't you want out of here? Didn't you have a life before? Isn't there anyone you miss?"

Sula sounded young. And incredibly naïve. Gail tried to pull back on the anger that had flared at the girl. She didn't deserve it. But it was hard. Gail felt so angry all the time, and now that she had real reason for it, the emotion drained instead of sustained.

As Gail fought against the old anger and the new exhaustion, another, softer whisper came. "I miss my dad. I was all he had after mom left him and moved out of state. I wonder if he looked for me. Maybe he didn't bother since I did the same thing to him she did. I left him." The agonized words were so soft Gail had to strain to hear them. "I ran away with my boyfriend, and things got so much worse. So terrible. On the streets, and then, here. I miss school, and my house. It was so clean and good. I miss my dad," she repeated with a catch in her voice.

"Hey." Gail felt uncomfortable. She had little experience with comforting people. "At least you have a dad. Mine took off when I was a baby, and my mom went nuts. She ended up in a state facility for the mentally unstable. I visited a couple times, but she was too out of it to know who I was." Gail shook her head briskly. "No sense dwelling on it."

"I miss him so m-m-much." The girl had turned on the waterworks.

Gail felt impatient. "Look, get over it. We've got a big problem here. You miss your dad? Good. Let's get you home. We'll all bake cookies and play board games and this will just be a bad memory. To do that, we have to get out of these metal cages. How do we do that?"

"We're not supposed to. This girl deserves to be punished."

"Fuck that. Snap out of it. You weren't always like this."

"I used to take gym classes. Mountain climbing was one of my PE electives."

Great, now the idiot was reminiscing. Gail gave up, crawled to the door, and started to dig with her short nails. One tiny spadeful at a time.

Suddenly something gonged the metal right next to her ear. Then again, higher. Gail froze, put her hands over her mouth to hold in a shriek. Kartane had returned. He'd come back to hurt her more.

She heard fast breathing from high in the air, then the thud of something heavy meeting packed dirty right outside.

Then the sound she'd quickly come to dread, the latch clicking and squealing as metal rubbed against metal. Her door opened.

The slender shadow wasn't Kartane. "I climbed," said the familiar soft voice.

"Atta girl," Gail breathed. "Oh, atta girl."

"Yeah?" Sula preened. "Thanks. But if we get caught, it will be bad. Very bad. Come this way." Sula groped for her hand, pulled her. "Oh," she said, noticing Gail's nakedness. "We have to get you a slave silk—a tunic—to wear. It's all he allows, here."

Gail peered at the girl's skimpy dress. "You climbed a wall in that?"

"I knotted it around my waist."

It fell barely below the waist unknotted. Gail raised her eyebrows when Sula found and gave her an identical one but said nothing. It was better than being naked.

"Here." Sula threw it over her head. The red silk settled simply, a sheer mini-poncho with slits all the way up the sides.

Gail plucked at the gossamer material. "At least it doesn't rub," she said pragmatically. Her lacerations might not be deep, but they still stung like fire. Her slacks and blouse wouldn't have draped so lightly on wounded skin.

She paused, looked again at Sula. "Are you okay?" She couldn't explain the odd, lingering concern she had for the much younger girl.

Her motherly instincts were kicking in at an inconvenient time, she decided. "Where's the exit?"

"I've heard there are two doors. But I'm only familiar with the tunnels to Kartane's building. My new master gave me to him to punish, tonight. But Kartane punished you instead. This girl is sorry."

"Stop talking like that," Gail said gruffly. "Is your name even Sula? Why were you being punished? You knee someone in the nuts?"

Sula gasped laughter, quickly stifled. "They would throw me to a sleen."

Before Gail could ask what a sleen was, Sula lowered her voice still further and whispered, "My name was Elizabeth. He made me . . . I had to discard my old identity and ritually beg to be made slave. Then he branded and collared me. Tonight he sold me."

"Branded? You begged to be a branded slave?" Gail's skin crawled. Maybe she had it all wrong. Maybe the girl actually was sick in the head.

"Yes. Begged." Sula's—Elizabeth's—voice was hard. "And you would've, too, after a few weeks. Believe it."

Gail rocked back as if struck. They'd tortured the girl. Jesus. "I'm so sorry."

"Some of the women come to enjoy the life of a kajira—that means 'slave.'" Elizabeth shrugged, a shadow against the darker shadows beyond. "I can't seem to perform as well as a kajira should. My master gave me back to Kartane to punish me for the crime of inattention at a gathering of masters. A slave's gaze is not free to wander." Elizabeth sounded stronger, almost hopeful. "I believe my master would like to trade me for a more dedicated slave. He is quite strict about such matters. But for some reason Kartane beat you tonight, instead. He will either break or destroy us both. After enduring the process once, I'm sure I'd rather die."

Sula cocked her head at a sound. Then: "We have to go!" She grabbed Gail's hand again, pulled with urgency. "If First Girl finds us, she'll—"

The lights turned on, flooding the cavernous room from its dirt floor to its unfinished, pipe-exposed ceiling. "She'll what?" A beautiful woman smiled with malice in her eyes. Her long red hair looked sleep-tussled and her own little red poncho was hopelessly wrinkled and clung to her curves. Her skin appeared bruised in places and scraped raw in others, but her smile didn't falter. "Do we actually have another escape attempt, Sula? Foolish, foolish girl." She looked curiously at Gail. "You're new. Not very young. Not a dancer or a pleasure slave. Destined to be a kitchen drudge most likely. You'd be wise to not bring attention to yourself." With that, she seemed to dismiss Gail.

"Sula, Sula, Sula. Your master will be most displeased. Kartane, too."

Sula wilted. "Please, Talia. Don't tell them. There's no need to tell Kartane. I . . . this girl didn't know what she was thinking." Her lips trembled. The brighter light revealed her youth. Coltish but athletic legs. Simple brown hair worn too long and straight. No makeup, or need for makeup with those pretty features and long dark lashes. She might be as much as eighteen years old. Maybe.

Talia grinned. "Hiding the truth from our masters would result in severe punishment for everyone. Whereas catching an escapee will result in my master's pleasure." She put her fingers to her lips and blew a piercing whistle. "Wake up, girls! We have an escape attempt!"

Gail watched with trepidation as first one woman, then another rushed into the room.

Sula pressed back, against her. Gail could feel her shaking, and it deepened her protective instincts toward the girl. Sula seemed terrified. But they were just women, fellow captives. Gail addressed them all. "What is this about? Why don't we all get out of here before the caveman comes home? Maybe tell the police so the asshole 'masters' can spend a good long time in jail?"

Sula whispered quickly, "Please don't make it worse."

The women didn't move. Gail whispered back, "What's wrong with them?"

"They are kajirae."

It seemed to serve as sufficient explanation for Elizabeth, but Gail noticed two women glancing at each other uncertainly.

Gail raised her voice to its most strident, argumentative level. "You're all stupid. You're gonna let them beat you, rape you, break you, and brand you? You gonna let them chop you up and eat you too, maybe, if they're in the mood? Maybe you are all better off down here, living like livestock."

A brunette answered with heat. "They don't eat us! You're the one who's stupid!"

"Oh, great. Welcome to third grade. Am I glue and you're rubber?"

The brunette looked confused.

"This is a chance, this is your gold-plated invitation, to get the hell out of this squalid prison. Remember the real world? The one where you're all equals in a relationship?"

"I . . ." One of the women started to step forward. Her friend held her back, whispering furiously.

Gail shook her head in disgust. "This is hopeless. We're going into that tunnel over there. Past the women who should know better!" She gazed at them with all the scorn she could muster. "Let's run for it," she added in a whisper to Elizabeth.

A tiny, gasping inhale. Then Elizabeth's slight nod. "Right." Gail felt her muscles tensing with readiness.

"Ready? Go!"

Trying to confuse matters further, Gail shouted as she ran, "This is the way out! Follow us if you want to live like a respectable human being! This is the way to civilization!"

With the lights on, Gail could easily see and dodge both women and the furniture and equipment. One woman's nails raked her skin, but she barely felt it.

More of the women remained frozen, and Gail dared to hope her shouts had intimidated them sufficiently to stay out of her way, and maybe even convinced others to follow: "Through the tunnel! Back to real life!"

When one shoved her, she abandoned the hope.

Determined to avoid any more encounters with Kartane, she recovered from her stumble and ran for her life.

She heard a gasp of pain behind her. They'd gotten Elizabeth. Stupid girl hadn't run fast enough.

Not her problem.

Gail made it a few dozen steps farther down the tunnel before slowing to a stop. She cursed. That dumb teenager. That crybaby, moron, weird-talking girl.

Tortured into cooperating with her captors, all but brainwashed into being a slave girl, Elizabeth had still tried to help Gail. She'd been brave enough to climb out and open Gail's door.

Of all the idiot things Gail had ever done in her life, going back into that slave pit of stupid slavish women, all of whom seemed to have a healthy case of Stockholm syndrome, would head the list.

Gail should go get the police. The police would rescue Elizabeth. Yeah. She took two steps forward.

Then stopped with another curse. Elizabeth had been convinced she'd be punished. Punishment meant serious pain. Or worse. The sleen thing had sounded ominous, whatever it was. Whippings hurt. They damaged. Gail's own seeping wounds still sent fiery reminders to her nerve endings.

And then, there was that head-honcho slave girl, what was her name . . . Talia. That one was bad news. She'd probably hurt Elizabeth out of spite. She'd certainly tattle to their "owners." Talia reminded Gail of a cruel cheerleader, the kind who wielded sex appeal and popularity with vicious glee. Then slept with half the football team.

Were the women playing some kind of crazy game? Or was it genuine slavery? If so, what made them stay when they didn't have to?

Gail frowned, torn. She'd be leaving Elizabeth at the mercy of slavers and their slut overseer. Not to mention a bevy of brainless women who didn't recognize a perfectly good escape opportunity when it slapped them across their collective face.

Gail turned back, angrier than ever. She walked back down the tunnel. She couldn't, wouldn't leave Elizabeth there alone. She had to try to convince the slave girls not to be such idiots. Maybe they'd listen.

19

"I'm sorry, ma'am. A dropped cell phone call is not sufficient evidence of foul play."

Charlotte tapped her short nails against the hard plastic of her notebook. She held her cell phone—warm from lots of recent use—to her ear. The police dispatcher's bored tone aggravated her.

Forty-eight hours, and still no word from Gail. Charlotte's many messages to her client went unanswered. She'd talked with Kartane for hours, too. She'd asked his advice.

She found herself trusting Kartane more than she had since before their marriage went sour.

She shook her head. Who would've thought they'd be good friends? Closer friends than before, after their adventures at Subspace then his building two nights ago. They had common interests. She'd prefer they didn't, and his involvement in Gorean play rankled, but she'd be dense not to recognize a certain kinship of interests.

She'd been wrong to keep him at arm's length this past year. When she needed friendliness and advice, he was there to help.

He'd advised her to wait to call the police. Said it'd be jumping the gun, and she'd just piss off her client. Charlotte would speak to Gail again soon, he predicted.

But though Charlotte patiently waited all of yesterday and most of today, when their three-o'clock matchmaking appointment passed without Gail calling, Charlotte called the police.

"If you believe the missing individual is a threat to herself or others, you should go to the local precinct to make your report."

The dispatcher was clearly used to fielding a variety of calls. Her blasé tone made Charlotte want to poke her with Martin's electrical prod. "You don't understand. If Gail missed our session completely, it means one of two things: either she's finally found Mr. Right without my help—unlikely, believe me—or she's possibly chopped into little pieces. Which is also pretty unlikely since she scares most guys away. See why I'm worried? Can't you just have someone check on her? I know where she was last seen, but I don't know where she lives."

"Ma'am, you're free to file a written report yourself, at which point the police department will determine if the individual is either a threat or is a vulnerable adult, for example, if she has severe mental health issues. If she is vulnerable, the person's name will be entered into the national database. Active searches occur only when there's some physical evidence of foul play. Do you have any?"

"No, but . . . no, I don't."

"Without that, there will be no active search. But you can file a report. If you have no other questions . . . ?"

Charlotte bit back a rude retort. The woman was just doing her job. "No, thanks."

"Thank you for calling Riverport PD; have a nice day."

Charlotte looked at the dead cell phone in her hand. "Okay." She stabbed it off.

A moment later it rang again. The police calling back, she thought, and flipped it open immediately. "Yes?"

"Charlotte?"

Charlotte gasped. "Gail? I've been worried sick about you! Why didn't you call me back? Why didn't you pick up? After your phone went dead I went to Subspace and—"

"I can't talk long," Gail cut her off. There was a new, subdued tone in her voice that silenced Charlotte more effectively than Gail's normal aggression. "I just wanted to let you know I'm, um, I'm doing fine."

Charlotte stared straight ahead, frowning. "Are you okay? You sound"—feverish? distraught?—"a little tired."

"That's right. I'm tired. I had to go on a sudden trip. I'm going to be taking a break from dating for a while. It's been a *subpar* experience anyway."

Charlotte blinked. She felt as if she were missing something. "But you'd wanted to ratchet it up. To go on even more dates. I don't understand. Am I doing something you don't like? I aim to make my clients happy."

In a flat monotone, Gail continued. "I just wanted to let you know I'm okay, so you wouldn't worry anymore."

In the background, Charlotte heard scuffling.

A gasp. Then Gail spoke again, her breath suddenly fast and unnatural. "I'd better go now. I'm feeling . . . very tired. Good-bye."

A click, then silence.

Charlotte tossed the phone onto her desk. "That's that, then." Gail clearly had had company. Just as clearly, she hadn't wanted to let Charlotte know it.

Gail hadn't wanted to take a so-called break from dating, she'd just wanted a break from her professional relationship with Charlotte.

She stared at the phone. It wasn't how she'd envisioned

Gail's call. Gail spoke her mind. She spoke her mind to a fault. She should have listed all Charlotte's inadequacies and bragged about how she'd found a guy with whom to get naked.

Charlotte shrugged. Maybe Gail was weirdly reticent about sex. Many people were. Or perhaps Gail had finally learned a little tact.

The woman still ranked as the strangest and most difficult client Charlotte had ever had. Charlotte was doubtless better off without such a moody client.

But against her will, a moodiness of her own stole over her. Gail had sounded well-occupied. Probably having fabulous sex while kicking Charlotte to the curb at the same time.

At least she'd had the courtesy to finally return Charlotte's phone call.

Of course, now Charlotte was client-free.

And sex-free.

She shifted in her chair, then winced. Martin had left her with a medley of lingering pains and soreness from two nights before. Her back. Her ass. Her scalp, where he'd pulled on her hair. Her whole body felt different, post-Martin. It felt alive.

Her body missed him, even if her brain didn't.

Okay, her brain missed him too. But it shouldn't.

Charlotte leapt to her feet. She'd get busy, clean the apartment . . . her gaze fell on the aquarium. Even with its dedicated light fixture, the cloudy water obscured her view of the fish and plants. She couldn't even see the coral tower and the little sunken ship with its tiny treasure chest and skull.

Her aquarium, normally a thing of color, movement, and beauty, looked like a toxic pond of silt and waste.

She equipped herself with gloves, scrubbers, tongs, and scrapers and began to work. After she finally cleaned the filter and pulled off the gloves, she smiled with satisfaction at the clear view of the colorful tank inhabitants.

But what was that? Her eyes narrowed, and she reached into the tank, disturbing the poor fish again. She rooted around behind the sunken ship.

She pulled out a dripping small, slippery, flat gray stone.

She turned it over. Yes, there was the *G*.

Kartane wanted this paperweight enough to specifically ask for it months ago. It held some sort of sentimental value. When had it gotten into the tank? Probably during the chaotic move.

Charlotte shrugged, dumped the wet, slimy rock back into the tank. Ugly thing. Why Kartane wanted it so badly was beyond her.

She'd jokingly tell him she'd found his pet rock, when she confessed Gail had finally called as he'd predicted. She'd bring it over to the old house with Hoagie's latest doggie toy that very weekend. She grinned, imagining the way her furry dog would whimper his joy and wag his tail so hard it moved his entire body back and forth. Hoagie liked his toys, and he loved seeing her. When she visited, it was almost like coming home.

Almost.

A pang of longing shot through her. How she wanted her own happily ever after, like what her clients got. To come home to a man she loved, to her own house, with Hoagie to greet her . . . the warmth and emotion of her desire shook her to her core.

It wasn't for her, though. She had to accept she'd never find a man who'd accept her for who and what she was.

Or would she?

Unbidden, an image of Martin rose in her mind. The hot movies and the thrill of lust accompanied his image. There was the man of her movie visions. Her X-rated gift paired her with Martin.

She tried to protest. To tell her visions that man all but threw her out of Subspace.

He touched a need within her nobody else had ever been able to reach.

Her body clenched pleasurably as if in confirmation. It ached with neglect as she thought about him.

She tried not to think about him. After what they'd shared together, the man had offered her and Kartane an escort off the premises, as if they might pick pockets and snatch purses on their way out. It was beyond rude.

With his image in her mind, she couldn't help remembering everything they'd experienced together.

She tried to think of more chores that needed doing.

The stupid movie in her mind started up whenever her attention wandered. The one starring Martin ravishing her brutally, thoroughly, deliciously. It was a dizzying emotional teeter-totter, taking her from anxiety to exhilaration.

He was bad for her, she told the visions desperately. Martin was violent. He didn't have to *punch* Kartane!

And yet, he'd done it for her. . . .

How perverse. More than a year after the branding trauma and finalized divorce, plenty of time to let her libido and brain reset to something resembling normal, and Charlotte found her sexuality awakened by another dominant.

A really, really good dominant. A compassionate dominant?

She'd all but begged Martin to use and abuse her. She'd craved it. Craved the depravity. Clearly she needed to keep her distance from Subspace.

"Have you wondered . . . just wondered . . . whether the fire of a slave girl burns within your belly?" Kartane had asked her while driving her home that night. She'd laughed it off, changed the subject, but inside she'd quivered.

She worried about herself.

How could she deny the truth of her body's response? At one point she'd felt *jealous* of the ravished slave girl.

How sick was that?

The rectangle of light at her living room window darkened. Charlotte looked at it. Subspace would open soon.

Martin, the hero of her movies, the man who complemented her so well, defended her so promptly, and frightened her so profoundly, was there.

She felt feverish with want.

She had to face it. He starred in her fantasies, but he was no figment of her imagination. He was real. He was there. And she wanted him more than anything in the world.

Charlotte rose to her feet, trembling at the decision she'd just made.

As if in answer, a lightning bolt of pleasure forked through her body.

"He's doing it again."

Martin looked at Amethyst. "Who's doing what again?" He didn't try hard to modify his tone. Couldn't Amethyst see he was busy?

He clutched the latest cell phone, delivered that evening through the mail slot of his locked office. The envelope had been waiting for him on the floor of his office, to be discovered after he'd opened his locked club, and that meant whoever was blackmailing him had a way into his club.

The only person he'd ever loaned a key, just the one time to cover the club while he was out sick, was Amethyst.

As if he didn't have enough to worry about.

His mom's sickness was holding steady, but the bills weren't. Oh no.

No stress here, nothing better to do than gossip with Amethyst. Who may or may not still have that key to Subspace. It could've easily been copied.

"What?" She stared at him. "See anything green?"

He looked at the woman without a word.

She simply placed her hands on black-latex clad hips and stared at him coolly. Her dark, black-lined eyes glittered dangerously. In her tight corset and with that careless sex appeal and attitude to spare, she certainly had the part of dominatrix down pat.

He felt a smile tug at the corners of his mouth.

Amethyst chose to play with Ratty, even though she had a waiting list of men eager to pay her for the privilege of licking her tall leather boots. No wonder Ratty was flipping over her. If only the guy could remain content as a bottom-leaning switch instead of striving for dominance, the two of them might have something.

Martin looked up into her eyes and felt his smile wither under her glare. "I don't know what is the matter with you lately, *Master* Martin, and I don't care. If you don't want to deal with that stinking scarecrow offending Subspace patrons, waving that stupid photo in everyone's face all night, that's your prerogative. Personally, I think it's a mistake. One of many lately," she muttered, turning away.

"Fine," he snapped, placing the envelope with its phone onto his desk. He strode past her without another look.

He cut his way through the night's bar crowd, then weaved through the goths and fetishists and adventurers and kinky tourists dancing to a remix of Ministry's "Everyday Is Halloween."

Sure enough, in the line just outside the front door, Peter shoved the battered photo of his daughter into the face of his next victim, a flannel-wearing guy who had numerous silver piercings from eyebrows to chin cleft. Peter's voice was raised, meant to be heard by as many as possible. "Please. This is Elizabeth. My daughter. Have you seen this girl? Anywhere?"

"That does it." Martin vibrated with fury.

He barely felt Amethyst's light touch on his arm. "Hey. I didn't mean to get you worked up. It'll be okay. Chill."

He shook her off, strode to Peter. Took him firmly by the elbow and hauled him away. "You're causing problems. I've asked you nicely. I get your pain. But you can't just harass people—"

"You get my pain!" Peter reared up. Straightened, he rivaled Martin's six feet. He wasn't as frail as he first seemed. Or as old. "You haven't a clue about my pain. She ran away from home last month. With a disreputable boy. She had every advantage, and now she's gone. Kidnapped. She's somewhere in your club."

"She's not in Subspace!" Martin exploded. "Don't you think I'd have seen her by now? After a month? She's not in there!"

"Last seen inside. Never came out." Peter began shaking. "Let me in to look."

"I did. Twice."

"I might have missed something," Peter whined. "Elizabeth is very young. You don't want me going to the police again, saying you let in a minor?"

"My permits are in order, as you found out."

"Just let me look—"

Martin seized him by his shirt. Shook him. "You are bothering my patrons. I've been more than patient. I've tried to help you. Over and over again. What do you really want, huh? Is it the club? Is it you, slipping those envelopes in the door, are you the one with the phones . . . ?" Martin shook him back and forth, until the sight of the trembling flesh on Peter's drunken, desperate face sickened him. Still, Peter stared, his eyes alight with determination, or avarice, or who the hell knew what. Martin didn't care too much at the moment.

Anger and resentment and frustration filled him. He pulled back his arm to punch the guy.

Amethyst knocked him off balance, making him lose his grip on Peter. "Stop it," she hissed. "You're making a fucking scene."

Peter stumbled back. "It's your fault!" he yelled. He turned, still shouting over his shoulder. "I know she's in there. You haven't seen the last of me!"

"He's a nutcase." Martin stared after him, the venom subsiding.

"A nutcase you nearly punched." Amethyst frankly stared. "Since when do you solve problems with your fists? This makes twice in three days. You slug the street people now? What the hell is the matter with you lately?"

Martin started inside.

She kept pace. "Well?"

"Peter was harassing the patrons. He'll scare them away." Martin pushed into the club with a nod to the doorman.

Amethyst followed, raising her voice to be heard over the music. "Well, yeah. But you think knocking him out in front of everyone will result in a collective sigh of relief? What is this actually about? Is it about Charlotte?"

When he wheeled angrily on her, Amethyst squared her shoulders and tilted up her chin. "Go ahead. Take a shot, asshole. The lawsuit will be very helpful. Can't think of an easier way to pluck this club from you. And the mandatory anger-management courses will do you good."

Martin checked his anger with difficulty. Normally he took Amethyst's bitchy, acerbic wit in stride, but she was pushing it. Really pushing it.

On the other hand, he hadn't been sure until this moment she wasn't the one blackmailing him. "Okay, Amethyst. You win. You want an explanation, so sit down and listen. The booth, there." He didn't quite shove her into it. He slid in opposite and spoke before she could take offense at his mild manhandling. "Shut up, please," he instructed as she opened her mouth. "I'm talking now. I'm being blackmailed."

He told her the details, about the mystery person's pressure on him to sell Subspace for next to nothing, about the delivered phones, about the threat to mail incriminating photos to his partner at Pavlov's Pet Joy. "Let me be frank with you. I need money from both that pet supply business and from Subspace for my mother's hospital bills. If Richard sees those images of me, all he'll think of is the negative publicity destroying both his reputation and our chance of selling the business to the buyer. But if I sell Subspace at a huge loss to the blackmailer, I'm screwed that way, too."

She started. "Richard? Richard Corvine, the Petclub tycoon?"

"That's one of his other companies, yes." Martin felt tired, suddenly. "Richard Corvine's about as vanilla as they come. An older, Bible-thumping, politically conservative country-club good ol' boy. Straight as an arrow. I checked him out."

"So all that's why you changed your mind about selling me Subspace." A small smile played about Amethyst's lips and her eyes twinkled.

Martin couldn't imagine what she had to smile about. "Yeah. So now you know. It's made me a bit short-tempered lately." He wasn't going to explain himself further. He felt stung. Why the hell was she smiling? "I'm sure I don't need to tell you to keep this strictly confidential."

"Yeah, yeah." She waved it off. "You should've told me sooner."

Tired of Amethyst's attitude, Martin stood. "I'll be in my office. Hi, Ratty." He walked away without waiting for a reply.

Ratty looked after Martin. "What's eating him?"

"Just about everything. But we're about to change all that."

"Are we?" Ratty remained standing even as he looked hungrily at Amethyst's well-displayed cleavage. "Maybe I'm not interested. Maybe I'm not at your beck and call anymore. Your fetch-and-carry boy. Your willing sex slave."

"And maybe you are, if I make it worth your while." Amethyst widened her eyes at him, mock innocent.

Ratty shook his head. "I'll probably regret asking. All right. What are we doing, and how will you make it worth my while?" He cocked his head at Amethyst, looking down at her crossed legs, then up to the purple streak in her hair. "Especially that last one."

"Ratty," she purred, snaking one long-taloned hand out to grasp his multicolored cloak, dragging him closer. "I'm so glad you asked. See these boots?" She uncrossed her legs, crossed them again in the opposite direction. "These boots were made for licking."

His reaction was explosive. "No way. Forget it. I'm not licking anything made of latex, leather, or rubber. If you can't see me as anything but a bottom—"

Her laughter stopped him. "Not you, silly. In fact..." She looked at his fierce expression, speculative. "If you help me with something very important, we can try a session together where you top me. Tie me up. Take out some of your problematic frustrations." She grinned at him. "I'll play along this time. Promise."

Ratty slowly grinned back. "That's more like it."

20

Charlotte's body moved to the rhythm, swaying to the music's throbbing imperative.

In her black jeans and faded black T-shirt, wearing dark eye makeup and bloodred lipstick, she knew she looked more like the other Subspace patrons: dangerous and ready to play.

She almost smiled as she made her way across the dance floor toward Martin's office, nodding her head and moving her shoulders and hips ever so slightly in time to the beat. Her hair, long and tamed to straight sleekness, gleamed in the low colored lights. Her black leather boots were old but serviceable.

Martin would be so surprised to see her. Pleasantly, she hoped. The doorman had given her a once-over and let her right in. But when she'd asked for Martin, he'd given her a strange grimace. He'd still pointed the way.

Tonight she meant to make the dirty movies with Martin come to life.

Shivering with anticipation, Charlotte remembered the last time she entered Subspace looking for Gail. Gail's phone call still struck Charlotte as odd. Odd enough that she found herself checking faces, still looking for her.

She tried to forget Gail. Now that the matchmaking business was stalled without her last client, Charlotte needed to find new ones. Maybe even here, at Subspace.

But first, she had unfinished business with Martin. Or rather, play.

At the end of a short hallway off the main floor, a crack of fluorescent light repelled the eye with its real-world business reminder. Martin's office, of course.

She made for it.

Though the bass still throbbed, she could hear his voice. Low and respectful. Caring.

A stab of jealousy speared her, unexpected.

Of course Martin had girlfriends. His talent, his charisma, hell, his position as manager of the club ensured he could have a harem of his own if he wanted. And why wouldn't he? What man wouldn't?

"I love you, too."

Her eyes narrowed when she heard the words. Love?

He hung up, and she saw him massaging his temples. Problems in paradise, she thought with mixed feelings as she pushed the door open.

As his gaze snapped to her, scanning her coolly from head to foot with no change in expression, her confidence deserted her. She consciously straightened her shoulders, walked in. "Hi."

"Back for more?"

It was such a change from his tone of voice on the phone that her back stiffened. Maybe coming here again was a mistake.

He looked down, rearranged paperwork. "I'm glad to see you're healthy, after leaving with Kartane. Being back with your ex seems to agree with you. But if you'll excuse me, I have important matters to attend to."

She poised on the cusp of fleeing again, this time for good.

She looked at his hands, grasping stacks of paper, sliding a finger into manila file folders to open them, tapping receipts with a slow, deliberate gesture.

Charlotte remembered his touch. "I am back for more."

"He get you all worked up?" he asked, his voice deceptively mild. "And now you're here to scratch an itch?"

"Don't be crude. I'm here because of you."

"I'll be crude when crude's called for. You left me for your ex. The one who branded you." He gave her such a cold stare she stepped back.

"True," she admitted. "But it's not the way you think. We're not back together."

"It's not your relationship status I question, it's your judgment. That man makes normal Goreans look benign. And believe me, that's an accomplishment. At least when Gail took off with him, I knew she'd tell him off within the first five minutes. He likes to own females 'for real,' but the smart ones don't stick." His look was pointed.

Charlotte stared at him. "Gail left with Kartane?"

"Just like you did. Even Amethyst did, for a while. And about a dozen others. Is it those big blue eyes? The blond good-looks thing? I don't get it."

She frowned. "This is important. Gail left with him?"

He nodded. "They went down into the dungeons. Lots of people around, nothing could've happened to her. Like I said, she doubtless left him in the dust as soon as he showed his true colors."

Charlotte reluctantly had to agree. "She doesn't put up with very much. She had to have ditched him right away...but where did she go from there? Why the weird phone call, then nothing till today?" Charlotte pondered. "Why did she want to come here at all? I don't know why she even gave you a chance, after your profile didn't complement hers. She wasn't looking for a dominant."

"What was she thinking?" Martin looked honestly curious.

"I suppose she figured she'd reform you." Charlotte looked at him. A smile threatened, but she controlled it. "Bring you to your knees, show you the error of your ways. That sort of thing. She must've been in the mood for a challenge. You're not a politically active vegetarian, you're not looking to start a family right away, and you're way too kinky for her."

"But not for you?" His voice was warm molasses. A smile quirked his lips, quickly hidden.

She made a show of considering. "I'm afraid not. You're not nearly kinky enough for me. You're just a tease, aren't you? There's rougher and tougher than you." Her blood surged and sang in her veins as she deliberately provoked him.

She gave him a ballsy wink.

Before she turned to leave, she was gratified to see his mouth fall open in surprise. "Bye-bye," she tossed over her shoulder, sauntering out. She gave a little extra sashay to her hips as she opened the door.

He was at her back, grasping a handful of her hair. "Not just yet." She felt her neck muscles straining as he gathered more hair. The large hardness of his body pressed against her, making his erection painfully evident against her still-bruised rear.

She tried to blink but her eyelids were strained open. "Mmm-hmmm?"

His fist moved up and down, making her nod. "Mmm-hmmm," he mocked. He flung her from him, making her stumble, then whirl to face him. "I know exactly what you need. The same thing I do, darlin'. But my way. Not yours." He gave her a wolfish smile, watching her pause in confusion, clearly enjoying the way she panted with lust. "I've got your number, little one."

"You think so?" She tried desperately to regain a sense of

control, even as she paradoxically savored his taking it away from her. Her heart beat so fast it seemed to want to burst out of her chest. Her nipples were rock hard, her pussy wet and wanting. Would he take her now?

He confused her more by simply leaning against his desk. Folded his arms. Smiled knowingly. "So you're a dating coach. A matchmaker. How do you stay in business, I wonder, if you make a habit of mistakes like matching up Gail and me?"

"Gail's a difficult case." Charlotte considered. "Was a difficult case. Business isn't so good now, partly because I am quite adept at the job. My movie visions never lie." She resisted an impulse to rub her scalp where he'd pulled her hair. Not because it had hurt, but because it tingled. Alive. She wanted that feeling deep inside, where only his most brutal thrusts would ignite her. But clearly he wasn't going to ravish her just yet. "I've matched up dozens of people. It's a gift," she declared, boldly meeting his gaze. "But because of it my clients only stick around and pay me for a little while before they go off together to get married and live happily ever after. Gail was my last client. Who knows what'll happen to her without my help."

Her clients' excitement and happiness when they connected with their soul mate rubbed off on her each and every time. She felt it in the crackle in the air around them at some of the weddings, their happiness conveyed by osmosis.

"What about the movies?" His voice prompted her.

She glanced at him guiltily. She'd just been thinking of the movies starring the two of them. His demanding, naked body. His face twisted with lust.

Now Martin's gaze, curious and skeptical, encouraged her, but with the graphic images of their violent coupling in her mind, she spoke with forced lightness. "I have X-rated visions, sometimes. Or maybe it's just a really good imagination."

When he only raised his eyebrows, inquiring, she continued.

"It works in person, and with dating profile photos. Sometimes I just, you know, see people together. I'll be working with a woman to help find her a date, and I'll see a guy's dating profile. And the movie starts. The two of them touching, kissing, making love. Sometimes—usually—it's pretty graphic. I can see them being intimate." She let her lips curl up in a smile. "When I see that, I make a strong case for the date, and most of the time they take my advice. And the rest is always history. They meet, they fall into each others' arms, I lose another client." She shrugged. "I got a lot of referrals for a while. But it's tapered off."

"I take it you didn't see Gail and I doing the horizontal tango?"

Laughter bubbled up inside her at the thought, but she quickly sobered. "I haven't seen Gail with anyone yet. She craves a bunch of kids and a husband accessory, but she's impossibly particular."

"And what about you?" he asked, his voice soft. "Are you particular?"

"Extremely," she breathed. "But not impossibly." He had no idea how appealing he looked to her, reclined like a lord, smiling like the devil.

"Did you see us together, Charlotte? You and I?"

When he levered himself up and started toward her, no power on earth could have stopped her from gasping.

He only grinned. "Let's go on a walkabout, shall we? Put your talent to the test here at Subspace. If you convince me, I'll introduce you to a bunch of single friends of mine who'll be very interested in your kind of professional help."

"I don't have to prove anything to you." She looked at him in dismay. This was not going the way she'd planned. She wanted to act out their movie, not watch new ones.

"You don't have to do anything," he agreed. "I'd never force a lady against her will. Unless she wanted me to." He winked, a mirror image of the wink she'd given him earlier.

She had to laugh. She let him lead her back to the dance floor and the bar beyond. Her gaze took in the grinding couples, the gyrations of singles, the clump of thirsty club-goers waiting for the bartender's attention. Her gaze snagged on the bartender.

"Him. That bartender. And . . . huh. Interesting." Charlotte peered from the whipcord-thin, long-haired bartender—more hippy than goth—to the enormous black bouncer who'd tangled with Ratty two nights before. "Yeah. Him and the big bouncer who wants to be his submissive. You should see what I'm seeing. Now there's a movie."

She felt Martin's body convulse with laughter before registering the sound. The movie was drawing most of her attention. How very odd to see the powerful bouncer on his belly, his large, muscular ass stuck up in the air like that. And the skinnier bartender covering him, handling him with a grace and strength that made the cords of his forearms stand out. "Wow. He's strong for his size. Huh," she said again, then focused on Martin. "What?"

He gave her an open-mouthed grin, wiping tears of mirth from his eyes. "I knew it. They've been hiding it from me. Afraid I'd think it's a conflict of interest and fire one of them."

"You won't, will you?" She rounded on him. "I don't want to get anyone in trouble."

"No. I won't. So long as they're discreet and it doesn't affect their work. They're so busy hiding it that they're my hardest workers." He smiled, unrepentant. "I took Tyro over there for a switch, though. All that bouncer bluster. He can be pretty intimidating."

"I don't think Amethyst believes in switches. Ratty is one, though. I've seen them."

"Ratty and Amethyst?" Martin stared. "Those two are meant to be together?" He shook his head with small, regretful smile. "I want to believe that, but I think you just blew your credibility. He needs more topping with her, but she won't give him the respect a top needs."

"No. I'm sure of it." Charlotte remembered the images. It was beyond doubt. Amethyst performing disciplinary moves on Ratty, and torturing him, but she'd seen Ratty working on Amethyst, too, in an undeniably toppish role.

She relayed the movie she'd seen of him with the Christmas-themed pins, and the other intimacies indicating a more flexible power exchange. Some of the back-and-forth and sexual combinations wouldn't have seemed possible to her if she wasn't watching them right there on the movie screen in her mind. "They might not know it yet. Couples often don't, at first. But they've got lifetime potential."

"Amethyst and Ratty." He smiled, wondering. "You're right, he doesn't want to be just a bottom. But can Amethyst hand him the reins, I wonder?"

"She will eventually."

"You sound certain. So, tell me. Did you ever see yourself with Kartane?"

The question was so unexpected, Charlotte answered without thinking. "Never." Was Martin jealous? Was he in any position to be jealous? Was he even available? His conversation she'd interrupted had sounded fairly intimate. "By the way, who were you on the phone with earlier?"

She immediately regretted it when he turned an amused gaze on her. It wasn't like they were in a relationship. Well, the movies in her mind said otherwise, but he might not feel the same way yet.

Before she could retract the question, he offered his answer. "My mother. She's very sick. It's a repeat bout with cancer. It's been a challenging year, financially and otherwise. Especially this month."

"Oh, my God. I'm so sorry." She felt her face flame with heat.

"Stop. It's life. And death. Age and sickness and medical bills happen." He seemed about to say more, but changed his mind. "Hey, let's grab a booth."

"Let's grab some quiet time downstairs. In the dungeons." Her instincts were taking over. Their talk of life and death, just as easily as if it were any other subject, inflamed a desire in her for life. For everything life had to offer.

She touched him, a hesitant graze of her fingertips against the silky cotton of his long-sleeved shirt. "You're one of the good guys, aren't you?"

"About some things, yes." He gave her a look that made her want to purr. He guided her to the stairs, led her down them. "I do my best to protect the things I care about." His fingers grazed her cheek, her smooth hair. She leaned into the caress.

"You're bringing out my irresponsible side," he growled, pressing his hard body against her briefly at the bottom of the stairs. "I'm really liking it."

She didn't tell him she thought he was one of the most responsible men she'd ever known. Running Subspace, making sure everyone played safely, defending her against harm, caring for his sick mother too. . . . He'd already had her interest and her lust. Now he had her admiration. Maybe even more.

But of course she wasn't about to wither his playful mood— or anything else—by admitting heavy things like that right now. She compromised. "I'm really liking you." She brushed her body teasingly against his. "Find us a private play space."

He grinned, steering her through the second interconnecting tunnel and beyond its smaller dungeon to a locked door. With a flourish, Martin produced the keys and unlocked it.

21

The room was bigger than the one made to look like a medical examination area. It had none of the doctor furniture or tools. The recessed lighting on the walls revealed what at first appeared to be a traditional, tastefully appointed woman's bedroom, as if the woman in question enjoyed a lot of pink, ruffles, and an ornate gilded mirror perched above a vanity cluttered with old-fashioned perfume bottles, cosmetics, and even a silver-handled brush.

Closer scrutiny revealed the walls, covered in a coordinating design of pink fabric, were lightly padded from floor to ceiling.

Martin watched her walk to the nearest wall and dimple it with one finger.

He closed the door behind him. He locked it.

"The padding's so people don't get hurt," he explained as she poked the other walls curiously. "This is the Rough and Tumble room. Currently decked out as a proper lady's boudoir for the upcoming Blood Orange Games." He looked at it critically. "It was a mental asylum last Halloween, but I wanted something different this year." He looked at her. "Something innocent to defile."

"I thought you didn't play."

"I've been living vicariously. Same as you, little miss X-rated visions. Please. Have a seat." He pulled out an antique-looking padded sitting chair for her. He handed her the silver brush.

She took it, feeling the wild humor rising in her again. "My hair needs attention. Hint taken." She looked at the ornate silver brush. Clean. Heavy. Its bristles trapped no stray strands. She shrugged, began to use it. The soft bristles stroked her scalp with a soothing, steady caress. She tugged strands of hair, brushing them until they gleamed. The old-fashioned brush offered a gentle touch.

Too gentle.

She was primed for something a bit more wild. No, a lot more wild. She sensed its potential building in them both. She remained just as she was, brushing, letting the energy hum between them. It crowded the air, nearly a tangible thing. The movies taunted her. It was as if he'd plugged into her deepest fantasy.

"Every part of you needs attention."

She froze at the deep sound of his voice, then continued brushing. "I'm alone, brushing my long hair. All by myself, fantasizing about sensuality. Daydreaming about the sudden appearance of a handsome, dangerous man who just won't take no for an answer. I'm so innocent, so vulnerable. I wonder what a man's touch feels like."

Martin made an appreciative sound. "You play the role well."

"Do I?" She paused teasingly, letting the brush drift to the table. Her hands slid up over her black shirt, brazenly circling her nipples. She leaned back, her eyelids drifting half closed, dreamy, even as her newly brushed hair slithered sinuously around her shoulders.

"Handsome, huh? I hope that part isn't a deal breaker." He spoke wryly, but she saw the real concern in his eyes.

"You're joking. Right?" She stared at him. She saw his crooked features and uneven lips anew. His piercing, intelligent eyes. His incredible body. The package of him simply worked. How astonishing he had no idea of it. "Martin. You're the most attractive thing I've ever seen. Not some airbrushed magazine cover model, but the real, raw deal. You radiate a primal magnetism. I'm sure you've seen how many heads you turn."

He looked uncomfortable. "You're sweet. If any heads have turned, I haven't noticed." He shrugged. "I hold my own with women, I suppose. None of that has seemed important since Mom got sick again, with no one to care for her except me. Death is real. Loneliness is real. That's about when I realized I wanted to get serious about finding someone to share my life with. Hence the dating-site profile you saw."

His solemn expression told her he spoke the truth. He honestly had no idea of his sex appeal.

Lucky her.

But she sat up. "You're attractive enough to make people walk into walls. You're certainly my fantasy man."

He grinned. His happiness licked out at her with an almost palpable sparkle. "That's what I wanted to know."

Her heart filled with a wondrous ache. It took her a moment to realize it was joy.

Martin spoke again, more lighthearted. "We'll have to get you a dress. Tight jeans are difficult to yank down. A dress flips up so easily, and panties are simple to push aside. Or rip off."

She tilted her head, intent. "Are you going to stop living vicariously?"

"I fantasize. Just like you."

Their eyes locked. She shuddered with frustration. "Then what are you waiting for?" she whispered.

"The proper time."

"When might that be? Halloween? Have you missed my not-so-subtle invitation to you?"

"A consensual non-consent scene must be negotiated in advance. No, I haven't missed your signals, you teasing little angel. I don't believe you've missed mine, either," he said with a wry smile.

She looked pointedly. "Hard to miss." He offered sizable tribute.

"To answer your question, Charlotte, the proper time is when I decide it is. Edge play can go very wrong. As you know."

"Fine." She stood, trying to ignore the sting of rejection. As if she, of all people, wasn't smart enough to realize things could go wrong. "I guess we can negotiate later. If I don't find someone else in the meantime." She tried to stare him into embarrassment, but his steady gaze beat hers down. The floor was covered by a much darker color than the wall, a glossy maroon. It was a large mat, she realized. She poked at it with the toe of her boot. The mat felt thin enough she hadn't noticed its discreet placement until actually examining it.

"Take your pants off."

Her gaze snapped back to his. "Excuse me?"

"Do we need to go over that again? I won't say it twice. Don't make me repeat myself." He noticed her glance at the door. "There's a 'Do Not Disturb' sign that comes on when it's shut."

Her fingers toyed with the waistband of her jeans. "You call this negotiating?"

"I can assure you that if you don't have your pants off within ten seconds, you are going to be one sorry girl. Ten. Nine. Eight."

Charlotte unbuttoned, unzipped, then remembered her boots. "Give me a minute," she complained, stooping to remove them.

"Seven. Six. Five."

She panicked when he walked toward her, stumbling back with her pants around her ankles. "Jeez, wait a sec."

But he wasn't walking to her. The dressing table with its carved mirror offered lovely painted drawers on either side of the sitting area. She'd assumed they contained more cosmetics, perfumes, hair ornaments and the like.

Of course, they didn't.

Martin opened the bottom one, drew out a large, lumpy velvet bundle. It clinked. Jewelry? No, too large.

He glanced at her. "Four. Three. Two."

She shimmied out of her jeans and stood in her black tee and skimpy white bikini briefs, self-conscious and awkward. "Am I supposed to . . . ?"

"One."

Martin placed the velvet bundle on the dresser.

Then he turned to her with his most forbidding look, walked her backward, and shoved her against the nearest wall. Its padding cushioned her from damage, but it knocked the air out of her. "I've always wanted to do that," he confessed. "And this." His large hands fisted the front of her panties. The edges dug into her flesh, climbed up her crack despite her clenching against it. With one violent tug, he ripped the material.

The sound of it echoed with the delicious violence of her fantasies, and Charlotte moaned as he flung the shreds of her panties from her. Surely now he'd take her. Here, up against the wall. Or the floor. She didn't care.

His body heat made her want to moan again with pleasure. The bulk of him nearly touched her. She hooked one slender leg around his still-clothed thigh. Tugged him gently toward her.

"Stop. Go sit in the chair."

She looked at him unbelievingly. "Now?"

He smiled. "I warned you." He flipped her around so she faced the wall. Her breath came fast against the papery wall covering. "I can still see the faded marks from our session two nights ago. Very nice." Her ass twitched as his warm finger traced first one pink marking, then another. "There's room for more."

"Wait—"

"Ten spanks for not obeying promptly. There has to be trust, Charlotte," he said with the infinite patience she'd begun to associate with him. "You need to trust me to take the lead. If I'm leading, you're following. If you're following, you do what I say, when I say it. You will count, please. Then we'll negotiate the rough stuff."

He landed a brutal blow on her ass.

She struggled, and he had to hold his forearm against her back. She heard his soft voice in her ear. "I'm waiting."

"One! This seems pretty rough to me." But she wiggled invitingly. It wasn't really that rough.

"Just the number, please. Since you're a slow learner, I'll let you start again," he said.

Whack!

The blow impacted even harder. "One." She heard her sullen voice.

"If you're not amenable to correction, or not into this, simply say the word 'red.' " His voice, bored.

Did he honestly think she wasn't into it? Couldn't he see the sensual thrusting of her rear after each spank? Couldn't he hear her rapid breaths? Was he totally missing the wetness between her legs?

"One!" she shouted, mock-cheerleader.

She heard a small noise, but before she could turn to see if Martin was laughing, he landed another blow, this one high on her thighs. Was it a coincidence his fingers trailed slowly up to her ass cheeks, probed gently at the crease between her thigh and the mound of her outer labia? It was fast. Too fast.

Whack!

"Two!"

Whack! Whack! Whack!

She counted, barely able to keep up with his strikes. It hurt, of course; skin abused from earlier in the week woke to the new chastisement and complained. And yet, it felt right. Like the itch Martin had mentioned earlier. An itch only he could scratch. If only he'd stop making it worse.

A pleasantly fuzzy heat began to suffuse her.

Whack! Whack!

After she called out the last, his hand lingered, then reached between her legs with unerring aim to circle her clit. The sensation shocked her to motionlessness, lest she inadvertently cause him to stop. She kept still, savoring, even when he altered his movement from circling to caressing with gentleness that stopped and started again, inflaming without satisfying.

She knew he could do it to her all night. Probably would, just to watch her squirm. The bastard.

"Haven't you punished me enough?" she finally gasped. "Don't I deserve . . . ?" She felt on the verge of begging.

"Deserve? Get your ass over to that chair. Sit down and spread your legs."

In a sensual daze, she stumbled from him, attempting to follow his directions. If only he'd tackle her, take her. The man was an unfeeling bastard, made completely of stone.

How she wanted that man, splitting her right up the middle with that one hard, defiling act, using his enormous penis as a weapon. Why wouldn't he match his actions to the movies looping with provocative insistence in her mind?

She managed to find the chair through blurred vision, sat. "Please," she finally said.

"No." Only that.

He smiled though. A flash of eagerness, a hint of anticipation. He crossed to the table, began to unfold the lumpy velvet package.

It worried her. What was it?

He noticed her look. A slight frown marred his face. "Close your eyes. If you open them even a crack, I'll turn you over my knee and give you twenty hard ones."

"All I want is one hard one." But she complied. "Tease."

He unwrapped the velvet. "I've always wanted to try this."

She peeked. Slithering out from the folds was a length of chrome-plated chain, as smooth and pretty as jewelry. He ran his fingers over each link.

"You're going to chain me up?"

"You'd best not have your eyes open."

She shut them quickly. "Nope."

"Liar." But she heard the smile in his voice. The sound of another drawer opening tempted her to open her eyes again, but she resisted, though the sounds intrigued her: the liquid squelch of lube? The faint cotton hiss of a towel?

Was that the tickle of his hair on her thighs? His mouth! She cried out at the hot, wet sensation of his lips and tongue between her legs, as intense as it was unexpected. "Oh, yes!" She gripped the carved edges of the chair, pushing herself at him.

He moved slightly away. More teasing. When he brought his talented fingers into play along with his gently flicking tongue, she moaned. He slowed, pushing her upper body farther toward the back of the chair. He lifted her legs, first one and then the other, placing her feet on the edge of the chair. She'd be visible to him completely, though her own eyes remained shut.

He tongued her again, massaging her with hands and mouth.

Right when she thought she couldn't restrain herself from grabbing the back of his head, making him satisfy her, he stopped. "Your eyes still closed?"

"Yes, damn it." She squirmed.

He shoved the cotton towel between her butt and the chair. "Good. Hold still."

His hands played between her legs, caressing, and spreading.

Suddenly, she felt a warm, hard link of chain being inserted. It went in so smoothly she knew it was heavily lubed. "What are you doing?"

She didn't expect him to answer, and he didn't. He inserted another link, pushing it deeply with his finger. As the remaining links followed, she felt the chain being pushed more deeply inside. It slowly filled and stretched her.

"Comfortable?" Martin pushed another link into her.

"I'm . . . wow. It's . . . intense."

He spoke in a lecturing tone. "Though there are few nerve endings in the smooth walls of the vagina, they're not fully stimulated—woken up—even during sex. I'm waking yours up. The stretching should introduce new sensations."

"I want . . . oh, God, it's amazing."

She heard the smile in his voice. "It gets better." His fingers paused their link-pushing to toy with her clit. "Just keeping you warmed up."

"I'm on fire!"

It was the wrong thing to say. He withdrew his fingers.

"Don't stop!" she complained.

"Patience." He pushed in another link.

As the chain slowly filled her, the sweet pressure of it touched places she couldn't have imagined. Similar to a G-spot touch with its deep and stimulating caress, the chain pressed against her more insistently and in more places. Martin was right. It was a sensation unlike anything she'd felt before.

"There. Hold still."

She stilled her squirming. "I didn't realize I wasn't. Martin, please . . ."

"Patience," he repeated. He flicked his finger against her clit and she cried out. "You're on the edge, aren't you?"

"Yes!"

"Good." He rubbed her clit skillfully and with purpose.

"Oh!"

218 / *Christina Crooks*

At the very moment her orgasm began, he pulled the chain out in one swift and continuous motion.

The throbbing bullets of ecstasy pummeled like multiple rapid-fire hits to her insides, intensifying her pleasure beyond anything she'd experienced before. She was aware of her scream and a gushing wetness only afterward, as the quakes shook her.

She became aware of his strong arms holding her steady.

She struggled for breath. "What . . . was . . . that?"

Her body continued to convulse with pleasure. She grasped the intricately carved wooden armrests and felt the pleasure going impossibly on and on. Her vision grayed out, and she had to tighten her grip on the chair to keep from sliding right off. Dampness wet the towel beneath her, and her inner thighs were soaked.

Charlotte didn't care. She slowly opened her eyes. "Please. What was that?"

Martin gathered the chain links, a smug smile on his face. "A simultaneous G-spot and clitoral multiple orgasm, unless I miss my guess. I do like you saying 'please' that way. It's sexy as hell." He dumped the lot into a bio-waste bin.

He turned to her. He looked at her sprawled position, took in her still-panting breaths. His erection strained at his pants. "Much too sexy."

Charlotte gathered her thoughts. They didn't take much gathering, as she wanted only one thing. "You said a consensual non-consent scene is edge play and has to be negotiated in advance. Let's negotiate. Now."

He stared at her for so long she crossed her legs, and her hot skin began to cool. Her body longed for his, but he seemed forever destined to remain aloof. It maddened her, subdued her, and excited her all at once.

The oddly exhilarating feeling was normal around Martin.

"Soon."

She stared at him. "Soon? Just 'soon'?"

His mouth quirked into a smile. "There's a bit more to it. There are hard limits and soft limits. There are safe words. There's pain and humiliation tolerances to determine, and safety considerations. It's a lot to cover. Probably best set up for another time."

"I don't think so." She straightened, belatedly realizing her arched-back, cross-legged position thrust her breasts forward. Then just as quickly, she smiled. Let her nipples signal him. Let her round breasts and the tiny glimpse of her dark triangle below drive him beyond all control.

She gave him her most challenging look. "You're all talk and tease. A bit of strong-arming, a wimpy little spanking, and relying on sexual toys? Though that last one was admittedly pretty amazing," she muttered. "You're adept with gimmicks. But you're not able to keep it up, are you? The old trouser snake gone to sleep? It's okay, there's nothing to be ashamed of." She gazed at his crotch pityingly.

He choked, spoke around laughter. "You're relentless."

She grimly fought back a smile. "And you're not relentless. Too bad for me." She rose, reached for her jeans. The panties were beyond repair.

She moved to pull her jeans on, hoping he'd stop her.

He didn't.

She buttoned the top button, looked at him with real disappointment. But she made herself speak with politeness. "Thank you for an incredibly pleasurable time."

He paused, then nodded. "Yes. I had a lovely time as well." He cleared his throat. "Ah, I'd promised to hook you up with a few singles of my acquaintance. Referrals for your dating coach business. Some of them are currently actively looking on fetish sites, others are older, wanting to settle down, more interested in vanilla-type dating. And there are a number of women and men who tend to use the weekly munches here at Subspace as a dating service, which is of course not the appropriate venue for such things. So you'll really be doing me a favor."

"A favor." She stared at him. "You're kind of babbling."

"Yeah, I know." When he slicked his hair back from his face she noticed how damp his skin was.

"Are you feeling okay, Martin? You didn't, you know, sprain anything? While you were doing that with the chain."

"No." He backed away from her. "You should probably go now."

Curiosity rose inside her. Then new awareness prickled her. He was nervous! Why?

"Martin?" she asked wonderingly.

"Just go. Get out."

"No."

"Just please do it."

"That's my line." She began to smile. "You'd like nothing more than to do me. Embedded to the hilt. Grunting like a pig at the trough. Until I cry with pain and shame, all wriggling and bucking unsuccessfully trying to get away. Gasping and begging you to stop, please, it hurts . . . yes?"

His lips pressed together. Then: "Charlotte . . . I'm very serious. Your safety is important to me."

"I know." And she did. Tender feelings shot through her, circled her heart. This man, the yang to her yin, the only one who seemed to accept and understand her, was trying to protect her. "You said there are hard limits and soft limits. And safe words—mine is 'red.' There are pain and humiliation tolerances. My tolerances are high. No permanent damage, like scarring . . . as for safety considerations, I assume you mean condoms. I further assume you will cover that issue. So to speak." She grinned.

"I can't believe I'm discussing this with you now. I swore to myself I'd take it slow with you. It's getting late. You should be basking in my aftercare. I give good aftercare." He sounded strained.

"I remember. But, Martin. That's not what I want right now."

She watched him swallow visibly. "Very well, Charlotte. I tried." He paced. "I didn't count on the anticipation making a mush of my brain where you're concerned." He took a deep breath. Exhaled. "All right. You forgot one thing though. Hard limits and soft limits. Do you know what those are?"

"I could guess. Hard. Hmm, let me see..." She smiled, lascivious.

"No, it's not funny time right now. I'm quite serious, and you should understand. Limits define the boundaries of what each person is willing and unwilling to do within a scene. Limits apply to activities, roles, intensity of dominance and submission, time duration, and physical activities such as bondage, whipping, or penetration." He stared at her. She had the feeling he'd assumed a teaching role, and it made her shift with impatience.

He continued. "Hard limits define something absolutely not okay with you under any circumstances. Soft limits mean boundaries that should be respected, but possibly pushed. Charlotte, what are your hard limits with me?"

The words burst from her. "A little late for those soft limits, don't you think? A lot of those things, we already did."

"You had a safe word." He sounded defensive.

"You got carried away." It was a revelation. "You wanted to play with me enough to bypass those formalities."

"You'd provoked me into it," he retorted. "And *you* had *me* at your mercy initially."

"Doesn't matter. Master Martin, owner of Subspace, skipped your 'quite serious' discussion of limits until now."

"Where we need them most. Tell me what they are. Or, I leave." He meant it. She'd pushed and prodded him into leaving, still sporting an erection that tented his pants into a mighty mountain.

"Yes, Martin." She smiled. She'd won! Exhilaration and lust surged and broke throughout her body, leaving her trembling with eagerness. Finally. Oh, finally. "My hard limits? No blood, no brands, no broken bones, no multiple partners, no unsafe sex. And as I'd already said, no permanent damage." Her hand crept toward her scar.

His hand went to her arm, stopping her. His smile was as warm as his honeyed voice, but his grasp all but ground the small bones in her wrist. "Don't even begin to consider I'd mar your beauty that way. Now. Keep your clothes on. I'm going to leave the room. Sit before the mirror and brush your hair as if you're the only person in the building. When I decide to, I'll come in. There will be a struggle. I will rape you. Is this acceptable?"

Her mouth went dry. Could she really do this?

His grip tightened. "I won't be merciful," he whispered. "Or kind. I'm going to fuck you in every possible way, and you will cry. You'll feel me shoving it all the way to your belly, pounding away, and I'll enjoy your struggle."

"Maybe I won't struggle." She realized she'd whispered, too. She spoke normally. "Maybe I'll enjoy it."

"And maybe you won't." He smiled. She shivered.

He released her wrist.

"So. I'm, what? The innocent victim of a home break-in?" She made her voice deliberately light, uncaring. "Completely oblivious, until I suddenly see the man who has invaded my room?"

"That will do." Already distant, he turned and crossed to the door. Opened it. Left without another word, which was somehow the most chilling of all.

"Oh my God, I'm really doing this." She paced for a moment, then sat down. The lump in her pocket reminded her of the phone she carried. Good thing it hadn't rung during the chain adventure.

Charlotte flipped it open, glad for the familiar routine as she glanced down at it to check for messages. Nothing more from Gail. Of course. Gail was otherwise occupied now.

Probably.

Charlotte frowned. Unease pierced the seductive haze. Gail'd said she was tired, but clearly she'd had company. And yet, she hadn't sounded hot and bothered during that last call, Charlotte realized with the memory of her own response to Martin fresh in her mind. She'd sounded exhausted rather than satisfied.

Charlotte should make one last quick call to make sure of her. It would probably piss Gail off, but now that the worry had entered her brain, Charlotte couldn't shake it.

Charlotte dialed, already impatient. She'd leave another message when Gail didn't pick up, then maybe her nerves would give her some peace. They had better things to do, Charlotte remembered with a return of her heat.

Finally, Martin would fulfill his role as her fantasy man.

Gail's number rang, and rang.

Charlotte saw the door swing open and Martin enter stealthily, but he'd forgotten to turn off his own phone. She grinned as he fished quickly for it, backing out of the room again to answer it.

Rapeus interruptus, Charlotte thought wryly. How modern they both were with phones to their ears. She couldn't blame Martin a bit. It might be his sick mom. It might be . . .

Her phone clicked as Gail picked up. Charlotte started with surprise. "Hello?"

"Yeah. Disguising your voice won't help."

It wasn't Gail. It was a guy.

Charlotte was too surprised to do anything but listen.

"I need more time." A male voice. A familiar voice.

224 / Christina Crooks

"Hello," she tried again. "I'm calling for Gail. Who is this?" But by then she'd placed the voice. Her body became rigid with shock. "Martin?"

The door swung open. He stood there, Gail's phone to his ear. He slowly clicked it off. Tucked it into his pocket. His features had turned to an inscrutable mask of granite.

The nauseating panic that surged through her made her realize how much she'd been simply playing at fear. Even when she'd been at Cory's mercy, she hadn't felt this level of betrayal. That was mere toying with dominance and submission and pain, compared to what she'd been about to do with Martin.

Martin, Gail's abductor.

He was the real deal, and it scared the shit out of her.

She leapt to her feet, her lips and her body numb. "You!"

"Charlotte. Sit down."

"I'm leaving."

"No, please. Not yet."

She bolted. She half hoped it was some horrible misunderstanding, that he'd let her go.

Right up until he moved to block her at the last moment. She ran straight into him, but the soft floor didn't give him the best leverage. She used his slight overbalancing to push him farther in that direction as she leapt the opposite way, out of his reach.

But he was quick, and as she jumped over him toward the door he grabbed her ankle, yanked.

She fell to the cushioned floor.

He threw the full weight of his body onto her. "Charlotte, stop. You don't understand."

She struggled. "You're crushing me."

He was. She had to fight for breath.

Easing up slightly, he began to speak.

She inhaled deeply, then shouted. "Red!" She struggled harder. "I said 'red.' Do you hear me?"

He nodded.

"Then get off me!"

"Not yet. Not until you understand—"

Her fears were true, all true. The Martin she thought she knew would've respected her safe word.

With tears in her eyes, she slumped ever so slightly, to lull him into raising his body off her a little more.

Just enough.

She brought her knee up, hard and vicious between his legs.

The wounded sound he made tore unexpectedly at her heart.

She still shoved him away, then crab-crawled out of his range as fast as she could force her limbs. She dug her nails into the soft wall to pull herself to her feet.

Then she ran.

22

As Amethyst ground her high heel into Richard Corvine's wrinkled, flabby neck, she yawned.

She looked down at the fully clothed executive and decided she'd quit the pro-domme business after this session. Desperate older men, like Richard here—she pressed down until he whimpered—who paid her to spank and humiliate them, gave her less and less joy.

At first, of course, the easy dominance had been the whole point. After Kartane, she'd needed to reestablish her sense of feminine power. That bastard and his corrosive sexist philosophy had left her shaken.

What galled Amethyst in retrospect was her willingness to participate for as long as she had. A few more weeks of Kartane's brainwashing about women having slave hearts, and she might've actually started to buy into it.

She placed her hands on her latex-clad hips as she posed before the kneeling man. She nudged his face with the toe of her boot. "I stepped in dog shit on the way here." She reclined on the hotel room's single chair, crossed her legs. Her boot stuck out. "Lick it off," she commanded.

"Yes, Mistress." Moaning with eagerness, Richard slobbered onto her thigh-high, lace-up stiletto boots. There wasn't really any dog shit on them, but he didn't know that. Or care about anything but his fantasy.

Amethyst pictured Martin's face when she told him about Richard Corvine's sexual predilections. It would be even better when she showed him the evidence of them. Martin had had too much bad luck lately, with his mom's illness and now the blackmailer.

How nice she could help out her friend in her own modest way. How nice that helping Martin helped her, too.

Amethyst checked on her client. Generous with his spittle, he tongued the leather until it shined. He glanced up at her face from time to time.

She didn't have to fake her look of contempt.

"I like your new mask, Mistress. It's very sexy."

"Did I ask what you thought? Lick."

"Yes. Anything, Mistress." He licked.

Once, she looked at the mirrored closet. The left slider door wasn't completely shut. She gave a nod to the sliver of darkness.

Richard's slurping sounds covered the faint hum of the video camera.

"You were right to come here."

Kartane picked up one chair, nestled it one on top of another. He moved on to the next.

Charlotte paced back and forth in the large conference room. She avoided the furs. "I just didn't know where else to go. It's a good thing you're so close to Subspace now, only a few blocks away. I'm glad to have a friend like you to trust with this sort of thing. It's so unbelievable."

She stopped against the wall, clutched at it for support. "He has her phone. He took her. He took Gail, and maybe others. He almost had me." Her hand fisted against the wall. "He lied to me. He has her phone!"

"You'd mentioned that."

She moved again, the tension within her making it impossible to remain still. "I trusted him." This was the most appalling thing, to her. "I believed him. When Martin claimed you went off with Gail, I should've known better."

From the far side of the room, she heard Kartane drop a chair.

She reached the end of the conference room, started back. "Sorry about all the walking back and forth, I've just got all this adrenaline." The aftereffects of both Martin's pleasuring then the shock he'd given her made her feel nauseated.

Kartane waved that away. He gave her a strange look. "Martin said I abducted Gail?"

She frowned. He'd left the chair where it had fallen. "Well, no. Not exactly. It was more what he implied. That you were crazy, a crazy Gorean, and therefore Gail had probably rejected you pretty quickly. I guess Martin figured I'd buy that you were the last one seen with Gail. Conveniently clearing him of being a suspect." She smiled a little. "Of course, you were kind of a crazy, once upon a time. And you are a Gorean. But you're not a crazy Gorean. You already got the woman-abducting out of your system."

He stared coldly.

She blinked. "Um, it's just a joke. At my expense, in a way. No offense." The florescent light of the large conference room gave his familiar face an unhealthy pallor. She looked at him curiously. "Are you okay?" His blue eyes were narrowed with the kind of concentration she hadn't seen since she'd lived with him. Since he'd tried to reach her libido via binding, torture, and branding.

She felt her flesh creep. She blamed it on Martin. If only he'd taken no for an answer. At least Kartane wasn't like that anymore, even if he was staring at her strangely.

She approached him, touched the fallen chair with uncertainty. "Hey, Martin's the bad guy. It's just that you know you have certain ideas about women... well, never mind. It doesn't matter. Martin despises you and Goreans both, which makes you a convenient target. He probably attacked Gail right away to subdue her. She doesn't put up with much male high-handedness. I hope she's okay."

At his continued cold stare and his perfect stillness, she spoke, defensive. "What? She doesn't. And I don't blame her one bit for it. Maybe she's difficult, but she doesn't deserve that fate. Oh, God, I'm talking about her as if she's dead. What if Martin actually killed her? She doesn't have any friends or family who know where she went. I have to go to the police, make a report."

His nostrils flared. "What? No."

"What do you mean, no?"

"They might search Subspace. And all around it, maybe."

She stared at him. "Yes. That's kind of the idea." She fidgeted, impatient, ready to go make the police take her seriously this time. Then she'd put all this behind her and start over again.

"Can you give me a ride to the local station? The one near my apartment will do."

He finally bent to the fallen chair. With slow, deliberate movements, he placed it with the others. Then he moved to the furs. He picked up a gilded velvet cord. Probably used on the evening's entertainment, Charlotte thought with curiosity. It intrigued her how some women could accept such servitude as a way of life. For play, maybe. But as a lifestyle? It boggled her mind. But, to each their own.

Kartane made his way back, stepping carefully on the furs. He moved with a slowness that showed reluctance until he stood before her.

"If you don't want to drive me, just say so," she told him. "I'll catch the light-rail. If they're still running this late. You don't happen to know the schedule . . . um, Kartane? What are you doing?"

With an economy of motion that spoke of long practice, he turned her while pulling both her arms behind her back. He wrapped her wrists together with a simple figure eight in the time it took her to realize she was trapped. "What the hell? Let me go!"

"I did, once. True masters don't release their slaves, any more than they'd give away another valuable possession. You'll probably be frightened and dismayed to learn I'm a true Gorean master now. But acceptance will come in time. I'll make you my First Girl." He sounded sorry.

Disbelief and confusion roiled her stomach. "Stop joking around." The tremor in her voice betrayed her. She knew he wasn't joking.

"I can't let you go now." He pulled her to the edge of the furs, scooped up another length of cord. He knotted it around her neck. "If you scream, I'll choke you unconscious."

She looked at her ex-husband. She saw the truth of his words.

But even so, when he led her to stairs leading below, she balked. "Please. Don't. We made this mistake before. You and me. It didn't work. I'm not cut out for the slave-girl role."

"It's not a role," he explained. "It's woman's nature."

"I know you believe that, but it's not true. I'm unnatural," she declared, inspired. "I'm a freak of nature, a free woman, a woman who wants to be like a man, no use to you at all."

He laughed at her. "Charlotte. I was married to you, remember? What's more, I saw your response to Talia's chastisement. I know what your body craves." He paused, shrugged. "It would be a shame to kill you."

She gaped.

"A captured woman who refuses slavery may be disposed of in any way the captor wishes, so as not to be a burden to him."

"Okay. Okay, honey? We're in America. On Earth. I'm a burden to no one." She remembered her current clientless state. "Even if I do have to work in fast food for a while. I can take care of myself."

"You'd prefer a strong master."

"Not at the expense of freedom."

"Words. Your body speaks a higher truth." He grasped a breast with easy familiarity.

She cringed away to the length of the rope. Her body was neutral to his touch. "We're just friends. We're friends," she repeated, willing him to understand it. "I'm willing to be your friend."

"I'm not willing to be yours. You have nobody to claim you now. No family, either." He looped the cord attached to her neck around his fist. Then again, dragging her closer. "No one to miss you."

Martin's face flashed through her mind. Martin would miss her. Then realization hit her. "You took Gail!"

He smiled. "Come with me."

"No!"

He stopped smiling. "Come with me, Charlotte. You're mine. You wear my brand."

"You said you were sorry for that! You cried!" She pulled back until her windpipe constricted. "It's not a brand, it's a blob of scar tissue. You let me go after you hurt me. Let me go now."

"I regret it took me this long to learn my business. Oh, no, not the magazine business. That was a means to an end. The business of owning women, the way they need to be owned, is my calling. I'll brand you properly, I promise. And then you'll be used properly. You'll come to love it. They all do." He smiled coolly. "Eventually."

"This is a nightmare," she said, strangling on her own words. "Wake me up." Between the lump in her throat and the tight rope, air couldn't reach her lungs. The world floated.

He loosened the rope. "Don't fight it this time, Charlotte. You won't win." She knew he didn't mean the rope.

"But I don't want you. I don't want this."

"It doesn't matter."

She knew he was stronger than her, and on guard, and between her bound hands and the choking collar, she didn't have a chance.

She could scream.

"Don't, Charlotte."

Her shoulders began to slump, obedient. He knew her too well. Yet not well enough. A lethal combination.

Lethal for her. He might do worse than brand her again. He might kill her.

She opened her mouth to scream, and his hand was there, sealing it shut, muting the sound.

"Bad girl," he breathed, when she'd stopped. "Do that again and I promise you you'll regret it."

She knew he spoke the truth.

He led her downstairs, then unlocked a heavy metal door, pulling it open and thrusting her through. A tunnel. Charlotte looked around. The rough, unfinished combination of concrete, metal rods, dusty bare lightbulbs, and the scene of dirt re-

minded her of the room at Subspace. So these were the undertunnels Ratty had talked about.

"How'd you get Gail down here? Rope and brand her like a
steer, too?"

"Submit, kajira. But not too much. A Gorean master com-
monly likes a spirited girl, one who fights the discipline and
collar, resisting for weeks or months until she is overwhelmed
and must acknowledge herself his. She comes to crave her master's smallest attention, and fears only that he'll tire of her and
sell her to another."

"Did you get that from those sci-fi novels? Dominant Wee-
nies of Gor?"

"Insolence will be punished."

"How about the truth? Is that punished?"

He yanked her forward, harder than necessary.

Suddenly they were at another door. He unlocked it with a
different key. When he nudged it open to push her inside, her
first impression was one of scent. Unwashed flesh. Tang of
urine. Copper of blood. A whiff of bleach. Food, too, though it
smelled oily, as if fried.

Then she heard the noise. Whips meeting flesh. Shrieks of
complaint.

"Punishment," Kartane explained helpfully.

"Great." She kept her voice light and sarcastic, but inside she
quivered with panic.

He led her to a metal enclosure, opened the simple padlock
on the outside of the door. Inside she could see more hard-
packed dirt, but not much else in the dim light. The scent of
urine was stronger.

"Go in."

"I'd prefer not to."

In answer, he merely removed her rope collar and thrust her
inside. The door clanged shut, locked.

She quaked, wrapping her arms around herself, listening to the shrieks of the woman being punished. The shrieks had grown hoarse, but the sharp impact of the whip meeting body didn't lessen. Charlotte shuddered.

Minutes later, the door rattled, and she leapt back.

It opened. A woman was thrust inside but immediately fell to the ground.

"Wait!" Charlotte said, but the door shut and latched again, leaving her in light still too dim to examine anything closely. Including the woman.

"Hey." Charlotte touched her with her boot, gently. The woman appeared to be naked, lying on her stomach, her white flesh catching the light in strips. Glints of sweat or blood pooled in divots and shallow grooves. Charlotte hoped they were shallow.

"Hey. I think you're hurt. Say something. Are you okay?"

The woman groaned. Then, "What the fuck do you think? Am I okay. Are you one of the lobotomized monkeys, or do you still have two brain cells to rub together?"

"Gail!"

The woman slowly pried herself onto her side. Charlotte felt the weight of her regard.

"Charlotte." Gail managed, with a grunt of pain, to rise to a sitting position. "You are so fired."

23

It was finally Halloween, and Martin sat where he could watch the front entrance of Subspace. He'd sat there since just before the sun went down, until now—hours later—and all he'd seen so far were far too many costumes of vampires.

If he saw another glittery fanged creature of the night, he'd stake it.

His mood was foul. Two days had passed since Charlotte had nailed him in the nuts. They still ached when he moved.

Not as much as the rest of him, though. His brain and heart especially. He should've handled her better. He should've handled everything better. Martin swiveled in his vinyl seat, winced. He scowled as he flagged the waiter.

Instead, Amethyst slid into the booth, across from him. "I have some good news. Want to hear it?"

"No. Go away." He paused, looked her over. "You're not in costume. They shouldn't have let you in."

"You're not in costume, either," she retorted.

"Owner's privilege. Besides, I'm scary enough naturally."

"Har, har. You'd make a good clown." She grinned.

In fact, his friend was all but dancing in her seat, her purple locks swinging to and fro. Martin sighed. "Okay. What's your good news?"

"I'm so glad you asked! I've found a way to buy Subspace."

He looked away with exasperation. Toward the door.

More sparkly vampires made their way past the doorman. Would he even recognize Charlotte if she came in costume? She probably wouldn't come at all. And he had no way to reach her.

He remembered Amethyst. "We've discussed Subspace a few times, Amethyst. It's no longer for sale at the moment."

She lifted a tiny flash drive on a lanyard loop, swung it back and forth as if she were trying to hypnotize him. Her gaze was certainly intense. "It's all here."

"What's all there?" He looked past her, glanced again at the entrance. His gaze went back to the small black rectangle. "I don't know what you're talking about. As usual. Where's Ratty? I thought for sure he'd come for Halloween."

Her smile lit her face up in ways he'd never seen before. It made him remember Charlotte declaring Amethyst and Ratty had a lifetime thing. It made him think of Charlotte's own bright smile.

It made his heart hurt and his balls ache.

"Ratty will come in his own time. Ratty's wearing a special costume."

"Not another vampire, one hopes."

"Will you please pay attention? Who are you looking for?" she finally snapped when he glanced again toward the door.

"Charlotte." His cock throbbed. His balls throbbed worse, of course, but that was to be expected. And was his own fault. "I have some things to straighten out with her. I think she thinks I kidnapped her friend. Well, her client. And it's true her client probably is actually abducted, since I have the phone. It's a long story."

"My story's better."

Martin glared at her, opened his mouth to tell her how wrong she was.

She spoke first. "You know I've done pro-domme work. The money's been great and I enjoyed men paying me for the honor of debasing themselves at my feet. Your boss, Richard Corvine, is a bootlicker. One of my regulars. I've got him recorded—right here—paying homage to my thigh-highs. On his knees." She grinned. "I made him state his name and occupation for the record, before declaring him a naughty boy. He's not a very thorough bootlicker, I'm afraid. He missed some spots. I had to grind him underfoot a few times."

Martin stared.

"So, Master Martin, you don't have to worry your scary little head any longer about any incriminating photos falling into his hands. He won't dare to take the smallest action with them once he knows you have this." She tossed Martin the flash drive.

He clutched it. "You're not kidding? No, I can see you're not. Richard Corvine. The same Richard Corvine?"

"Petclub tycoon? Yep." She grinned, smug.

"I don't believe it." He saw her look. "I investigated him from every angle, but everything slid right off the man. He was as pure as a man of God." Humor bubbled up inside him. "Damn. He's your boot cleaner, huh? I looked everywhere to pin something on him, then you go and find his dirty secret. It was right in front of me the whole time."

"Everyone has secret fantasies. He's just like most people out there: good at hiding them. Especially the super naughty ones."

The black square of plastic rested in his palm. It held the power of freedom if Amethyst was telling the truth. "You're amazing," he said with awe. "Relentless and amazing. Mistress Amethyst."

He saw her shudder. "Not 'Mistress' anymore, please, at least for a while. I promised Ratty a shot at topping me tonight. Can you believe it? So." She flicked a finger against the flash drive, her nail clicking against it. "This means I get to buy Subspace, yes?"

"Yes. Yes, gladly." He cast another glance at the door. A tall man wearing a rubber mask entered. Something about his posture seemed familiar.

Martin sighed. "I'll gladly unload this place on you. You offered a fair price."

She looked at Martin, her gaze keen. "What's wrong then?"

"Charlotte is what's wrong." He gave Amethyst an abbreviated version of the scene two nights before. "It ended as badly as it gets. She jumped to the conclusion I'm worse than Kartane." No wonder she hadn't returned to Subspace. "He's the one who took Gail downstairs to the dungeons, he's the one who hurt Charlotte when they were married, but I'm the one who gets all the blame."

"Kartane took her downstairs. Hmmm." Amethyst nodded, taking it all in. "You still have the phone?"

"Yeah. All of them. Now that the blackmail threat's gone, I can bring them in to the police." He started to rise.

"Hang on a sec." A deep frown furrowed Amethyst's brow. "Kartane wanted Subspace, too. I don't think he meant to say it out loud, but he once talked about the club as if it was going to be his own personal hunting ground. Soon."

They stared at each other.

Martin's pulse sped. "You don't think . . . ?"

"That Kartane's your blackmailer? Sure."

"How'd he get into Subspace? You're the only one besides me with a key and the security code."

She gave him a slow smile. "Ah, so that's why you've been weird lately. You thought I was blackmailing you. Silly boy."

"If I've been weird lately, it has to do with more than just you. Self-centered girl. Since you're so smart, answer the question. How'd Kartane get inside Subspace to deliver the phones?"

"I have a better question for you. Where's Gail?"

Martin swore, rose to his feet. "Of course. We've got to get those phones to the police." He had a thought that chilled him. "What if Charlotte ran to Kartane that night? Jesus, I'm an idiot. He might have taken her just like Gail. We do have to go to the police right now."

"I don't believe it."

Martin turned at Amethyst's tone, and just stared, open-mouthed at the man who stood before them.

"I am Ratty of Gor!" Ratty had a cloak thrown back, showing his scarlet tunic, sandals, and the sword in its scabbard slung over his left shoulder. The knife attached to his leather belt looked real. His metal helmet, with its Y opening, covered his tattoos of rats. A pouch at his waist bulged with its unknown contents. "Fear me!" He grinned at them both. "What do you think of my warrior costume? The tharlarion boots were kind of challenging, but I know a place that does soft leather work."

"Ratty?"

"Yes?"

"We're kind of in the middle of something."

"Ah."

Amethyst took in his expression. "Maybe you can help us. We were just wondering how someone might enter and leave Subspace without being seen, or tripping the alarm."

Martin could tell from her voice she didn't really expect an answer, had in fact only asked to make Ratty feel included, but the slender man was nodding. "Easy. The Blood Orange room, the really old dungeon? It could be connected up to the Riverport undertunnels. They're a network of old tunnels that reportedly go from nearby businesses to the river. Or, they used to before being bricked off."

Martin and Amethyst looked at each other. Martin shook his head. "Kartane took her downstairs, and nobody saw her again."

"Saw who?" Ratty wondered.

Amethyst nodded. "It makes sense. We have to look."

"Agreed." The two rushed off.

Amethyst hurried back, grabbed Ratty by his leather belt, and pulled him along.

24

Charlotte finished using the bucket, unable to help grimacing in distaste. The odor cleared her sinuses. The bucket hadn't been changed since she'd arrived two nights ago. As she made her way across the hard-packed dirt floor, she stumbled over Gail's bare feet.

The woman's lack of reaction showed how much of her spirit had leached away during the past days. "Hey," Charlotte said as she settled against a metal wall as far from the bucket as possible. "Are you okay?"

"I want to hurt him." Gail spoke in a monotone. "Then lock him in a dark cell. See how he likes it." She moved slightly, and Charlotte heard her bite back a whimper. "He thinks he's some sort of king. A 'Ubar.' He's crazy."

Gail didn't have to say who she meant.

Charlotte nodded, then realized Gail might not be able to see it in the dark. "Yes, he is." Gail's condition frankly worried Charlotte. Yesterday Kartane took Gail out for another session with something that made an ominous thudding sound. A brick? A rock?

242 / Christina Crooks

He'd ignored Charlotte, except for the hot, spicy drinks he watched her swallow. Caffeine? An aphrodisiac? He'd called it slave wine. It wasn't poison, but neither did it make her warm to him. Quite the opposite.

What was he thinking? He hadn't touched her at all. Saving her for something special? Or did he prefer to break only one woman at a time?

For that was clearly his intention. Gail had told her everything the first night, from Elizabeth's help trying to escape to the inventive punishments meted out by both Talia and Kartane upon their recapture. "He won't stop until we beg him to enslave us. Beg for his brand. Beg for his use." Gail's tone had revealed the depth of her horror. "We have to get out of here."

When Kartane had flung Gail back into the cell, the woman couldn't do more than curl up into a ball and shudder.

She sat listlessly now. It frightened Charlotte as much as anything else. Gail wasn't the listless type. "Talk to me. Are you okay? Can you walk? Can you run?"

"I want to hurt him. Brand him on the forehead with a big *G* so everyone knows he's a Gorean pig. I want to hear him scream."

"Gail, you have to snap out of it."

"He kidnapped Elizabeth. She's just a kid."

"Gail, please."

"I want to hurt him." Shadows moved as she turned her head. Charlotte could feel the weight of her gaze. "I believe I will get a sperm donation. I'd rather do that than have anything to do with men. Not ever again. And if I'm pregnant with a boy instead of a girl, I'll abort it."

Charlotte felt tears gather in her eyes. "Gail," she began helplessly.

The lock rattled.

Both women scrambled backward, as far from the door as they could get. They huddled together.

The door swung open, admitting enough light to make them squint. "Hello, slaves."

He waited.

Charlotte remained silent as long as she could, but fear rose quickly in her. Whatever he'd used on Gail, it had left her incapacitated for hours.

It was only their words he wanted. For now.

Gail moaned her rage and defeat.

Both of them finally replied with reluctance, "Hello, Master."

"Very good, slaves." His tone carried triumph.

Charlotte tasted bitterness in her mouth.

"Charlotte. I placed you here with Gail so you could learn your place relatively painlessly, by proxy. But it occurs to me I've been neglecting you. Do you feel neglected?"

"Yes." She ignored Gail's gasp of surprise. "Why don't we go grab a cup of coffee and talk this over like civilized people?"

Kartane laughed. "Oh, certainly. In time. First, however, I have a question for you."

Charlotte heard the familiar jingle of her keys, the ones he'd taken from her the first night.

"Your apartment contains something of mine. I can't seem to find it."

"You went into my apartment?"

"It's much easier with keys," he agreed.

Realization hit her. "That was you last week! Picking my lock, trying to break in. What on earth were you looking for? We split everything in the divorce."

"A piece of property is missing. A very important piece. I've looked everywhere. I've asked you about it before. I'll describe it again. It's a small, flat stone, very plain-looking, with the initial *G* formed on its underside." He looked at her. "You've seen it."

"I remember your asking about it. You said it was a paper-weight that had sentimental value."

"You know where it is." He approached her.

"Don't tell him where it is!" Elizabeth shouted.

She'd been so quiet after being punished for the escape attempt, Charlotte had all but forgotten the girl in the cell next door.

Kartane was on Charlotte, hauling her up and forcing her against the metal. "You'll tell. If you know what's good for you, you'll tell."

"It's his Home Stone! The Ubar's Home Stone! Without it he has no power!"

"Shut up!" he snarled.

"The Ubar has lost his Home Stone!" Elizabeth called out, her voice echoing through the darkness. Shocked murmurs came from all directions. "The Ubar of Gorr is outcast! We're free!"

"You're free when I say you're free!" But Charlotte felt the tremble in Kartane's grasp. She could smell his fear-fouled breath. He muttered, "God damn it."

Suddenly Gail attacked, more viciously than Charlotte would've expected. It loosened his grip on her, then broke it. Charlotte slipped away easily, gaining just enough distance. Then turned and, with one still-booted foot, kicked him in the stomach. It drove him back, off-balance and gagging. The two women edged past him and rushed to make their escape. They shoved the cell door shut. Metal clanged as they threw the latch. They looked at each other over it, then shrieked when Kartane threw his body against the door. "Talia!"

They backed away. "Talia will let him out. We have to go. Now. But . . ."

"But nothing!" Charlotte pulled the naked Gail back toward the tunnels.

Gail grabbed her arm to stop her, completely unself-conscious about her nudity. "Not that way. And we have to let Elizabeth out."

"Okay. Crap. Okay, yes." They rushed around the metal walls to Elizabeth's cube, opened the latch. "Oh, baby." Elizabeth lay on her side, her legs and arms tied behind, drawing her body into a bow so tight her red silk poncho bunched underneath. Gail hurriedly untied her, her hands swift and compassionate on the thin young girl. Charlotte helped them both to stand.

Kartane threw his body against the door again. They all heard the cracking sound. "Come on!" Gail cried. She led them away from the tunnels, but before Charlotte could object, Gail explained, "Talia and Kartane's other favored slaves are that way. The rooms are more comfortable, with lounge chairs and tapestries and large beds. Elizabeth described it. The asshole's got himself tiered slave pens. We're in the ghetto section. We don't want to go uptown. I know there's an exit in this direction—a tunnel to Subspace—I'm just not sure where." Gail stumbled.

Charlotte supported her and Elizabeth both. "You guys are in bad shape," she despaired as they limped forward too slowly.

Gail shoved at Charlotte weakly, anger without strength. "You two go ahead by yourself then. Maybe you'll find the exit without me."

"I'm not leaving without you," Elizabeth promised.

Charlotte tightened her grip on Gail, hauling her forward more quickly. Did Gail get some kind of perverse energy from being obstinate? "Stubborn bitch, aren't you?"

"It works for me," Gail replied, gasping for breath. "Bitch," she added.

Elizabeth's arms draped around both Gail and Charlotte. The young woman pointed with her chin. "Is that it?"

An enormous tapestry of a warrior slaying a dragon dominated the wall.

"Behind it," Gail said.

They wasted no time shoving the tapestry aside. They saw the door made of plank wood so old it was rotted in places.

"They're coming." Elizabeth said it calmly, but her face blanched of color. "A lot of them. I really thought the loss of Kartane's Home Stone would make them rebel against him. Please hurry."

"Okay. The door's sticking. I'll have to kick it. Let go for a sec." When their arms dropped from her, Charlotte raised her leg and kicked the wood. Dust puffed into the air. She kicked it again, but it only rattled in its jamb. "They don't build them like they used to," she muttered.

A strong grip pinched her shoulder painfully. "Got you."

Her heart skittered into panic as Kartane's fingers dug in cruelly. A wild fear sealed her throat and made her limbs heavy and stupid. She moaned, inarticulate, her mouth instantly drying out, her tongue clumsy.

He had her again, and she wouldn't get another chance at freedom. This was what she'd tried so hard not to think about. His cruel possession brought her back to the unspeakable time when she'd been the focus of his sadistic attention for two days. Being tied and tortured and branded, being betrayed, all the while with him convinced it was what she wanted.

He still believed it.

She'd wondered, during the worst of the pain and humiliation, if she'd brought it all on herself. If she deserved it.

If she'd created the monster he'd become by being one herself.

Knowing the depravity he'd sunk to, and with a repeat of the same or worse fate facing all three of them, and the same questions plaguing her now more than ever, Charlotte finally found her voice. She shrieked her horror.

25

Martin and Amethyst followed Ratty down into the old dungeon room.

It seethed with bodies. At any other time, Martin would've been delighted by the thick crowd.

"This room rocks!" Ratty waved his sword at a Renaissance-garbed beer wench in front of the tall iron maiden. The blond woman grinned at him, licked her lips, and thrust out her cleavage. Even with her costume, she looked impossibly modern and soft next to the metal coffin door hiding its dangerous spikes within. "You should let people play here every night, not just on Halloween."

"The liability's too high and the extra manpower's too steep," Martin replied, scanning the old dungeon pieces and peering behind piles of ancient bedsprings. He waved off the dungeon monitors who looked at him inquiringly. "It's a madhouse tonight," he muttered.

A half-naked man wearing only antlers, a loincloth, and moccasins stumbled past, laughing. Another man painted as a zombie paddled a woman costumed in a strange, gelatinous blob of see-through gray Martin couldn't place until the man explained. "I'm tenderizing some brainzzz for dinner!"

"Eat me," the woman begged. She wriggled artfully, but the manacles enclosing her wrists kept her pinned close to the old post.

"A really fun madhouse." Ratty looked around with more purpose. "All right. Let's try ... over there." He led them to the brick archway and the cabinet placed under it. He opened the cabinet. "That's what I suspected."

"What?" Martin itched to shove him aside. "What is it?"

"The cabinet is backless. You clear away these old hanging clothes, and, see? That's a door."

"How did you know that?" Martin gently pushed him aside.

Amethyst looked at the slender man with approval. "Good job. How *did* you know?"

Ratty preened. "I took one of those Riverport undertunnels tours once. The doorways were always under the brick arches."

Suddenly a heavy blow landed on the wooden door. Then another.

They all looked at each other.

A piercing shriek of terror cut through the door as if it were made of silk rather than wood. The music played on, the bass continued thumping its beat into their bodies, and none of the club-goers paused in their play.

But Martin, Amethyst, and Ratty stood in a frozen tableau for a long moment. Had they really heard the bloodcurdling sound?

"Jesus," Ratty finally said with reverence.

Breaking the paralysis, Martin shoved dresses aside to fling himself at the door, hitting it with his shoulder. It cracked under the blow, but held. He tore pieces off, splinters stabbing his fingers and lacerating his palms.

How had he not noticed this going on in his own club? Re-criminations lacerated his spirit far more deeply than the pieces of wood did his flesh. How could he have been so blind? What was Charlotte enduring to sound like that? She had to be terrified out of her wits or in an extremity of pain or in mortal danger to scream that way.

Whatever was happening to her was his fault.

Panic and fury gave him near-superhuman strength.

He threw himself at the door again, helpless rage fighting through healthy and rotted wood alike to reach her.

26

Kartane saw the door buckling. The bright, colored lights from the Subspace dungeon spilled through the ever-widening cracks, cutting through the tunnel's darkness as they tore through his dreams. The door was coming apart.

So were his plans.

He bared his teeth, desperate. His gaze dropped to the hands reaching through the door.

He had to do something.

"Talia."

No answer.

"Talia!" He turned.

The slaves were standing loosely, comfortably, without the usual deference of crossed wrists before them. Rather than downcast eyes, theirs pinned him accusingly. Talia was the only one who approached him. "Master? Is it true your Home Stone was stolen?"

Deep unease skittered through him. They weren't letting it go. "It wasn't stolen. It's been misplaced. I'm going to reclaim it."

The women looked at each other.

Talia nodded her acceptance, crossing her wrists.

The others didn't.

"Go. Back to your slave cribs, all of you."

They didn't. "I want to go home," one of them whined.

Kartane lifted his hand from Charlotte to slap the other slave for insolence.

At that moment the door crumbled under the onslaught. Martin burst through it, his eyes blazing with wrath.

"Martin!" The tearful relief in Charlotte's voice grated Kartane's nerves.

Martin ran straight to Charlotte and Gail. Kartane's muscles bunched in preparation for battle. If he could subdue Martin, he might salvage the situation.

"I think your game's about played out, big fella." Amethyst smiled sweetly at Kartane.

Amethyst! The one he'd hoped to make a favored slave. The one who made him feel anything but masterful. How dare she insult him before his slaves! Kartane snarled, his anger diverted from Martin. He lunged at her. How sweet it would be to break her slender neck.

He had her in a headlock, where she struggled, helpless in his grip. He grinned, a baring of teeth. Let the others take the warning that Kartane of Gor wasn't to be trifled with. Let them realize a Gorean warrior feared nothing, least of all a woman.

Out of the corner of his eye he saw more people pushing through the destroyed door. A strange, tall man wearing a Halloween mask. And most oddly, another Gorean warrior. A slender man, but properly dressed. He shouted something, but the red haze of fury sealed Kartane's ears to all but the sweet music of Amethyst's strangled breaths.

The strange Gorean threw aside his sword, fumbled at his waist pouch. The slender man raised his hand to him and attacked!

The blow that crashed against his skull knocked Kartane to the ground. He tried to move, but the warrior kneed him in the chest, threatening him with another blow using the stone held in his hand.

"I lay my sword at your feet." Kartane offered the symbolic words of surrender.

Instead of accepting his surrender, the man shrugged. "I don't see a sword. I do see some abused women and an over-grown gamer who takes his Gorean shit way too seriously." He hefted the flat gray rock over his head.

But before he could use it, the women shouted. "The master has a Home Stone!"

Amethyst looked, and started laughing. "Ratty! Where'd you get that?" She pointed to the stone.

He shrugged, then spoke for her ears only. "It came with the outfit."

Kartane had to watch, with amazement and humiliation, as Talia and his slaves abased themselves before their new master, Ratty of Gor.

Ratty looked down at all their crossed wrists and bowed heads. "I could get used to this."

"Don't even think about it." Amethyst folded her arms across her chest. Then, as Kartane watched, she uncrossed them . . . and crossed her wrists before her. "I prefer not to share."

Kartane felt a sickening sense of loss, hearing that soft voice come out of Amethyst. Ratty had eyes for only Amethyst. After placing the stone back in its pouch, he claimed her, right in front of Kartane, with a long, firm kiss.

27

Martin cradled Charlotte. She was stunned by the power of the relief and regret shining in his eyes. His large fingers touched her with fast, investigatory touches that would have set her aflame if she weren't so distracted.

Her thoughts whirled and swirled, stirred by more emotions than she could name. She clung to him. "I'm so sorry I ran from you. Sorry for believing the worst of you. Thank you." She lifted one hand his face, tracing his features, reverent. "Thank you for finding me. I'm fine. Gail, though. She needs a doctor. And clothes. And, Elizabeth..."

"Elizabeth!" the tall man called out, his voice muffled by his mask.

"Who's that?" Charlotte asked Martin.

Martin gently nudged her aside, rose to his feet. "I intend to find out."

"Elizabeth, where are you?" The man ripped off his mask. His tufted hair and wild gaze made him look different, but Charlotte recognized him. So did Martin.

So did Elizabeth. "Daddy!"

She struggled to her feet. By the time she'd managed it, Peter swept her off them. "Elizabeth! I knew it, I knew you were alive, I knew you were here, Elizabeth. Oh, thank God."

"Daddy." She snuggled into him, crying. He locked his arms around her, cradling her as gently as if she were made of porcelain. The weight of years seemed to come off him. Charlotte realized with surprise he wasn't old at all. The lines on his dirty face were etched in a pattern of tiredness and grief, but they didn't show the same elderly scarecrow who'd assaulted her outside of Subspace that night.

Peter murmured to his daughter, "Who did this to you? Was it Martin? Is he a white slaver?" Peter's look when he turned to Martin could've drilled holes through steel.

"No, Daddy. It was him." She indicated Kartane. "He kept me in a cell and hurt me. He hurt the others, too."

Peter turned to Kartane. "Did he?"

Gail answered with a venomous look of her own aimed at Kartane. "Yes. He did."

Amethyst explained. "He's an extremist, for a Gorean. They're all sexist and irrational, but he's way beyond the pale. He likes breaking women's spirits. Don't you, sweetie?"

"I see." Peter kissed Elizabeth on the top of her head. "Maybe you should leave. Go with this nice lady outside, and wait for me there." He caught Amethyst's eye, nodded to the broken door he came in.

Amethyst took the hint. "Let's go, luv. Your daddy will be along shortly."

"Okay." Then Elizabeth surprised everyone by walking up to Kartane and spitting on his face. She cocked her head at him. "You didn't break me. You never could, asshole."

"Language," Peter chided.

"Sorry, Daddy."

Amethyst and Gail laughed, then helped Elizabeth through

the broken door. Gail clung to her hand for a moment, then came back.

Ratty held the jagged edges away from the bruised girl, then followed both Amethyst and Elizabeth.

Gail glared at Kartane. "I'm staying."

"So am I," said another of the slave girls.

"And me." The red silk-clad woman had her hands on her hips. She smiled at Kartane. It wasn't a submissive smile.

Kartane looked up at Talia. "Talia? You, too? I demand that you assist me!"

She shook her head, but after a moment, a look of sadness crumpled her face. Her shoulders slumped, as if Kartane's predicament stole her strength. "A weak master is a sad thing. But I cannot hurt you." She turned her back on all of them, followed the others through the door.

Martin and Charlotte rose. He addressed Peter. "This"—he indicated Kartane's undertunnel den—"is emphatically *not* part of Subspace. Subspace is only about consensual play. I want you to know I had nothing whatsoever to do with Kartane's illegal activities here, and no knowledge of it."

"Then you probably don't want to know what's about to happen here." Peter didn't take his eyes off Kartane, who rubbed his head where Ratty's stone had landed. "You both probably should leave. Now."

Martin nodded, but Charlotte balked. She spoke to Peter. "Promise you won't kill him. He wasn't always this way. I can't allow . . . he doesn't deserve to die, is all. I'm calling the cops, you know. They'll lock you up if you kill him. Gail, you too."

"Spoilsport." Gail bared her teeth at Kartane, who shuddered.

"I wouldn't dream of murdering him." Peter looked a great deal less desperate and more purposeful now that he'd achieved his goal of finding his daughter. He looked powerful and almost handsome. "I won't do anything to him that he hasn't done to my daughter."

Gail looked at Peter approvingly.

Kartane paled.

Charlotte nodded. She looked from Gail to Peter, then back again, suddenly distracted. "Oh."

Of all times for it to happen. Of all the impossible times. Charlotte nearly laughed as the film in her mind rolled. The X-rated movies, finally playing for Gail.

Fit and frisky, a nude Peter embraced Gail. He didn't use a condom, Charlotte noticed. Gail might actually get the baby she craved, as well as the partner.

"Gail," she began, her voice choked up. "You won't believe what I've just seen."

But Gail still glared at Kartane.

Charlotte swallowed her emotions. Time enough to tell her later. If it proved necessary. "Just don't kill anyone," she repeated, talking to the air between them both. "Either of you. You'll be glad you didn't." She edged toward the broken door. "Good-bye, Kartane. Don't ever contact me again. Assuming they leave you in any condition to do so."

"Charlotte, don't go! Please!"

Martin propelled her firmly away when she wavered. She was grateful for his strength, as her own seemed to have temporarily deserted her. She had the shakes again.

"I just can't believe it. He'd whipped Gail, hitting her and hurting all of them. Like he did to me when we were married. He was going to do it to me again."

"Shh. It'll be okay. You're with me now, and you're safe. Everything is as it's supposed to be, now." Martin spoke in a deep, reassuring voice. They climbed into the Blood Orange room, and it was as if they'd entered another dimension. The rust, dust, and wet rot of the undertunnels gave way to faint smoke and sweat scent that tickled her nostrils. The music throbbed underfoot, smoothing Charlotte's pulse to a more regular beat in time to it.

It seemed impossible that she should feel better so quickly.

And yet she did. Not perfect, but better.

She clung to Martin, relishing his muscles, remembering his strength. Savoring his faith in her. Appreciating his patience. He'd led the rescue. Without him she'd be lost.

She gazed up at him, all her love and lust offered up to him, if he wanted it. "Almost everything's as it's supposed to be," she finally corrected. "There's one small thing still missing."

He stopped. He raised his eyebrows, then gave her a speculative look. "I see. In that case, three things must occur. First, we call the police, get that mess in the undertunnels dealt with. But not yet. I believe the victims will benefit from the catharsis of some minor vengeance. I figure we can give them"—he indicated the shattered door and those on its other side—"an hour of time. Or, two hours? Will that be enough to do what they need to do?"

He was actually asking her? She nodded slowly, the weight of judgment making her limbs heavy even as the fairness of such rough justice caused an aesthetic and cathartic shiver of appreciation.

Of course Martin was asking her. She'd been a victim once. Of Kartane. "Yes. Two hours."

"Second, you let me give you a luxurious bath in back."

Her entire body clenched with pleasure at the thought, and she all but moaned. "Yes!" She snuggled more deeply against him, breathing him in. Her savior.

"Third. Third . . ." He held her away from him. He bestowed a look of such knowing sternness, her knees weakened and her insides fluttered. "Third, we conclude our own unfinished business, Charlotte. In the same room, where the walls are padded. I'm going to give you some new bruises inside and out, my sweet. I'm going to terrify you in the best possible way, and I promise you'll remember every moment of it for the rest of your life."

She looked into his dark eyes. She believed him.

She nodded, a formal agreement.

They both ignored the revelers swirling around them, the laughter and the violence both. He nodded, contemplative. "Be sure. Be sure I'm the one you want."

"Are you kidding? I just need to know if you're willing to do the dirty deed."

He smiled his answer. It was a happy smile and a cruel smile, and her muscles twitched pleasurably and her nipples hardened at the sight of it.

"Very well, Charlotte. Let's begin soon so I can hear you scream just for me."

28

Martin would soon tear her panties off again.

Charlotte's belly plunged in excitement.

A warmer, more tender feeling snaked through her as well. She let her fingers trail over the padded wall of the room, remembering the bath. It went faster than ideal, since they both had other things on their minds.

Even so, Martin's hands as he'd bathed her had touched her skin and scalp with reverent gentleness. As if he couldn't bear to press too hard or accidentally pull her long hair. He'd acted as if she were made of fragile glass.

His soft touch had caused the tender warmth to bloom inside her.

Such gentleness from Martin was a little funny when she thought about it.

She whirled around, carefree, laughing. Her hair streamed out, mostly dry, and the scent of flowers filled the air around her. She probably glowed with the delightful emotions. Plug her in, she'd light up the entire club. Martin commanded her heart as well as her body. She knew the signs, having seen them in her clients often enough. Infatuation.

Maybe even love.

Certainly lust.

The thought of Martin's imminent "home break-in" had her almost painfully excited.

She mentally blessed whatever detail-oriented decorator saw fit to fill the games room cabinet with ladies dresses.

Jeans were problematic for the game they were about to play even if she had been willing to put on the filthy things. The time in the cell had rendered them unpleasant.

Charlotte smoothed her hands over the unfamiliar garment, glad the flowing ivory selection fit her as well as it did. After Martin had deposited her into the room wearing only her towel, then left, she'd pulled the dress out from the cabinet. It had to be a hundred years old. A miracle it fit and that the fragile fabric didn't fall apart.

She felt the lacy edging at the wrists and neck prickle her flesh. The mild discomfort stimulated her. Everything stimulated her. Where did all this energy come from? Was it as simple as Martin's delicate, healing touch?

She stared in the mirror. The dress would be nothing but rags when Martin was through.

She smiled.

She watched a woman from another century smiling back, seated there before her boudoir, gazing into the ornate gilded mirror. Surrounded by delicate things like perfume bottles, with a silver brush in her hand, Charlotte felt as if she'd stepped into another body. A newer, braver one.

A vulnerable, innocent-looking one.

A happy one.

What does such a woman do at such a time? Why, she brushes her hair, of course.

Charlotte brushed her hair.

Martin walked in without knocking and the noise of Sub-space intruded. He eyed her dress. He slowly closed the door behind him.

With the door shut, her own fast breathing was all she could hear. He looked serious. His face was that of a stranger.

Pleasure spiked in her. A stranger had broken into her home.

She dropped the brush, which clattered on the marble table-top of the dresser. She stood up while backing away, so that the chair she'd sat in fell over. "I don't . . ."

"Shut up." Martin took in the way she clasped her arms around her body protectively. He unbuttoned the top of his shirt. His hand traveled down, hooked into the pocket of his black pants. "Aren't you a sight in your pretty dress."

Her expression of dread must've pleased him. He gave her a coldly lecherous smile. "Take it off."

She moved slightly, in preparation for a mad dash.

He raised a blocking arm. "Sorry. You're not going any-where until I'm finished with you."

"Please leave." She tried to stare him down, intimidate him. It failed utterly. To her surprise, real tears sprang into her eyes, blurring him to a stranger. She tingled with fear and anticipa-tion. "You can't."

"Watch me." He crossed to her, fought for control of her arms, finally lifting them above her head. He kissed her, and his lips were unfamiliar. His scent reassured her even as the hungry disregard of his mouth made her heart lurch wildly in a panic.

"Stop!" She struggled, turning her head away.

Instead of answering, he pushed her to the padded floor, then fell atop her. It knocked the breath out of her.

She tried to wriggle away, but he pulled her back, ripping her dress and baring her breasts. "Very nice." When she tried to buck him off, he wrapped one hand around her neck. "No." With the other, he explored her body, ripping cloth as he trav-eled down her body.

He tweaked one nipple, then the other. When she whim-pered, he grinned and moved his hand from her neck to her mouth. "Go ahead. Scream if you want."

She bit his hand instead.

He pressed harder in response. "You're going to pay for that." He sounded happy.

She could relate. His rough treatment had her on the verge of orgasm, but as he twisted one nipple punishingly, she did scream. He gave her the beatific grin of a sadist.

Then he ripped her panties—they came off only after he pulled hard enough to bruise, making her yelp again. He fumbled at his pants as she bucked frantically.

He pushed her down brutally, using his weight to keep her legs pinned as he fumbled between her thighs and his. Then she felt his warmth and heft and hardness, and she panicked anew, twisting in desperation, trying to keep her legs sealed shut against him.

He thrust once. The feel of his head bruised her sensitive swollen flesh, the crown parting her. He thrust again, forcing himself in, penetrating her defenses. Her walls stretched as he filled her. He pushed his cock into her.

She screamed at the invasion. Then again as it dug even deeper, seemingly splitting her apart. He was in her to the hilt, and she could feel the hard muscles all up and down his body dominating her, trapping her. He forced himself in again and his balls pushed against her spread inner thighs and ass as he pounded into her very center. The hardness of him bruised and stretched her further, pinching and hurting, and she screamed against his hand.

He thrust again and again. After a time all she could manage was a moaning grunt in time with his thrusts.

The friction of his brutal movements ignited her. The unspeakable pleasure at what he did to her, at his domination and his contemptuous use of her body, spiraled up and up. All she could feel was him.

"You're all mine, aren't you."

She looked at him and saw the bestial pleasure on his face as he used her. It matched the movie visions perfectly, and she knew he was about to come.

Her pleasure swelled ever higher. Against his rutting thrusts, she shook her head. She had to be defiled this way. She embraced her fear as she tried frantically to buck him off. She failed to budge him even slightly. Her body began to tremble with the uncontrollable onset of orgasm.

"That's what I thought," he told her with gentle scorn even as animal lust contorted his features.

He increased his rhythm to please himself.

It sent an enormous, shuddery wave of pleasure through her, tipping her over the edge.

When she screamed against his hand, it was in mindless ecstasy.

"You're going to have bruises," he said, cuddling her afterward. "Here, and here. And here. Oh, and here." He touched her gently, reverently. "Let me kiss each of them. And all the new ones I'll be giving you."

"Can I give you some, too?" She snuggled into him, covered only in a welcome cooling sweat and his large, protective body. Her body tingled and throbbed with a pleasurable sensation of sated lust and a deep contentment. She was well used, she thought with satisfaction. She'd never felt so at peace. "I mean, fair's fair."

"If you want." He gave her a lazy smile. "Could be fun, once you learn how to do it properly. And if you promise not to abandon me again in the middle of a session." He looked at her with the stern look that turned her insides to jelly.

"Okay. I promise." She kissed him on his stubble-covered jaw. He'd forgotten to shave. He'd been worried about her.

She settled deeper into his comforting embrace. Martin was right. Everything was as it was supposed to be.

She was crazy about him. She traced Martin's muscled chest

with one investigating fingertip. Martin was nothing like Kartane.

Which reminded her. "What about the police? It's probably time to call them. Do you think Kartane's okay?" She fretted. "I wonder what they're doing to him."

"Nothing he doesn't deserve, I'm sure. They'll keep him busy for a few more minutes." He held her close, nuzzling her hair with his chin. "Are you really worried about him?"

She thought of the past week, and all it had revealed. "Not too much. He hurt a lot of people. Badly."

"Including you," Martin reminded her.

"I'm all better now, thanks to you. You know who I'm worried about? Hoagie."

She tilted her head up for a moment to watch Martin's forehead crease into a small frown. "Hoagie. Not the sandwich, one presumes. The name sounds familiar, but I don't remember a Hoagie. Is it a club name?"

She giggled, still a little high from their violent lovemaking. "Not exactly. Hoagie's my dog. My adorable mutt, raised from a puppy, living with my ex because my little apartment doesn't come with a backyard. I should go check on him. Kartane has a nice house, but he's shown enough lack of empathy that I'm a bit worried about Hoagie."

"Charlotte."

The seriousness in his voice stilled her, made her look up again at him curiously. "Yes?"

"I have a backyard. And a very nice house. Would you and your dog like to share it with me? I can keep Hoagie in more dog toys than he'll ever need." Martin's light tone didn't match the steady intensity of his gaze. His fingertips grazed the flesh of her arm, then shoulder, raising delightful shivers. It was his most gentle touch, again. He had so many touches to offer her.

They had so many to offer each other. "You're serious. Move in with you?" She checked his face again. "You're really serious."

He nodded. "With the Subspace sale proceeds plus turning my share of Pavlov's Pet Joy into big cash, even after my mom's bills I'll be doing quite well. Plenty well enough to make investments. I'll take care of overhead while you ramp up your matchmaking business. The western wing of the house can be my office. The eastern wing can be your office. You have a gift and passions that should be used. We both do. Don't you agree?"

Eastern wing? Did she agree. What a foolish question. Visions of a house so big it had wings danced in her head, making her feel giddy. She could live and work in such a house. With Martin! Her naughty matchmaking movies could play every day and night, and not just for others anymore. "Yes. Okay. I'd love to."

The force of his arms clamping around her conveyed the depth of his relief, as did his low voice growling in her ear. "Good. You won't regret it. I'll help you move tomorrow."

"Okay."

"You say 'okay' a lot. Did you know that?" The smile in his voice when he spoke brought an answering one to her lips.

"Really?"

"Uh-huh."

She pondered, then turned a cheeky grin on him. "Does it bug you? Okay, okay, okay. Okay?"

He chafed her hand with the gentleness that thrilled, and the promise of roughness that thrilled even more. "I believe that is what they call 'playing with fire.'" He dumped her off his lap.

"Okay," she taunted.

He ignored it. "And you're going to get burned. Again and again. I hope that's *okay*." He returned her cheeky grin. Only his was decidedly sadistic.

"With you, yes." When his hands grew much less gentle, she shuddered with pleasure. "It is definitely okay."

29

Gregory guided the enormous Halloween tour down into the farthest reaches of the Riverport undertunnels.

He'd forgotten the superstitious nonsense of the last tour days ago, and tonight's festive crowd—many in costumes, many who'd begun drinking early during the holiday evening—helped keep the heebie-jeebies away. With such a record-breaking crowd, he'd make enough money to advertise nationally. Business would boom. Maybe he'd complain again about the fetish club next door, get that seedy place shut down. Their goings-on were an offense against decent society, he thought indignantly.

He provided the group with running commentary about each room. He described in lurid detail the tortures endured by abducted men and women a hundred years ago.

The inexplicable dread that had gripped him last time was all but forgotten . . . at least until they'd all crowded into the room that always felt so much colder than the others. He could see his breath in the flashlight beams slicing through the dusty air.

His arm hair suddenly rose with gooseflesh.

Gregory abruptly decided to skip the Lilli story, and all the rest of the stories for that matter, and expedite the tour. [?] cided he'd earned a drink. "... And this simple storage roo[?] was a long-ago pit for abducted recalcitrant women, who were dropped through the trapdoor you see above your heads, to a fate unimaginable down in the very bowels of the earth. They ended their lives right here, alone in the dark on the rotting mattresses, after falling from what must've seemed like heaven in comparison."

As he'd expected, many flashlight beams joined his to highlight the old wooden square of the trapdoor high above.

The trapdoor moved.

Gregory peered, uncertain he'd really seen it. But the sheep were gasping and murmuring in awe, so it wasn't just his imagination. It really had moved.

The spit in his mouth dried up. The cold in the room seemed to swirl around him with sinuous fingers, like a freezing lover. Or was he seeing things? Dust in his eyes? The bad air in the room, he told himself desperately.

It was Halloween. The night the spirits walked.

He stared up, petrified. The trapdoor opened.

"Lilli?" he whispered.

The dark square above was replaced by white flesh.

A body pitched through to land on a dusty old mattress.

Gregory screamed, which started the stampede. Someone knocked him down, but he managed to crawl off to the side, clutching his flashlight.

He raised it with trembling hands.

The nude body on the mattress—a man?—seemed uncomfortable. Gregory supposed it had something to do with the whip marks all over his body. Or possibly the tight ropes binding his wrists to his ankles, making his body arch backward into a painful-looking tight bow. Most likely it was the brand on his forehead, still oozing from recent application, but deep and distinct enough Gregory could see the letter *G* clearly.

elled rose perfume. Gregory tightened
ht as all the muscles in his body seemed
e moaned as he heard a woman's amused
s precisely what I've been waiting for, all

"None ___ n the soft tone he heard the satisfaction in her voice.

Gregory looked but couldn't see anyone there. No evidence of the woman who spoke with such a faint, whispery voice soft as embers settling. He turned back to the man on the mattress, who'd begun to emit an unearthly shriek...just as he felt the cold grip of a woman's slender hand over his, clicking off his flashlight.

Gregory scrambled to his feet and ran blindly, finding the stairs up by pure luck. Or perhaps he'd had guidance. As the sound of approaching police sirens filled his ears, Gregory also discerned the peals of feminine laughter echoing in the cavernous spaces as if from a distance of decades, laughter that would echo in his mind for as long as he lived.

The tour operator fled the Riverport undertunnels and could never be convinced to return.